Nasty, Very is Julia
his previous novels
Prize: *King Fisher*
the author of *A Spy*
Panther Books.

Rathbone lives in the New Forest and travels widely.

NASTY, VERY

'Nasty, Very is as good as its word . . . Bags of period detail here to enjoy, incidentally, shown best of all in the label-conscious bravura of Charlie's final apotheosis as a Thatcherite diehard election winner.'
The Observer

'As a savage parody of the Britain that is no longer great, his novel deserves attention.'
Daily Telegraph

'This brisk and biting novel.'
Sunday Telegraph

A SPY OF THE OLD SCHOOL

'Scintillating addition to the fiction of school-tie-and-Cambridge espionage . . . History made savagely incarnate.'
Sunday Times

'Intelligent, sophisticated and brilliantly cynical, as only the best British espionage novels can be, this deserves consideration right up there with Le Carré and company.'
Publishers Weekly

By the same author

Diamonds Bid
Hand Out
With My Knives I Know I'm Good
Trip Trap
Kill Cure
Bloody Marvellous
King Fisher Lives
¡Carnival!
A Raving Monarchist
Joseph
The Euro-Killers
A Last Resort
Base Case
A Spy of the Old School
Watching the Detectives
Wellington's War

JULIAN RATHBONE

Nasty, Very

A Mock Epic in Six Parts

GRAFTON BOOKS
A Division of the Collins Publishing Group

LONDON GLASGOW
TORONTO SYDNEY AUCKLAND

Grafton Books
A Division of the Collins Publishing Group
8 Grafton Street, London W1X 3LA

Published by Grafton Books 1986

First published in Great Britain by
Michael Joseph Ltd 1984

ISBN 0-586-06742-6

Printed and bound in Great Britain by
Collins, Glasgow

Set in Times

The extracts in Part Six from the House of Commons debate of 3 April 1982 on the Falklands crisis are reproduced from *Iron Britannia* by Anthony Barnett, published by Alison & Busby.

This book is for:

Danny
Jeremy
Nick
Tony

All this the world well knows; yet none know well
To shun the heaven that leads man to this hell.

Part One

1

Dark cloud, purple, a gust of rain on a light breeze, snatches of blue, then suddenly the blessing of warm sun swirls a brief swathe of light across a water-meadow; buttercups heavy with water-drops sparkle, nod and beck like so many crowned, coroneted heads, with cuckoo flower intermittently more stately amongst them.

Through the meadow two lads saunter, loiter, towards the willows and alders, bosky, bosomy with new foliage. The sunlight glides on ahead, brushes the copses, silvers the tiny brook, and fades between the tumbled warehouses and workshops of an abandoned factory. The square clocktower in the middle is briefly ochred, then turns black again.

Charles Bosham, fourteen years old, grey Viyella shirt over baggy flannels, gold-dusted with buttercup pollen above wet shoes, mop of curly fair hair cut short up the back of his neck and above his ears, but left to flop a little ludicrously on top, exaggeratedly freezes, one hand thrown back to halt his companion behind him.

'Look, Terry,' he hisses. 'Look. Down there. Toad. Fat toad.'

Six yards in front of him, heavy with unlaid spawn, she laboriously pushes, paddles herself in slow, slow motion, obeying a palaeozoic impulse to carry her load to the still water where the brook swells briefly into a pool. She has trouble with a broken stick across her path, lifts her snout on to it, one three-toed hand, drags up her haunches, and then heaves.

'Ugh! How positively foul.' Terry Mead is taller, thinner, a year older than Charlie Bosham, with steel-rimmed spectacles perched on a nose that will one day be beaky, but his uniform is the same. 'How very positively foul.'

For a minute they watch her. As her left-rear hand gets a hold over the twig, it rolls back beneath her, and she presses on.

Behind her, Charles, Charlie Bosham, snaps open the breach of his BSA air rifle, pulls back the levered barrel, thus driving a plunger into the cylinder above the stock, compressing air. Then he fingers a tiny lead slug out of his trouser pocket, and fits it snug. Carefully he closes the breach, carefully lest the slug drop out. He smells machine oil, caresses the satiny pistol grip with its intricately lettered trademark so satisfactorily embossed in the dark wood, hefts the solid, pre-war gun to his shoulder. His eyeballs burn with excitement, a pleasurable, almost ecstatic constriction blooms at the pit of his throat across the top of his chest, his scrotum tightens. Terry, blinking, snaps into place the barrel of his tinier, feebler if newer Diana pistol, and nods.

The guns clang. Fumblingly reloaded, they clang again.

Toad dies, but will not stop twitching. Unlaid spawn spills from a rent between her haunches, glistens as the sun pays another fleeting visit. Embarrassed, not by guilt, but by intensity of feeling – intense feeling is always something to be mocked – the two lads move off, on, down towards the copse and brook, for a moment not quite ready to reaffirm each other's presence.

Reeds with little crisp black flowers on their stems intermittently pierce the turf, which becomes soggier; dragonflies flit by on jewelled wings (Charlie tries a shot but misses); the first swallows swoop along the brook, and house martins weave arabesques with their flashing white rumps against the shifting clouds. Between the budding lilypads more toads slither on and off each other's backs, copulating, spawning, unheeding at first as the pellets plop, then diving or sinking out of sight, leaving one white-bellied male amongst the heavier leaves.

'I've only got five left,' says Charlie. 'How many have you?'

'Three.'

'We should have brought the tin.'

'Yes.'

They push through red dogwood, muddied shoes squelching in the bog, the BSA rifle snagging on the whippy branches, past a briar rose just showing pink petal through its swelling buds, then up a bank where willows, once neatly pollarded now long neglected, trail new leaves above a drier carpet where daffodils recently died. It's almost an island, notorious to the local gangs as a den or fort to be diputed with clods of earth hurled in the air to simulate hand grenades, but today, this special day, deserted. The sun is out now more constantly, warming the air, promising a balmy evening after the chill, showery day. Charlie throws down the air gun and sprawls beside it; Terry squats close by. Charlie swats irritably at a fly. His thick shirt feels sticky now, his skin itches, his eyes sting; suddenly he sits up, scratches ferociously in his thick thatch of fair hair.

'Fleas, fleas, Charlie Bosham has fleas,' chants Terry.

'Oh, put a sock in it,' says Charlie

Silence, except for the low movement of water, the gentle sussuration of the leaves.

He adds, fiercly, 'I want to shag.'

Terry turns abruptly away; then, his face scarlet beneath his spectacles, turns back. 'So do I,' he says.

'I'll do you, if you do me.'

'All right.'

Afterwards Terry buttons up (no zips) and then kneels at the foot of the largest of the willows, rummages amongst its roots, pulls out a packet of Du Maurier filter tips and an American Zippo lighter. The packet is damp but not wet. It does not have the push-up inner section of an ordinary cigarette packet, but a lid that lifts like that on a cigarette case. For the children this makes the brand a posher fag. The Zippo is flipped in imitation of the usage of GIs in American war films, and flares; the boys lie back and self-consciously inhale.

'I'd like,' says Charlie, 'to do it with a girl some time.'

'Yes.'

'I wonder what it's like.'

Terry considers. 'Quicker, I should think.'

'Yes. Less . . . brought on.' He searches for the word. 'More *natural.* I think if I put mine in a girl's hole and just moved, then it would just come.'

'Yes.'

They both consider this effortless proposition with great satisfaction, and, in the warm sun, smoke on.

'Old people they were,' says Charlie.

'Who?'

'All those people in the church. Abbey. I mean they were dressed up . . . like . . . I don't know.'

'Like Stewart Granger or James Mason?' suggests Terry, whose parents have taken him up West to see the remake of *The Prisoner of Zenda.*

'I suppose so. Carrying swords and all that. Dressed up. But they were all old. Really old. Not like Dad, even. More like Grandad.'

'Normally speaking, nowadays,' says Terry, wisely, 'you have to be quite old to be somebody important. I mean before the old ones will let you . . . I mean people live longer now.'

'I shan't wait. I'll get on.' Charlie stubs out the diminutive filter of his Du Maurier.

A distant hum starts below the horizon but crescendoes into an appalling roar with quite unbelievable speed, so quick that they are hardly on their feet, eyes up and hand-shaded as the leading bunch of four, pursuing and almost catching their own sound, hurtles across the sky above them, out of Kent, and arrowed into the heart of the city, four followed by five more goups of four – cigar-shaped planes with screaming jets slung from stubbier wings than the old planes had.

'Meteors,' shouts Charlie. 'Wow!'

Hardly does the roar fade than it begins again – twice more they come, each time a flight of twenty-four Meteors in six groups of four, black against the blue sky above them, briefly silvered in the sun against lilac clouds stacked above the city, then black again as they slip beyond the low ridge above the meadow.

'Holy Smoke!' says Terry. 'Now, that was something. Positively. Actually wizard.'

They push back through the dogwood, out into the meadow, and up the slope to the pair of cottages that separates the fields from the council estate beyond. Two nearly old women, born before the city reached their garden walls, daughters and wives of farm labourers who worked the swallowed land, talk laconically across the fence. The boys negotiate a bramble patch, climb a low tumbled wall, and for a moment look back over the meadow and the deserted factory where once gyroscopes and similar devices were assembled for Soviet tanks.

Beyond stretch the suburbs of Bromley and Orpington and, blue on the horizon, the North Downs draw the line to suburban sprawl. Above them the receding cumulus is piled into high and airy palaces of marble built on granite foundations.

There's a choice now for the boys. On their own, both would move off along the side of the hill, taking a longer route than necessary to their respective homes; together, neither will admit to the other their fear of what lies ahead. They walk on up Daffodil Road and into the Flowers

Estate, so called because each street is named after a flower. Blockish redbrick houses, set in terraces of four or six, no pebble-dash or timbering or bay windows, march up to a small green near the top of the hill. There are sounds of laughter, shouting, clattered crockery, and the smell of food fried in lard. Two boys, about the same age as Charlie and Terry, or a little younger, swing suddenly out of a cut, halooing one after the other, and deliberately cannon into Charlie as they pass.

'Yobs,' says Charlie, suddenly a touch pale, his knuckles whitening on the stock of his air rifle.

Terry corrects the slang: 'Oicks.'

They move on up to the green, which is really a square with eight terraced houses on each side. The road runs over the hill here and is metamorphosed into Violet Lane. On the green there is a trestle table supporting cakes, tinned fruit, salads, sandwiches, and under it a crate each of screw-top quart bottles of light ale, and Guinness, and lemonade secured by wired-down porcelain caps. They had wanted to roast an ox, but the Ministry of Food had ruled that the meat should be cooked the night before, given away in sandwiches, and that there should be a tradition of ox-roasting in the village.

The table is hung with red, white and blue swags of crepe paper which the breeze, sharper up here, is already shredding. Small children, rather grubby by now, but dressed in starched frocks, hair braided and ribboned, or shirts and pressed trousers, hair Brylcreemed, eye the coming feast with more curiosity than anticipation – most of them are too young to remember VE or VJ day. Their mothers add the finishing touches to the table; four or five men smoke at a corner, hands cupped round their tiny Woods and Weights. Suddenly they all laugh raucously, slap at each other's shoulders, and one calls out, 'Come on, Bess, when do we get to open the beer?'

'The hoi polloi are not debarred from the national

celebration,' says Terry. 'Their antics are curious but not refined.'

Charlie is not prepared to admit that this is beyond him, but has taken the point that 'oick' not 'yob' is the right word.

'A yob' he says, 'is someone who sniffs the saddles of ladies' bicycles.'

With relief and no further incident, they reach the end of the green and the crest of the hill. For a moment they pause. In front of them, Violet Lane threads its way down through the rest of the Flowers Estate, and the hill drops away to lose itself in the monstrous megapolis that is spread out in front of them – still by and large a city of two-storey buildings, so that on a clear day you can see the giant cranes of the docks just below Tower Bridge, the bridge itself and the dome of St Paul's.

At the end of Violet Lane, Terry heads on down to a spacious Edwardian villa set in an avenue of acacias. Daddy is senior partner in a local law firm. He is quite well known in the area since at the last election he almost gained the constituency for the Conservatives for the first time ever.

Charlie moves east, heading into a waste of straight roads flanked by thousands of semi-detached houses, all identical: bay windows, pebble-dash, timbered eaves, front doors with half-lights stained in debased art-deco flower shapes, each with a scrap of lawn in front and a rockery, and a strip of garden at the back with a shed, a fruit tree, and a lawn. Some have H-shaped television aerials. 263 Goldsmith Drive is one of them.

2

'Children's viewing, then how young people have been celebrating, then edited highlights,' his father is saying as he comes in, 'nothing important until five to nine when good old Winnie gets his say in.' He puts by the *Radio Times,* peers up over black-framed spectacles. 'Where have you been then, young feller-me-lad?'

'Down Skerrit's Meadow. My eyes had begun to ache'. This is still a good way of getting out of watching the magic box when adults feel you ought to. There is much concern about the possible effect excessive viewing might have on young eyes. 'I met Terry Mead.' This also was a good move.

'Young Mead is a good lad. A very good lad. You get in with classy sorts like that at your new school and you'll get on all right.' Solidly built, greying hair well greased, good solid moustache, spreading stomach, his father is almost as old as the century. Now he looks up and around the assembled company. 'The Philip Sydney is a fine old school, and our Charlie did well to get his scholarship.' The assembled company, who have heard it all too often before, ignore him.

They include: Elizabeth, Charlie's aunt (a well-worn joke she hates), a thin desiccated spinster, assistant matron in the local chest hospital; Charlie's mother, who is fat, docile, defeated; Charlie's sister Anne, who is eleven years old, fat docile, but not quite defeated; and Charlie's grandad, Joseph Bosham, who is fat, beery, triumphant, and confused almost to the point of senility. That concludes the home team.

The visitors are as follows: David Alderson, a thin dull

man who manages the second of Edward Bosham's hardware shops; Margaret Alderson, his wife, frenetically bright, and still affecting the slacks she learnt to wear in the war; their son George, dull and spiteful, two years older than Charlie; Elizabeth Coleman, an attractive war widow who works as cashier for Bosham; her wildly attractive daughter Jane, twelve years old; and bright young son Peter, aged ten.

It is a large gathering, the largest the house has ever seen since it was built in the early thirties, and the reason for it is the presence of the large black box that stands beneath a fringed standard lamp in the corner by the leaded bay window, its screen now dead. It has been made clear that it is the patriotic duty of those who have television sets to invite those of their acquaintance who have not to view the day's events at a Television Party.

The front room is a mess. Almost every easily moved chair in the house has been put down in it, arranged originally in concentric semi-circles round the set, with father Bosham's armchair moved from its usual place by the fireplace of yellow glazed tiles to the centre of the front row – but now, after seven hours of uninterrupted viewing, during which television snacks, luncheons and teas have been eaten off paper plates, and endless cups of tea, coffee, squash, and bottles of pale ale drunk, and perhaps over a hundred Capstan, Senior Service, and Players smoked, not to mention Grandad's noisome pipe, it is . . . a mess. A midden, Charlie's mother has called it, before bursting into tears and waddling off to the kitchen, where the women now comfort her and brew up yet another pot of tea. The men and some of the children stay on, restlessly wondering what to do next. The problem is that the day will not be properly over until the Speech, due at nine o'clock, a fact which everyone knows and for which no one has prepared.

A desultory argument continues between Mr Bosham

and Grandad Bosham '*Sir* Jack Hobbs,' cries Grandad. 'Whoever heard of a Jack being a Sir. No. No. Let me finish. Mark my words. It's derogation of standards. I mean, once you let a sportsman in, then anyone can get in. Any rag, tag and bobtail.'

'Gordon Richards I grant you. But Jack Hobbs is a gentleman,' repeats his son.

Charlie's aunt, however, has resources. She comes in now from the dining room, briskly, as if inspecting one of her wards, claps her hands for attention and announces, 'Right. You must all amuse yourselves for an hour or so. Charlie, take the children up to your room. Play one of your silly games. Edward. Take the men out into the garden while we clean up in here, or, if you must, to the Duke of Wellington.'

Charlie is surly: 'Anne's a baby. Can't play properly.'

Anne cries, 'I don't want to play in Charlie's room.'

'That's all right. You can help in the kitchen.'

High above a cardboard London whose streets are littered with green wooden houses and red hotels, a plastic Spitfire on a fishing line hunts an Me 109 out of the skies. Dice rattle in the box, land; one die rolls off the board and on to the quilt. As he sees it stop Charlie exerts pressure on the bed near it and topples it over one more quarter-turn. 'Total of six,' he says. 'You land on my Mayfair.' He draws breath. '*If,* if you sell back *all* your houses, and *if* you then mortgage all your properties, you might be able to pay me.' Pasty George Alderson listens dully. Charlie goes on, 'But then you might just as well get out of the game, because the next time you land on anything to pay rent, you *will* be out.'

'But,' says Peter Coleman, who is really very bright for only ten , 'if you do have another go, then it might be me you lose to and that would give me still a chance of winning.'

George looks from one to the other. He is utterly

confused. From high up on pillows covered with the yellow box-pleated imitation-satin bedspread, Jane watches the three boys squabbling over the death throes of the game. She has lost out intentionally to her younger brother quite early, knowing how wretched he will be if he is the first to be bankrupted.

'What,' asks George, 'can I do else?'

'Well,' says Charlie, and there is no excitement in his voice – he has won the game too often, too certainly, to find it any longer exciting, 'if you give me just Oxford Street, Bond Street and Piccadilly Circus, I'll take them for the whole debt, and then you can go on.'

'Instead of mortgaging them and selling them back to the bank?'

'Yes.'

'That would be cheating, wouldn't it?'

'Not if we both agree. Who is being cheated if we *both* agree?'

Jane intervenes: 'Peter, Peter is being cheated. That way you'll get all one side and half the other, and Peter is bound to be caught each time he comes round.'

Silence. The westering sun puts in the last call, picks out dust motes that dance above the bed beneath the Spitfire and Messerschmidt, touches with gold the tawdry toys and comics that litter the room. It is the largest bedroom, at the back of the house. Mr and Mrs Bosham have the front room, which is only slightly smaller, Anne the tiny boxroom over the stairs. Charlie flushes a little, looks hard at Jane, begins to pick his nose.

'Perhaps we should vote on it.'

'It'll be two each.'

'You don't count. You're out.'

She tosses her hair, which is naturally straight, once blonde now darkening richly, but waved for the occasion like Deanna Durbin, and smoothes her skirt over her knees towards white ankle socks.

'Anyway, it's the rules. You should play to the rules.'

George has been thinking it over and the message has at last got through, the penny has dropped. 'You mean, if I give you these, you say I can go on.'

'Yes. And you've still got houses on Pentonville and Euston. You could still get some rent and . . .'

Not win, no. But at least not to be beaten into third place by a snotty ten-year-old who still wears shorts.

'Done,' says stolid George.

'Just a minute,' says Jane. Her voice has a strange note now, and the three boys pause. She looks straight at Charlie – sees a lanky, but strong-looking boy, thick fair hair above the short back and sides, pale blue eyes, puffy-lidded, and the skin slate-coloured towards the nose, which is stubby and a touch squashed; the mouth is large, lips plump but often sulky; his chest is broad and strong for his age, and there is already a down on his arms beneath his rolled-up shirtsleeves. He looks at her, and she smoothes down her dress again, so for a moment all he can see is the pressure of her breast buds beneath a child's brassière whose fasteners and adjusters are outlined just below her collar-bones. Then he sees cool serious eyes, greenish brown – they are gazing so intently into his that involuntarily he shudders.

'Well?'

'Come here. I want to whisper.'

'I can't. If I do, the board and everything will be upset.'

He looks across the litter of title deeds, hotels, chance cards and the satisfying solid lead charms, each trapped in its place awaiting the dictates of the dice, except the Top Hat George anxiously sucks. He slides his feet to the floor and awkwardly picks his way from the foot of the bed to the head.

'Well?'

'Head closer. Much closer.'

She grasps his upper arm, pulls him down.

He feels her hair on his cheeks, her breath in his ear. His own blood now roars there too, and for the life of him (and it now seems as serious as that) he cannot make out a word she says.

'Say it again. Slower.'

She gives the impatient toss to her hair, draws breath, and mouths the words with irritating slowness. 'Play . . . the . . . rules . . . Give . . . Peter . . . a . . . chance . . . Play . . . the . . . rules . . .'

'And? Why?'

'And . . . I'll . . . let . . . you . . . in . . . the . . . bathroom . . . with . . . me.'

He swallows. Straightens.

'When?' he asks hoarsely.

She shrugs teasingly. 'When the game's over.'

Laboriously, they liquidate George's assets according to the rules, Jane, as banker, counting out the money. George sulks. Peter, back with a chance, is flushed, excited, wants to get on. Charlie is at the foot of the bed, chewing his nails as if he has not eaten for a week.

Downstairs the front door slams, adult voices echo up the stairwell.

'Get a move on' says Charlie. 'For God's sake, get a move on.'

With George satisfactorily stripped, Peter rolls the dice and the game restarts. Jane, prey to more excitement than she knows she should show, picks up a book from behind the bedside locker where it has probably been for years, since it is *The Jolly Jump-Up ABC*. It has a separate little story on each page. She has never seen a pop-up book before. Awkwardly she fingers up the heavy paper into little tableaux and through misty eyes reads.

Harry is galloping on his horse across the prairie with Red Indians after him. Jane is pressing her dollies' clothes with her iron . . . Tea is ready, says Jenny, as she carries the tray into Richard's tent . . . Frank was given a bus conductor's uniform at Christmas, and Mabel a nurse's uniform . . .

The adults arrange themselves again in front of the box, chairs collide, elbows nudge, knees get in the way. In the confined spaces these accidental brushes are acutely embarrassing, for any physical contact that cannot be construed as definitely aggressive is thought to be sexual. Thus, if Mrs Coleman (Jane's and Peter's mother) touches fingers with Mr Bosham as she hands him the packet of crisps he has asked for, he will smile inwardly to himself, knowing that she has long been a widow and yet takes care of herself, while he, even at fifty-three, still retains a lot of that Cagney magnetism his wife claimed he had when they were courting . . . too long ago.

He finds the scrap of blue paper, unscrews it and noisily shakes the spilled salt through the packet, wriggles his bottom more deeply into the deep brown brushed moquette.

'Them, those, coronets and that, in the Abbey, were all made of brass, you know. Not gold.'

'Get on with you,' says his fat wife, jolly now the house is relatively clean and she has a couple of surreptitious gins inside her. 'They was, were, surely gold. I mean, they has to be gold, don't they?'

'Brass. Every last one. Five quid people were offering for seats on the route,' he goes on, not for the first time that day. 'Five quid. And I reckon we got a much better view here. Much better.' He reaches forward and switches on. The set hisses, buzzes, flashes a snowstorm and clears itself to reveal an open carriage with an enormous black woman under an umbrella, waving, waving royal acceptance of cheers that seem more raucous than loyal. Margaret Alderson, passing him a glass of light ale, asks, 'Will you see the fireworks from here, Mr Bosham?'

'This is the recording. Highlights. In a minute you'll see

that notice some git put up on a tree saying Lover's Nest. I don't think so, Mrs Alderson. Maybe the big ones from the upstairs window.'

'They will show them on the television, I think . . . Isn't that right, David? The fireworks are to be on television.'

Gloom, bad temper, swells in Mr Bosham's chest. The fireworks are scheduled for ten twenty . . . Will these people never go? They'll eat him out of house and home, and nothing but salad all day, with lettuces at one shilling each . . . his wife must have been mad to have bought them at that price.

'Well, we shan't be staying that long,' says attractive Mrs Coleman – big woman, good shape. She's got some sense anyway, he thinks, and handsome too, got a bit of bottom, something to get hold of, but firm-looking, not a load of lard like Charlie's mother. He usually thinks of his wife as Charlie's mother. Mrs Coleman goes on, 'That will be long past Peter's bed time, and Jane's too for that matter. In fact, Mrs Bosham, we'll be off soon, so I hope you won't mind if I just ask you again, those of you who haven't contributed . . .' She lifts a collecting box and gives it a shake. Not much in it.

'Come on, Grandad, get your hand in your pocket. All the rest of us have.'

'Eh? What? What for?'

'You know what for. We told you before. It's for handicapped ex-servicemen, that laid down their limbs for our heritage. All this that's been on all day.' He waves his glass at the television. A young lady, overdressed, with a very large crown on her head, waves back. 'Mrs Coleman very properly has asked us to contribute because this is a Viewing Party. And she sends it all to some general . . .'

'General Sir Bernard Paget, Mr Bosham.'

'I'm giving no money to no bleeding general.'

'Dad, I'll lay one on you if you use language here. These are respectable people. We are respectable. You may not be, but we . . .'

'You'd be nowhere without me. I built up that business. And I'm respectable too. Titled ancestor. Shouldn't be suprised if I'm not a . . .'

'A viscount. Yes, Dad. We've heard it all before.' Edward Bosham raises his eyebrows and throws in a collusive grin at Mrs Coleman. I'd like to get my hands on those tits, he thinks. He turns back to his father. 'And that makes me the son of a viscount. Come on, Dad. Cough up or get out.'

He shakes the box under his father's nose.

'Got no change.'

'Good. Put in a ten-bob note.'

'You're joking. Here. Here we are.' A coin clunks through the slot.

'Oh, thank you, Mr Bosham. It really is a good cause.'

'Yer, well. I'd've done my bit too, you know. But I was already too old, even in 'fourteen. I'm seventy-three, Mrs . . .'

'. . . Coleman.'

'Coleman. Seventy-three. And I've seen some changes. *Sir* Gordon Richards. *Sir* Jack Hobbs.'

'All right, Dad, all right. Come on and sit down. Look there goes those jet aeroplanes again. It'll be time for the speeches any minute, better get the kids down.'

'I'll tell them. Got to go to the bathroom anyway.'

'OK, Dad. But don't be long.'

But in the hall, the old man, who is now really in a hurry, and trying not to hold on to himself, is confronted by a blockage, a slow-moving procession on the steep stairs above him. In front comes Jane Coleman, her head up, tears in her eyes, a bright touch of scarlet on each cheek; then Charlie, thick lips pulled in, white-faced, the dark rings round his eyes yet more pronounced; and behind him and above them all, with the mein of an avenging angel, comes Elizabeth Bosham, Virgin Warrior.

'Out of the way, Father,' she calls. 'Let us through, if you please. Come on, you little chit. Get a move on. And you, sir, if you please,' and she gives her nephew a sharp push on the shoulder so that he has to grab the banister to avoid falling into Jane. Reluctantly the procession gets under way again, but not quick enough for Grandad, whose mottled hands are now clamped to his crotch and on whose face is an expression of ecstatic agony such as old painters depicted on the faces of venerable martyrs.

At last they get into the front room, except Mrs Coleman who, unaware of impending doom, has slipped out into the back garden for a last breath of fresh air.

Mr Alderson and Mr Bosham are peering at the screen, which is now the main source of light; perched on a chair beside them is fat Anne, bemused but pleased that she is allowed to be up still; and at that moment, from the back room, in come bright Margaret Alderson and Charlie's mother, bearing the sixth and seventh plates of lettuce and salad-dressing sandwiches they have made that day. With the doorway to the hall behind them, painted chocolate brown against embossed coffee-coloured wall-paper which matches the heavily fringed pelmet and curtains, Aunt Elizabeth and the two children form a momentary tableau – with the children's formal clothes still smart, the emotion thick on their faces, they resemble a Victorian genre painting.

'Turn that thing off,' commands Aunt Elizabeth in the tones that send Irish orderlies carrying enamel bedpans skidding over polished tiles.

Mr Bosham does not turn his head. 'I will not.'

'Edward, turn that thing off. I have something very important to say.'

'Of course I won't. Winnie's on in a minute.'

Crowned heads, uniforms loaded with bullion and stars, page boys with lace, a little blonde girl whose head just peeps over the balustrade, all smile and wave with jolly gentility.

'Edward. Charlie and this girl have been in the bathroom

together.'

This achieves an effect on everything except the television set. The tableau is perfect – they could all be waxworks; then Jane breaks the spell, by tossing her waves again; clearly she is more angry now than frightened, and properly angry – an emotion quite unlike Aunt Elizabeth's righteous wrath. The latter continues.

'I found the bathroom door locked. I knocked. I said I would wait. They came out. First the girl. Then Charlie.'

With his eyes still glued to the screen, which now shows film of the Union Jack billowing, then Big Ben, then Number 10 Downing Street, Mr Bosham begins to undo his belt, the broad belt that circles his spreading tummy. Charlie's mother resorts to the only strategem she knows for such occasions. She drops her plate of lettuce sandwiches and flees through the back room to the kitchen to have hysterics. Margaret Alderson puts her plate more carefully on the sideboard and goes after her to assist. Anne Bosham puts her thumb in her mouth and leans closer to the screen. Mr Alderson goes bright red and begins visibly to sweat.

Mrs Coleman, also Elizabeth, comes in through the french windows from the back garden where she has been admiring the display of the Bosham's Lilibet Floribundas. She had hoped to miss Churchill. Her husband was one of the Few, had been burnt to death in a Hurricane three years later, but the noise of Mrs Bosham's hysterics had signalled crisis. Her daughter displays relief with the slightest of dimpled smiles.

'They had,' Elizabeth Bosham goes on, 'been in the bathroom together. I think we can . . . hazard a guess . . . I mean . . .' Suddenly she goes scarlet and tears spring to her eyes too: 'It is disgusting, disgusting, horrible . . .' but she gets a grip on herself, holds on.

Still with his eyes on the screen, Mr Bosham stands and

unthreads the rest of the belt from the loops round his trousers – which not so miraculously do not fall down since he wears braces too; perhaps the belt has never been more than a weapon.

'They're not showing him,' he says. 'Just the voice. But it is live. Still. No better than the wireless really.'

He turns at last, faces his son.

Who, bruised-eyed, as tall as he, outfaces him with a stare that combines challenge, hate, and almost no fear at all. He has not been strapped for eighteen months, and he's a lot bigger now.

His father takes in this fact, as the familiar, measured, patrician yet idiosyncratic tones, the s's slightly lisped, drop lapidary phrases on the floor at his feet. Vaguely, but none the less fiercely, Mr Bosham senses the possible fracas if Charlie should put up a fight.

'Well. Young feller-me-lad. What do you have to say?'

Charlie takes his measure and visibly relaxes, runs stubby fingers through his nodding forelock.

'Jane went to the bathroom. I thought she had come out. I went in because the door was unlocked. She was just combing her hair. Then we came out. Isn't that right, Jane?'

Jane, relief blossoming proudly in her face, nods assent, but Elizabeth Bosham blazes out, 'Then why, young Charlie Bosham, was the door locked? Pray tell me that, young Charles. Why was it locked?'

Elizabeth Coleman tries: 'It's natural to lock the door as soon as you get in. Perhaps Charlie did that before he saw Jane was there.'

In the gathering gloom the sub-aqueous light flickers ghastlily about their faces.

It ish. Our dearesht hope. That the Queen. Shall be happy. And our resholve unshwerving. That her reign. Will be ash glorioush. Ash her devoted shubjectsh. Can help her to make it.

It won't wash. They all know it.

Charlie shrugs. 'She asked me. It was her idea.'

The assembled company see immediately the road he has signposted for them. All but the Colemans rush off down it. Jane does her best to bar the way, and blurts out, 'Yes. He was cheating. At Monopoly. Pete wanted to win. He should have won. I told him, I said, yes, yes, I'll go to the bathroom with you if you don't cheat no, any more. There.' Jane holds her defiant pose for a moment, realizes she has dug a pit for herself and so drops into it. 'It was my fault.' Her mother meets her halfway across the floor and folds her into her arms, letting her sob against the bosom Mr Bosham so much admires. George Alderson and Peter Coleman now join in the throng, standing wide-eyed and thumb-sucking in the space Jane has vacated.

Mrs Coleman moves her daughter towards them, brushes past minatory Elizabeth Bosham, takes Peter by the hand, and shuts the hall door carefully behind them.

We pray to have rulersh who sherve. To have neighboursh who comfort each other. And have peoplesh who thrive and proshper. Free from fear. May God glant ush such bleshings.

The front door bangs. Through the leaded bay window they see the Colemans fleeing down the short path to the gate set in the low privet hedge. They are still trying to sling on their raincoats.

'Mark my words,' says Elizabeth Bosham, 'that girl will be a hussy or worse, like her mother before her. Edward, if you have any sense, you'll fire the mother tomorrow.'

Massed orchestras and bands. God Save the Queen. What a din as it crescendoes into the second strophe! The men and boys are shiftless for a moment, then see how Elizabeth Bosham has straightened immaculately, head up, hands pressed flat to her box-pleated skirt. Awkwardly they adopt similar poses, then Mr Bosham leans forward, tweaks by the ear fat Anne from her chair and holds her thus upright as the last chords crash into silence.

'I will,' says Mr Bosham. 'If she has the cheek to come into the shop again, she'll find her cards waiting for her.' Secretly he is relieved, for he has recognized that with her around he will inevitably make a fool of himself with her sooner or later. Especially with the hot weather coming and not much business.

Margaret Alderson comes brightly through the back. 'Listen. We've put out a nice supper for us, and since the Message is voice only, why don't we all come through and listen to it on the wireless.'

The young tones are as limpid as pearls dropped in clear Malvern Spring water:

When I spoke to you last, at Christmas, I asked you, whatever your religion, to pray for me on the day of my coronation . . .

They sit themselves round the sandwiches, the Royal Doulton, the cup cakes, fruit cake, the biscuits, and the cosied pot. Mr Alderson picks up Mrs Coleman's collecting box.

'She left this behind.'

Throughout this memorable day I have been uplifted and sustained by the knowledge that your thoughts and prayers were with me . . .

Charlie takes a cup cake, bites off the icing and slip of angelica without bothering to ease it from its corrugated paper. His mother, still tear-stained, but much recovered, and smelling of gin, playfully slaps his wrist. 'Naughty boy. Sandwiches first.'

Mrs Bosham takes the box from Mr Alderson, shakes it and puts it down. 'Well,' he says, 'I don't know where to send it.' He picks up a knife and slits round the top, spills a handful of change on to the linen of the tablecloth.

I have been conscious too of the millions of others who have shared by means of wireless or television in their homes . . .

'I put in half a dollar.' He slips the half crown to one side.

'What about you Dave?' Since he has claimed the largest coin, he is now pleasantly conscious of having put others on a spot. His manager claims a florin.

The ceremonies you have seen today are ancient . . . origins are veiled in the mists of the past . . .

The ladies claim shillings, the children sixpences that had been provided by their parents. A new bronze hexagonal threepenny bit remains.

'Who's's that then? The thrummer. It must be Dad's. Mean old git. Just a thrummer.'

Parliamentary institutions, with their free speech and respect for the rights of minorities, and the inspiration of a broad tolerance in thought and expression . . .

'Where is Grandad?'

. . . part of our way of life and outlook.

Elizabeth Bosham stands, pushing back her chair so it tips against the wall behind her. 'Dear Lord. He went to the bathroom. He's been there ages.' She wags a finger at Charlie. 'If he's had a stroke . . . I'll never forgive you.'

As this day draws to a close I know that my abiding memory of it will be . . .

'She's going to mention Everest,' cries Margaret with glee. She has a cousin in New Zealand . . .

. . . not only the solemnity and beauty of the ceremony, but the inspiration of your loyalty . . .

Elizabeth returns. 'He's all right. But he wet himself and won't come out until he's got a change.'

Charlie's mother stands. 'I'll find something of Dad's.' Meaning her husband.

. . . thank you all from a full heart. May God bless you all.

Part Two

Baird and Skeffington, Estate Agents, High Street, Woolingham, not apparently a large establishment, but, apparently, prosperous. The Georgian bay windows were newly painted in glossy black, each small light neatly filled with a notice and – for Baird and Skeffington liked to be pacemakers in the art of selling houses – each notice embellished with a black and white but glossy photograph, well snapshot, of the property advertised, *Secluded freehold house on hill-top, large garden, exceptional views, 4 bed., 2 rec., central heating, 10 mins. London Bridge, £5950.* Half timbered, two gables framing a heavily studded door that would not have disgraced a castle.

Giles Marsh thought, five and a half if they're lucky, and pushed open the glossy eight-paned door. A bell chimed, and on the other side of a glossily varnished desk, with matching wooden filing cabinet behind her, a young girl looked up from the nails she was lacquering. Her hair was spun white gold, parted low on the right-hand side, puffed up a bit, but falling in curled underswags whose ends just touched a dainty chin. She was wearing a pleated Crimplene dress which clung nicely to her artificially rounded but probably attractive breasts.

'I have an appointment with Mr Bosham.'

Carefully not smudging the lacquer, using the sharp tip of a long nail, she swivelled in a leatherbound diary.

'Mr Marsh?' Her smile was that of an angel welcoming a particularly highly rated martyr at St Peter's Gate. 'Do step this way.'

Charlie Bosham, rising from a grey steel and leatherette adjustable office chair, stood to shake hands over an older, darker, larger desk than Doris's, and stubbed out with his left hand the Three Castles he had been smoking. He was faced with a man still in his twenties, but older than him, who, he noticed, with a sort of minor chagrin, was dressed with a sharpness – shirt striped in dove grey and white, knitted black silk tie, square-ended – that he, with limited means, aimed at but could not achieve. The face was open, smiling, the teeth gleamed again, the lips suggested generosity, but the skin was pock-marked and pale, the hair too black. A yid, thought Charlie. He was wrong. Giles Marsh was a Maltese, son of a wholesale and retail greengrocer and fruiterer.

Giles Marsh, on his side, registered with pleasure the presence of sweat on Mr Bosham's palm – it suggested insecurity. He took in the solidly built young man in front of him: the eyes too small with puffy lids, the hair fair but greased and combed into a not too competent version of a duck's arse, the large-boned physical strength that he had come to recognize as the essential characteristic of the Saxons he usually had to deal with. On the mental side he had learnt to respect their ignorance, stupidity, greed and capacity for malicious cunning – respect, yes, for these characteristics helped them to function as businessmen with quite respectable efficiency, although ultimately they remained almost always manipulable; especially, they were vulnerable to both flattery and the pinpricks of insult.

He sat down in one of a pair of Parker Knoll Dunsters, refused one of Charlie's Three Castles and lit a black Sobranie. But he complimented Doris on the aroma of the coffee she placed on a low glass-topped table at his elbow which had been painted, splattered and dribbled on in imitation of a Jackson Pollock. She spoilt the effect: 'Glad you like it, Mr Marsh; it's the new Nescafé, Blend 37. I thought you'd appreciate the continental flavour.'

'I'm sorry Mr Baird isn't here to see you,' Charlie began, leaning back in Mr Baird's swivel chair. 'He has a villa near Marbella which he always visits at this time of year.' This apology was word for word what Mr Baird had told him to say whenever a new face appeared in the office. Oddly enough for an estate agent, it was only one word of a lie. The villa was brand new. For the six summers before 1959, Mr Baird had taken his wife for ten days to the Royal Hotel at Bognor Regis.

'I am sure,' said Giles, 'Mr Baird's absence will present no problems, none at all. Now.' He unzipped a pig-skin document holder. 'As I told you on the phone, I represent people who for the moment wish to remain anonymous, but who are very interested in a property to the south of Woolingham. For reasons which will become clear, we are anxious to employ an agent with knowledge of the area in the preliminary stages of the matter, and you seemed to us to be ideally situated for that function . . .'

Charlie was by now both flattered by and in awe of the style of all this. One day, he determined, he would master the lingo, and use it with just such ease.

What remained of Skerrit's Farm consisted of two empty barns, an empty hen run, a very old sheep-dog, a younger tortoiseshell cat, a neglected and drought-ruined cottage garden, a farmhouse, parts of which were unrenovated Jacobean . . . and Mr and Mrs Skerrit.

'Doomsday Book, they was a Skerrit on this land,' old man Skerrit said, 'but they call him Sceret, S-c-e-r-e-t, in them days. But none to follow me. None now to follow me.' He glanced balefully across the table at his wife, who sat opposite him. She was a very large, pallid woman with horribly swollen legs. She looked as if she had sat in the high-backed, unupholstered wooden armchair for months if not years. 'Not much left for 'un if they was.'

Pale blue watery eyes glazed into a dream of the past as the old man stared out through uncleaned, diamond-leaded windows. 'Just a meadow now, that the council pays me rent for to use as an amenity, and they two cottages. Mrs Cartwright and Mrs Jackson. Widders both. Five shillings a week I get from each, and I can't put it up, not even to cover the slates that come off.'

Charlie leaned towards him. 'History,' he murmured. 'That's real history, Mr Skerrit. And I know my principals have deep respect for history. The development will be called Skerrit's Industrial Estate. I can promise you that.'

Mrs Skerrit stirred, smiled wanly. 'Estate, eh. There, that's grand isn't it? Skerrit's Estate.'

'Do you have,' Charlie went on, 'the contract with the council about you? I mean, here in the house? With regard to the use of Skerrit's Meadow and Brook as a public amenity.'

'Aye.' The old man got to his feet and lumbered across the room, which was cluttered with dark or black furniture, to a heavy bureau that stood in the corner. He rummaged behind the lid for some minutes, muttering to himself, 'Danged bills. Water rate. Electricity. Grandad never had no need of piped water. Used the brook and the well. Never did no harm. Candles and lamps. Here it is. No.'

'Try the secret drawer,' said Mrs Skerrit.

'Yes. Yes, this dooz be it.'

'There'd be no wireless nor television without there was electricity,' said Mrs Skerrit, then added with self-satisfied glee, '*The Archers* tonight, then that *Emergency Ward Ten*. I like that. You see, Mr Bosham, when I were in the Woolingham General, they had . . .'

'Mr Bosham don't want to hear nothing on your legs.'

'This is all right,' said Charlie. 'Fine. No problem.' He lurched back into the rocking chair they had put him in, steadied himself with both hands on the heavy oak table. What a load of junk, he thought. You'd have to pay a man to take it away and burn it. Not more than a fiver's worth in the whole room. In the whole house probably. 'Well, there you are, Mr Skerrit. That's the offer. And a very generous one it is too, I think you'll agree.'

A grandmother clock ticked like a slow drip of water. It

had a sun and moon that were meant to rise and fall appropriately, but since the moon was now up Charlie assumed that the facility had failed. The old dog stirred on the hearth rug, and its smell became briefly more nasty and obvious than before.

Mrs Skerrit cleared her throat: 'I've always wanted a nice bungalow. At Peacehaven. To end our days.'

Mr Skerrit was apologetic: 'Maud is not really country. Never was. Born in Woolingham.'

Charlie contrived cheeriness. 'Well, that's fine. A nice bungalow at Peacehaven would come at about three and a half, maybe four. That would leave you a nice nest-egg over. I could put you in touch with a very sound company that would give you an attractive annuity on the residue of, well, let's say, fifteen pounds a week . . . minimum.'

'Three and half?'

'Thousand. Three and a half thousand. Then buy an annuity to give you fifteen pounds a week.'

'We already get five pound a week from the bank from what I got compulsorily purchased off of me just as the war broke out. Where they put up that factory.'

'So with twenty pound a week, plus pension of four pound, you'll be very well off indeed, and no upkeep, like you have here on the farm and cottages.' Charlie hesitated . . . Twenty-four pounds a week was getting on for double his own income and he began to feel he'd offered too much, though substantially below what Giles Marsh had suggested. Too late now. He went on. 'It really is a very good offer. Mr Skerrit. Mrs Skerrit. I do hope you will give it very serious consideration.'

Charlie lit a black Sobranie, using his Ronson.

'Who'd like a cup of tea?' asked Mrs Skerrit, and to Charlie's astonishment she heaved herself on to her tree-trunk legs, which then, one after the other, ponderously carted her bulk to a dresser varnished deep brown to make pine simulate mahogany, from which she took three cups and saucers. The best in the house presumably, but with their old-fashioned sailing barges and windmills they looked pretty awful to Charlie. Then on she went towards the kitchen.

'Mr Marsh?'

'Yes.'

'Bosham here.'

'Who?'

'Bosham.' A moment's panic, then . . . the bastard, he's caught me again. Charlie injected irritation into his voice. 'Of Baird and Skeffington, Woolingham.'

'Of course. Well. How did it go?'

Heart pounding now, this was it, must keep very cool, must sound very cool indeed. 'Rather well, actually.'

'Jolly good.'

'You mentioned a figure. I think I can get Skerrit to accept a sum substantially lower.'

'You can? Jolly good.' Pause.

Hold on. Hold on, don't say anything.

'Bosham?'

'Yes?'

'Still there?'

'Yes.'

'Ah. You want to know what's in it for you?'

'Ye . . . urrmph.'

'I see. Well. Let's say twenty per cent of the difference between what we offered and what Skerrit will accept.'

'Fifty.'

Pause.

'Thirty.'

'Thirty plus the fee we agreed.'

Pause.

Marsh laughed. 'All right. So what is the figure?'

'Twelve.'

Pause.

'Well. Quite the little operator, aren't you? With the fee, you net yourself a round grand. OK. OK. But now listen, Bosham. I'm going to move on this quite quickly. Our solicitors will be in touch with Skerrit right away. You got the name of the people who act for him?'

'Mead and Mead, High Street, Woolingham. A chap called Dickson does the conveyancing.'

'Good. We'll have a deposit paid down by Thursday, and contracts drawn up as soon as possible after that. Understand?'

'Of course.'

'What about those tied cottages, then?'

'I've got it in hand.'

'Really?'

'Really.'

'OK, then. We'll be in touch. Ciao.'

'What?'

'Bye bye, Bosham.'

Charlie, sitting in Doris's chair, replaced the handset as if it were centuries-old precious glass, leant back and wiped sweaty palms on his trouser legs. He had not been so excited since that glimpse of the fresh brown haze of hair round the slit between Jane Coleman's legs six years before, and much of the physical reaction was the same: eyes that smarted hotly, a tightness in the throat – only the erection was missing, and that wasn't far off.

The office was still, warm, lit by a golden twilight that filtered through the slats of the almost closed Venetian blinds. Behind them one of the last flies of summer buzzed intermittently. He noticed a hair clip in the ashtray. Doris's. Doris. He began to go through the top drawer of her desk, the narrow one in which she was allowed to keep her personal things.

More Kirby grips. A lipstick. Nail polish, nail file, a small vial of Tabu eau de toilette. A photograph, postcard-size, in a black plastic frame, of a fresh-looking, chubby-cheeked boy with curly hair and glasses. Her boyfriend? Perhaps. Written across the bottom a date, 3/2/59, and the words: *That'll be the day.* Then right at the back a white compact and the sort of long box toothpaste is sold in, only thicker. Not a compact, although embossed on the lid with a gold filigree pattern. He opened it. A rubber dome mounted on a springy circle. Then the box. Ortho-gynol with applicator. Instructions. Sit with feet up, knees apart, squeeze the cap, and insert lengthways . . . With one hand he loosened one of her paper hankies from its packet.

One aspect of playing Rugby for the Old Sydneyans that Charlie did not like was the communal showering after the game. The bonhomie, the shouting through the drab, echoing chamber from whose ceiling drably grey shower heads were suspended, the swirling grey suds at his feet carrying tight little curls of pubic hair, the scum, other people's scum, swirling through his toes: all this offended, not his fastidiousness – no one could ever accuse Charlie of being fastidious – but his sense of his own privateness, his separateness.

It was the horseplay that he minded most – the flicked wet towels, raising a welt on an unwary rump, the bar of cheap soap tossed about the echoing room, the laughter of the other chaps when one tried to push a fist into a shirt sleeve that some cunning sod had knotted. Behind it all he sensed, though never verbalized, the latent homosexuality, the unmentionable secret they all shared.

He put up with it for a variety of reasons. He liked the game. As a prop forward, first in the colts, then in the second team, and now on trial for the first, he enjoyed pitting his weight, his bones, his muscles against his opposite number in the set scrums, the solid jar of shoulder against shoulder (catch him wearing a shoulder pad!), the horse-like heave of back, thighs, shins, the toes of his boots scrabbling for a hold in the mud, then the release as the other side gave and then broke, and the opportunity came to trample and heave aside the torsos out of which the push had gone. Better still were the scrimmages and rucks, where flying elbows, raised boots, lowered shoulders could be used even more ruthlessly, a hand could be pushed into the face of an opponent with the thumb searching for his eye, and the cleated boot hunt for an exposed thigh.

But there were other factors. After three years as a scholarship boy who had achieved entry through success in a purely mechanical 'intelligence' test into the state-aided. albeit still largely fee-paying, ancient grammar/public day school, he had become bored with almost every aspect of the curriculum except Rugby football. He achieved five 'O' levels – in English, Maths, Religious Knowledge, History and Geography, but failed the rest. Failed them not because he lacked the ability, but because where the body of knowledge to be mastered was boring, and the method by rote, he just would not be bothered. And so, against the advice of father, teachers, friends, he abandoned, commendably early, the road to success via the professions or related trades.

However, he had realized too that by dropping out he was in danger of cutting himself off from the network of 'old boys' in influential positions – doctors, solicitors, senior civil servants in local government, and so on – and so he had paid up his subs to the Old Sydneyan Soc., bought the appropriate tie, and earned and kept his place in their Rugby teams.

In the event it proved to be a poor investment, but that's by the way.

To begin with, the going had been tough, since, while he was sixteen, most of his team-mates were eighteen or more, but now, at twenty, he was accepted as a very competent player, and was on trial for the first fifteen. Some of his colleagues had been ready, too, to treat him as an 'oick' but had soon learnt that an elbow in the eye, followed by a fulsome apology, was the consequence of overt snobbery on their part. And the selection committee began to recognize his usefulness: particularly his ability to intimidate and occasionally injure the opposition without drawing the referee's attention.

So, on Saturday, 5 September 1959, he turned up at the alma mater to play for the Possibles against the Probables and had, by 5.00 p.m., sufficiently lifted his aggression potential to a level that indicated a Probable. Knowing that he had badly bruised the opposing hooker's toe, and opened an old scar on the opposing fly-half's eyebrow, he assumed that that was why Terry Mead, who was hon. sec. of the Old Sydneyans, singled him out under those awful showers.

'Have a jar later?'

A moment to remember the right way to answer, then: 'Why not?'

He watched Terry, who was now tall and thin, a wing three-quarter, and even beakier nosed than ever, soaping his scrotum and circumcized prick with exhibitionary enthusiasm, and then repeated, 'Why not indeed?'

Except in the depths of winter, Rugby Union played at the adult level kicks off as late as reasonably possible, anyway not before half past three. This may be to give the teams time to sober up after the lunchtime session; more probably, the aim is to keeping the gap between showering and evening opening time as narrow as possible.

On that particular evening then, most of both teams sauntered up from the Philip Sydney through the leafy sun-soaked avenues of the posher part of Woolingham, timing their arrival at the Prince of Wales at dead on six o'clock. They were dressed in flannels or cavalry-twill drainpipes, with old school ties knotted below unbuttoned shirt collars, or silk scarves in the same colours tied like cravats, and, for the evening was warm, they either trailed their jackets near the ground or wore them slung across their shoulders like capes.

The Prince of Wales had many bars, a restaurant with help-yourself carvery, and a small ballroom with a sprung floor where there were still dinner dances every other Saturday night, though telly had cut the clientele by half. It smelt of sour beer, cabbage and cigars – a mixture which, though objectively horrible, is generally recognized at a subconscious level by aficionados as the very warm, welcoming essence of such places. They are wombs for the infantile regressive in all of us males, places where the responsibilities of existence can be shrugged off, anxiety and guilt drowned in alcohol, nicotine and bonhomie.

On the way up, Charlie speculated. The invitation to a 'jar' had been superfluous – Terry knew that Charlie would be amongst those present. It meant therefore that he had something particular to say or ask. Perhaps, as hon. sec., he was going to sound out Charlie as to his availability to play first-fifteen rugger before the selection committee made a formal offer of a cap . . .

For the first hour or so it seemed Terry was avoiding him. Five pints had been sunk, the rowdier element were already carolling the obscene version of 'Old King Cole' so loved by rugger players for the felicity of its wit and its adaptability to local patriotism:

'Push it in and out, in and out, said the tailors,
Merry men are we,
But none so fair as can compare,
With Sydneyans' RFC.'

But it was the fact that Charlie had stayed near the centre of a small caucus that represented the minority lower-caste element in the teams – chaps who were already making their way as sellers of used cars, insurance, or as local government clerks, bank tellers – that kept Terry away. At last he leant into the group and tapped Charlie on the shoulder.

'A word in your shell-like, old boy.'

'Of course.'

'In the snug, if that's all right with you.'

'Sure.'

The small private bar was almost empty – a couple canoodled without actually snogging over Babycham and pale ale, and two men, perhaps thirty years old, put the finishing touches to a deal: 'It's swings and roundabouts, old chap, I grant you that, but I aim to win on the roundabouts – the other buggers can lose on the swings.' They lowered their voices as Terry and Charlie came in.

'Aye, Aye, Aye, Aye. In China they do it for chilli
So let's have another one, that's worse than the
other one . . .'

Terry placed a jar each on the marble-simulated top of the table.

'I'm not too keen on this stuff from pressure barrels, are you? Shame all the pumps have been taken out. Still, if it saves you a bob or two in the evening, then it gets my vote. Bung-ho.'

They drank, put their mugs down on the Watney Mann mats.

'I'll not beat about the bush. You know Lissie, Felicity, my sister.'

'There was an old man of Madras
Whose balls were made out of brass
In windy weather
They clanged together
And sparks came out of his arse.'

Charlie had met her twice, but not for three or four years. Dimly he remembered a thin girl, not tall, pale, a year or so younger than him. Even at the height of adolescent randiness she had not seemed attractive.

All the more surprising then when Terry leant forward and, in a much lowered voice, almost a whisper, went on, 'She's bought one. Copped it. Got a bun in the oven.'

Charlie steadied himself, said nothing, waited.

'Well, the chap doesn't want to know. Can't blame him. Lissie admits she led him on. Get a chap too far on and there's no stopping him. Anyway. Got to do something. Don't know what. Chaps up in Harley Street cost a bomb. Fifty notes. More, sometimes. Can't raise that sort of lucre.'

Charlie still waited, though his slightly puffy eyes narrowed a little, perhaps his normally thickish lips looked thinner. Then he felt in his pocket, took out a box of black Sobranie, lifted the lid and pushed it across to Terry, who said, 'No thanks. Prefer my own,' and lit a Players.

'Well,' he went on. 'I thought perhaps you could help.'

Charlie's pale eyebrows lifted a fraction.

'I mean. Well. Dash it, Charlie.' A touch of pleading bonhomie injected now to soften what might have been construed as an insult. 'At Sydney you were always a bit of a fixer. And you've got a sister nursing at St Chad's. Well. You know, she might know someone, needy medic, that sort of thing, in need of a bob or two, who would undercut the Harley Street mob . . .'

Raised voices from the larger bar. *All right, squire. All right. No need for the Boys in Blue. I take your drift. We will remove our valued custom to pastures new.*

'I'll look into it,' said Charlie at last. 'I'll see what I can do.'

'Oh, you're a good scout, Charlie, Always were. See. Between you, me and the gatepost, there's going to be a general election soon. Very soon. And the male Dop'll be having his last fling for Woolingham with the best chance he's had. Now if it got out that his daughter . . .'

'I take your point,' said Charlie. 'I take take your point. I'll do my best, see what can be done. Can't say fairer than that.'

'Of course you can't, old chap. Of course you can't.'

On his way back to Goldsmith Drive through the warm September gloaming, Charlie took a detour round the outside of the Flowers Estate to Skerrit's Meadow. There, in a clump of brambles with fly-brown blackberries under his nose and used contraceptives under his feet, he had a lengthy piss and looked over the bushes at the two flint-stone cottages that stood between him and his first grand.

On both sides, television light glimmered through net curtains from back parlours; on one side, four or five bits of washing hung luminously above bolted lettuces and cabbage stalks, and four scraggy hens clawed at the grit beneath.

Something had to be done. Something must be done, but what! He shook himself, zipped up. Almost his first zip, his first Terylene-mixture slacks. No matter how you shake your peg, the last drop's down your trouser leg. He pushed through the brambles, right up to the low paling fences, and heard, as it were in stereo, from two sets at once, the closing chorus of *The Black and White Minstrel Show*. Oh dem Golden Slippers. He stooped, rummaged in the dried grass and thistles, and came up with two white and grey flint cores, each of which fitted snugly in the palms of his hands. Then, Billy Liar-like, plucked with his teeth the imaginary pin from the first of his imaginary hand-grenades, and lobbed it easily over the fifteen yards to drop satisfactorily onto the bottom pane of the first back-parlour window. He did the same on the other side, sprinted, vaulted the wall into the road, and sauntered back to the fronts of the cottages.

Two angry old ladies at their gates.

'You seen 'em mister? You seen 'em? Which way they go?'

'Two youths? Yes, I saw them. They went that way.' In his poshest accent, pointing up Daffodil Road. 'Teddy boys, I deh say they were. Yes. Teddy boys.'

'Dang them, the varmints. The bloody varmints.'

He peered through the gloom. One old lady was thin, beetle-browed, the other plumper, rosier. Both wore shawls, black skirts, thick stockings, bedroom slippers.

'Why don't you ring the police?' he suggested with malice, for he knew they'd have no telephones, and they wouldn't go up into the Flowers Estate to the nearest public box.

He walked on, quietly whistling a Cliff Richard number, and feeling better. At least he'd had a sight of the enemy.

'Someone's been in my drawers,' said Doris, pouting and frowning. 'Sure they have.'

'Wish I had.'

For a moment, the enormity of this froze both of them: she, head bent over the desk so that her hair fell forward, almost masking her face, the turned-in ends meeting in front of her mouth; he, standing just inside the street doorway, pulling at the poppers of the parka he wore when he was on his Vespa. They both blushed, then he strode across to Mr Baird's door, past the empty desk he usually occupied in the front of the office opposite Doris's, and was, as far as she was concerned, gone.

She stared for a moment at the shut door, and composure returned – cheek! she thought. But he might be quite nice, never thought of him in that way before. Then she returned to examining the evidence.

Twenty minutes later, having recombed her hair,

checked powder and lipstick, and given herself a squirt from the Tabu atomizer, she knocked and went in with the mail.

In fact there was very little – in early September the house-buying season is generally closing down, which was why Mr Baird used to pick these weeks for Bognor and now Marbella. There were a couple of requests to be put on the mailing list, two cheques from solicitors – fees on sales concluded at the end of the previous week – and a letter from Giles Marsh with the letterheading 'Belgravia Properties':

With regard to our conversation and correspondence re Skerrit's Farm, I am pleased to inform you that a cheque representing a returnable deposit of ten per cent of the agreed purchase price has been placed with Mr Dickson of Mead and Mead, High Street, Woolingham, and that contracts will be drawn up. I take leave to remind you that these will be on the basis of unoccupied freehold throughout.

Get those old bags out.

'There was, you know,' said Doris.

'What?'

'Someone in my top drawer. I know 'cos there was an unopened packet of hankies in there and now it's opened and one gone.'

'I expect you forgot you opened it.'

She shrugged, tossed her hair in a way that momentarily, and for a reason he could not quite place, recalled that haze of soft, pale brown hair between Jane Coleman's legs.

'Well, maybe. But perhaps you should make sure that nothing's gone from here.'

That afternoon, before the bank shut, he paid one of the cheques that had come in the morning into the petty-cash account. The next morning, Tuesday, he used one of the petty-cash cheques Mr Baird had left signed but otherwise unfilled-in to draw out four hundred pounds cash. He spent most of the rest of the day rehearsing how he would conduct the evening's interviews; he went to the public library and found on the electoral roll the names of the occupants of Skerrit's Cottages; he got Doris to type out two forms of receipt for two hundred pounds each. He did all this with a heavy, dull sense of resentment. A grand was what he'd been after – he could see now no way of getting more than six hundred.

As he walked up the short garden path – the gate swung to and relatched itself with a click behind him – he could hear the signature tune and chimes of Big Ben announcing the evening news. He had chosen to visit Mrs Cartwright first – the smaller, plumper of the two women – simply because he believed small plump women are more easily bullied than tall thin ones.

'I don't know who you are, or what you want, but you'll 'ave to come and watch the news out before I'll speak to you.'

The General Election will be on Thursday, 8 October . . . The Prime Minister, who lunched with the Queen at Balmoral . . . flew back to London to chair a cabinet meeting at 10 Downing Street. . . an hour later the following statement was issued . . .

Charlie, bored, looked around him. A tiny parlour, not much more than eight feet by eight feet with a low sash window, the bottom pane patched with cardboard. A dresser, black and heavy. A mantelpiece with two yellow and white pottery dogs, not at all life-like, pop-eyed, flop-eared. Brass spoons, horse brasses hung on leather straps, a couple of candlesticks. All junk except a small serviceable Formica-topped table that might fetch five bob.

. . . The opposition leader, Mr Gaitskell, and shadow foreign minister, Mr Bevan, are in Moscow visiting the Russian leader, Mr Khrushchev. However, a spokesman

from Transport House welcomed the news. Labour are eager to go to the polls, believing that policies for social justice, fair distribution of wealth and solid retrenchment in the economic sphere are what the people of Britain now want . . .

Mrs Cartwright half turned back to him, peering up through thick, ugly glasses: 'You come about the house then?'

Charlie nodded.

'Yer. Old Man Skerrit come up yesterday and said how he were selling and like the new owners will want no tenants. We'll see this out, then I'll get her next door in and we'll see what's what. Sit down, if yer want.'

Charlie perched on the edge of a high-backed chair by the understairs cupboard. There was a strong smell of gas and old newspapers. Toss a match in, that would sort it all out quick enough. He swallowed, blinked, knew he lacked the nerve.

On show at Farnborough is the front line of Britain's defences for the sixties – and the technical revolution on our doorstep is as evident here as in any other aspect of our lives. The two-stage guided Black Knight rocket is capable of delivering a two-megaton nuclear warhead; the tactical Thunderbird and Sea Cat . . .

Her next door? He'd planned to see them separately, but . . . well, why not. Get it all over quicker.

After some scattered showers today the weather tomorrow will again be generally warm and bright . . .

'We got no showers love, did we? Could have done with it too and all. Right, that's that.'

Mrs Cartwright reached forward, turned the set off, picked up a large black poker from the fireplace and rattled it on the cast-iron fire-back, which figured St George and the Dragon. A moment, then the rattle came back from the other side.

'She's coming.'

Charlie had got it wrong about their characters. Not that it mattered. Mrs Cartwright was the leader, the one to be dealt with. Mrs Jackson was thin but wispy, not tough, older or less well preserved than her neighbour, with hands knotted by arthritis into knobbly claws that could barely cope with the mug of milky tea Mrs Cartwright set down in front of her.

Neither wanted to move or be moved, but both seemed unaware of their rights in the matter, at least not fully aware. They spoke of not wanting to cause trouble, they never had, but there, when all was said and done, a roof over your head, you could call, in a manner of speaking, your own, was not to be given up lightly. Mrs Cartwright admitted, when pushed, that her Billy would take her in for a time, till she found somewhere else, but Mrs Jackson had nobody. Mrs Jackson recalled that there was talk of the council building flats especially for the elderly, and they both brightened considerably at the thought. 'I'd like a nice council flat,' said Mrs Jackson, 'and no garden to worry about.'

At this point, Charlie produced two large manila envelopes, unsealed them, and deliberately but quite quickly counted out of each forty five-pound notes. Mesmerized, the two old ladies watched the large blue sheets, each with Britannia and St George, flicker by, then Charlie pushed them together, turned each stack over – a lion passant regardant holding a key – and placed one in front of each on the Formica-topped table.

'There,' he said. 'Earnest of my principals' good faith and their awareness of their responsibilities, both legal and humane. Not yours when the deal with Mr Skerrit is finalized, but yours now. To cover your expenses and tide you over until you find somewhere else. If you'll just sign these receipts . . .

With the callow optimism of cowardly youth he now hoped

that would be that – that things would take their course, that Jackson and Cartwright would move out, and that all manner of things would be well.

What did bother him was that, as things stood, Mr Baird was going to be able to detect that four hundred pounds had gone out of petty cash, and, hopefully, back in again. Even if Charlie had made no entry in the petty-cash book itself, the bank slips and statements would eventually arrive and show four hundred in cash out and four hundred in cash in. This led Charlie to think about book-keeping, in particular and in general, in a more positive way than he had before: hitherto, he had made entries and carried out the simple calculations required with bored ease, not fully understanding the significance of what he was doing. Now he sensed possibilities, and with the aid of *Teach Yourself Book-keeping* began to master simpler intricacies of the science. It didn't help his immediate problem – though he realized that, if he kept his eye open for the quarterly statement of accounts with ledger slips from the bank, he should be able to subtract the two relevant ones without Baird knowing. Doris, though, might have to be enlisted when the time came, either to do it herself or provide a diversion.

That would leave only the typed entries on the actual statements. Well, generally, the petty cash was his responsibility and if he simply followed his usual practice of preparing a quarterly digest – so much in, so much out, balance stands at – the chances were he'd get away with it.

And if he didn't, so what. The money had gone out, the money would come back, why should Mr Baird worry?

So long as it did come back.

Monday, 14 September, at about 11.00 a.m., Doris was polishing her nails again, and Charlie was sitting in his own, identical desk, opposite hers, drinking Blend 37. At first, during Baird's absence, he had enjoyed the status of having his coffee in the boss's grand, grey-steel, adjustable office armchair, but more recently, as he had begun to appreciate Doris's charms more clearly, he had been able to forget that she was an 'oick' from the Flowers, and therefore definitely touchable but not to be talked to. Above all he had a sense of her potential as an ally, and so he spent more time with her in the front office.

'They reckon the Odeon's going to be one of them bowling alleys,' said Doris.

'Yes?' Charlie was looking at an ad in the *Sketch* for the new Hillman Minx. It had a nice American look to it, like a Chevy in a way. Wrap-round fenders, tail-wings. Seven hundred and sixty-four pounds, sixteen shillings and tuppence. Perhaps old Baird would get shot of the Wolseley he used to drive punters around in and get something a bit slicker.

'It's daft really. You can spend twice what you do in a cinema at a bowling alley, and you can't snog neither. Well, that's what my boyfriend says, anyway.'

She has a boyfriend. Of course. That class of girl always does. Watch out then. The Dutch cap not just for the off-chance, but special purchase. That new family-planning place over in Lewisham.

'I don't know why they call him 'Supermac, do you? I mean he's so *old*.'

Bored now with Doris's serendipitous line of unconnected chat, Charlie was about to return to his master's office and *Teach Yourself Book-keeping* when the telephone rang.

'Baird and Skeffington,' chirped Doris. 'Yes, yes, he's here. Do you want to speak to him? I can take a message. The Prince of Wales. At twelve. And the name, sir? Giles Marsh. Yes, I have . . . Ooh! he's rung off. That must have been that fancy dark bloke come in ten days ago . . . '

As Charlie kicked down the stand of his Vespa, a voice called to him across the hot tarmac of the carpark.

'Bosham!'

There he was. Greasy yid. Sitting in a low Austin Healey Sprite, racing green, hood down. Bastard.

'Ah, Bosham. There you are.'

'Shall we . . . ?' Charlie was about to say, 'Shall we go in?', expecting at any rate to have a pie and a beer with Marsh, if not a steak lunch, but he sensed in time that lunch was not on.

'Listen, Bosham. I can't stop. But I'd just like to know what you're playing at. That oaf Skerrit says he knows nothing about those two old bags moving out. I sent a chap round the other day and he says they look dug in there for ever. So. Well, Bosham, I just have to tell you this. Those cottages must be vacant possession on Monday, 5 October, or the deal is off. That gives you just three weeks. So get your skates on.'

He gunned the engine of his sports car, backed into his own exhaust, and was gone.

Charlie was ready to burst with anger, frustration and fear, and he knew the last of these was the killer. If he let his mind dwell on the deficit of four hundred pounds and Mr Baird back in the office on 12 October, fear would give way to despair and despair would numb him into inaction.

He kicked his Vespa back into life and, helmet-and-goggleless, parka flapping like a mad thing behind him, whipped his way down and up the leafier avenues of Woolingham, over the top and through the Flowers, and so to Skerrit's Cottages.

Mrs Cartwright was in her front patch of garden pulling up the dead, sticky ends of petunia and lobelia plants. In a basket on the path beside her she had some well-established, in some cases already budding, dahlias.

She straightend, wincing slightly, palms on her fat buttocks, then wiping them on her apron.

'Ah. It's you back, then, is it?'

'Yes. Now, if you don't mind I have a word or two to say to you . . .'

'And I to you, young man.'

'I gave you two hundred pounds . . .'

'Which, if you give me that receipt, you can have back.'

Hope there. Yes. Get back the four hundred and duck out of the whole awful business.

She saw his hesitation and went on, 'And glad to. Mind, I don't say I shan't move. Very probably I shall. But when I'm properly fixed up with somewhere to go. Them are me rights. My son, Billy, says so, he's been into it all. And meantime you can have your two hundred back, and I'll get my dahlias in. Billy give'm me, he's got more'n he wants in his allotment, and they last through nicely to November and beyond if the frosts ain't bad.'

'And what about Mrs Jackson?'

'Her next door? Ah well, that's different, see. She's out, gone already, went yesterday afternoon. Into a council transit home they call it, but it looks like the workhouse to me. Pending transferral to one of them new single-person flats. Which, by the by, she will have that fitted carpet in, she tells me, in that Bri*-Lon, floor to floor, on your two hundred quid, and a three-piece suite too, she tells me, and made-up curtains, though what she wants that for I don't know. I shan't miss her, never fear, always whining on about something . . .'

'Mrs Cartwright, if she's gone, you have to go!' Charlie was shouting, almost screaming now. 'Can't you see? The cottages go together. If she's gone, you've bloody got to go yourself. By October . . . in a fortnight. You'll be hearing about this, I promise you. Yes. I'll have . . .'

He stopped. Ten paces away, pasted to Mrs Cartwright's front-parlour window, was a picture of a benign, smiling, kindly, quite elderly gentleman, and the legend in blue: *Vote for Freddie Mead and the Next Five Years.*

More quietly, but with yet more menace: 'You'll be

hearing from our solicitors on this matter. That I can assure you, Mrs Cartwright. You'll be hearing from them.'

In 1959 the nurses' home at St Chad's was more like a house of correction than the expression of the Nursing Ideal its designer had intended. Outside, the Ruskinian polychrome terracotta and brickwork had been ruined in a variety of ways – by bomb-blast, by an accretion of fire escapes and steaming pipes (the hospital laundry had been built on as an annexe), but most of all by smog and pigeons. Black grease and guano smirched everything. Inside, bedrooms that had been planned for two now held four student nurses; the once proud refectory which had had mosaics based on designs by Lord Leighton depicting Seven Wise and Seven Foolish Virgins and of Mary Magdalene washing Jesus's feet had been painted over in two-tiered shiny cream and shiny green like the wards in the hospital itself. What had been the library with oak carrels and a substantial collection of standard medical texts, selected in the first place with the approval of no less a person than Nightingale herself, was now an echoing common room with stackable leatherette chairs and two ping-pong tables. It was the only place in the whole building, indeed in the whole complex of St Chad's, where a student nurse could talk to a male from the outside world, even a brother.

Anne Bosham at eighteen was as attractive as she was ever to be. The spots that had afflicted her from her tenth year had gone, leaving a tracery of shallow scars; the brace too had gone, the dentures were to come; she was not as fat as she had been, nor as she would be again. Still, she had Charlie's puffy eyes and thick lips, but lacked his florid colouring – her mousey hair had none of the reddish touches that lit his; where his complexion shone with reasonable good health, hers was grey and tiny blackheads crowded over her snub nose. At best, even when taken care of, it was the sort of face we are prepared to find not unattractive on a man; women who are born with it and further compromise it with bad diet and despair are denied for ever any pretension to good looks.

This was one cause of the solid core of resentment which was to be central to Anne's personality for the next ten years. There were others. Whatever cisterns of affection their parents had had, or even concern for anyone other than their separate selves, had been drained, squeezed dry, on their first-born male before she even appeared. Whatever talents, inherited or acquired, he had she shared, but while the caste of the society into which they were born took some pains to develop his, albeit with the sole aim of turning him into a greedy, small-minded, but cunning businessman, hers were suppressed or warped. Eventually her cow of a mother realized that she had an unmarriageable daughter on her hands: she then followed the already often given advice of her sister-in-law Aunt Elizabeth, and pushed Anne into nursing.

She went quite readily. It was an escape from home, promised some sort of independence, her contemporaries at school declared they envied her her 'vocation'. Anne had never been envied for anything else before, or praised. She had no idea what a vocation was, and took no pains to find out.

No love was lost between her and Charlie, but at least they had no illusions about each other. Their relationship was the most honest and open either had ever had. When he came into the echoing drab room, empty apart from two Nigerians who played table tennis with unacceptable skill, they did not kiss or touch or even greet each other. Anne simply led Charlie to two chairs by a grubby window that overlooked the black tarmac of the carpark, the steaming pipes, the high windows of St Chad's, and the tall chimney whose smoke signified the passing of unwanted bits – cancered lungs, smashed legs, unwanted or malformed foetuses.

'Well, Charlie.'

He hesitated for a second, then plunged straight in: 'Friend of mine. His sister's in trouble. You know what I mean?'

He glanced sidelong at her. She nodded.

'Silly cow,' she said.

'Yes. Well. Her GP is a friend of her father's, and she's a minor. Anyway, he's not the sort to cook up a certificate on psychological grounds. She, they, that is she and her brother, who came to me in the first place, can't afford the Harley Street cowboys. They wondered if you knew a medic here who would fix her up.'

She bit her nails.

'You're not the father?'

'Hell, no.' This was said so laconically that she knew he was telling the truth. Machismo would have crept in if he had put a girl in the club.

She chewed on, then: 'How much?'

'Twenty.'

'And for me?'

'Five.'

'Ten, and I'll help.'

Could the Mead kids get together thirty? Probably not. If you can't afford fifty your not going to find thirty. Never mind. If necessary, and if he got what he needed out of it all, he'd pay Anne her whack himself.

'Done.'

For a second their eyes met and the faintest glimmer of a smile was shared between them, an expression of recognition rather than feeling. They had each other's numbers and knew it.

For a moment Charlie hesitated at the gate of The Rowans,

Acacia Avenue. It was a large Edwardian villa with big sash windows on either side of an imposing porch, substantial oak door, featuring a large, fluted brass knob. Brick-built, stuccoed to a grey finish, original slate roof, laid in the front to easy-upkeep lawns with well-established laurels. Recent double garage to the left of the gravel drive-in and a new Jaguar Mark II. Grace. Space. Pace. Very nice, but plastered with those posters: *Vote for Freddie Mead and the Next Five Years.*

In he went and found a ceramic bell-push, brass-ringed.

A girl. Thin, dark, dressed in a blue, figure-hugging suit with three-quarter-length sleeves trimmed at the cuffs and lapels with deep blue velvet. High heels, also blue. A girl less thin would have looked curvaceous in it, a curvaceous girl fat.

'Hullo. You must be Mr Bosham. Charles. Terry said you would call about now. He rang. He's awfully sorry but he's held up, some teribly boring student-union thing, should have been over by two, but they're recalling the president or something and he's been made a teller. Too teasing. Come and meet the Dops.'

Fortunately Charlie already knew from the classier clientele of Philip Sydney that this signified Dear Old Parents.

To wipe his feet or not? Buggered if he would. She almost had a figure from behind, in that suit. Perhaps after all not so surprising that some sod had bothered to get his leg over.

A large room, green and white. Feature: polished marble fireplace, the real thing. Pictures in gilt frames. Glazed polished cupboards, there's a posh name for them, can't remember it, full of plates and glass, much of the glass whirly and strange. Large, oval, mahogany table, with six chairs to match.

Mr Mead, tall, heavy, Terry's conk of a nose, in baggy grey suit, complexion to match, looks tired, hair lank and dead-looking. Mrs Mead, thin, mother of Lissie, pale grey woollen dress, pale bluish-grey hair, good hairdresser, pearls, black court shoes.

'This is Charles Bosham. Old Sydneyan. Come to see Terry.'

'How do you do's all round. Very well, thank you, *not* pleased to meet you. And madam certainly isn't. A touch haughty. Just finished tea. Could have another pot made. A hint's a hint. No, thank you. I had mine before I came out.

Suddenly Charlie was alone with Mr Freddie Mead.

'Awkward hiatus, actually. The ladies want to tittivate,' he murmured. 'Big night tonight, you see.'

'Oh. Really? Sir.'

'Yes. Actually.'

'Really.'

Freddie Mead drifted away from the fireplace to a sort of chest in a corner with very thin drawers. He pulled one out.

'My father collected these.'

Obediently Charlie stepped to his shoulder. Rows of chips of stone.

'Flint arrowheads. He picked them up on Woolingham Down. Where the Flowers Estate now is. He was quite something of an antiquarian.'

The drawer was pushed shut. It left an attractive though musty smell in the air. Spiced wood.

'Big meeting tonight, you see. The PM's coming. Well, he's in Bromley tonight, so it isn't much of a chore for him. Jolly decent of him, all the same. It might be just that bit extra we need.'

A door clicked. Madam.

'Freddie?'

'Yes, dear.'

'I think you should change. You have time.'

'If you say so, dear.'

‘I do say so.’

‘Very well.’

For a moment Charlie thought he was on his own. He wondered: what are flint arrows worth, then sensed a presence behind him. Lissie. Still in the same suit but now with a high-crowned cloche with a big-bowed ribbon on her head, and a huge blue rosette pinned to her flat chest.

‘I’ve just been out in the country, actually,’ she said brightly. Her voice was high, almost grating. ‘Gloucestershire. The Cotswolds. Eric drove me back. We came over that new flyover. Chiswick. Quite the thing, really. Did the Dop tell you the PM is speaking for him tonight?’

‘Yes.’ That was bald. He added, ‘Actually.’

‘So we are in a bit of a tizzy. You must excuse us. Terry will be here. Directly. I’m sure.

A long silence. Long enough almost for one to become conscious of dust-fall.

‘I believe you’re to fix me up.’

More dust fell.

‘I think that’s right. You’ll fix me up. Isn’t that it?’

‘Yes.’

‘Well, that will be a relief. Point is. Not much . . . brass around. Well, I’ve spent my allowance, nothing now till Christmas – I mean, these rags cost forty guineas, would you believe? And poor old Terry’s up to his eyes with his dinners and all that, and he’s had trouble with his car. So?

‘Twenty-five.’

‘As much as that?’

‘Guineas.’

‘Oh dear. Oh well. I suppose you won’t take a rain check until I’m twenty-one? I’ll have thousands then, all of my own.

He knew she would cry if he didn’t say something, and he hated women to cry. It always seemed like a demand for something – a hankie at the very least. ‘Your grandfather’s arrowheads. Very interesting. Your father showed them to me.'

She gave a huge sniff. 'Yes. I think he thinks you're interested and that's why you came. Another friend of Terry's did that.' She gave another sniff, walked over to the case and pulled out another drawer. 'He collected coins too.' He stood behind her. A subtler scent that Doris's. As she bent over for the coins, her short dark hair lifted to reveal the nape of her neck. A sudden rush of emotion swept over him. This upper-class chick was a broad, a hussy, no better than she should be, no better than Doris. And this one was vulnerable. Doris had her defences. This one was already penetrated, the enemy had got in and sacked her, left behind a bun in the oven and signposts for those who might want to come after.

She turned, brushing her body against his, lifted her head.

'You may kiss me if you want to. Most men do.'

He did. But Charlie was not good at kissing, and he did it rather awkwardly, giving an entirely spurious impression of gentleness. He also gave the cloche a rakish tilt.

'Thank you,' she murmured. 'And thank you for getting me fixed.' She moved a step off, having heard a sound, a stair creak perhaps, that he had not detected.

Her mother came in, she too now wearing a hat and the same blue rosette.

'I was showing Mr Bosham Grandad's coins. This is a Kruger half a crown. Issued by the South African rebels in the Boer War. Rather interesting, don't you think? And this is . . . '

'Your hat's crooked. Isn't your father down yet?'

'We haven't seen him.'

'I do wish he'd hurry up. We have to be at the Conservative Club at six to meet the PM. His secretary particularly asked Daddy to have a briefing chat with him on local issues and it will look awful if we're late.'

'It's only half past five.'

Daddy came in. This suit was darker, cleaner, better pressed.

'There you are. Well. I think we can be off,' Mrs Mead straightened the Old Sydneyan tie, flicked dust off his shoulder. 'Aren't you wearing one of these?' She touched her rosette.

'I don't think so.'

A chill.

'Very well.' Pause. 'Well, everyone, time to be off.' Mrs Mead included Charlie.

God, she doesn't want to leave me in the house on my own. Afraid I'll walk off with arrowheads and Kruger half-crowns. Twirly glass.

Without a word Charlie followed Mrs Mead and Lissie out on to the gravel by the new Jaguar, and Mr Mead closed the heavy, brass-fitted door behind them. It clunked with the solid precision of a space vehicle's hatch in a science-fiction film.

'I'm sure Terry will be here directly,' said Mrs Mead from inside the lovely car. Grace. Space. Pace.

'Please do wait,' pleaded Lissie, large brown eyes filling again.

Bastards, thought Charlie, as the deep gravel crunched beneath the broad tyres. He sat on the low brick post that marked the entrance to the drive, and smoked.

Fifteen minutes later, Terry arrived in his 'banger', a 1951 MG Midget.

'Hullo there. Sorry to keep you waiting. Are they all out?'

'Now. Yes. They've gone to some meeting.' Charlie stubbed his cigarette on the brickwork, making as large and black a smear as he could.

'Oh Lord. And they turned you out to wait for me here.'

He straightened from popping up the canvas hood. 'Really, the Dops are the loveliest people, but just a touch insensitive at times. Never mind. Come on in and tell me all about it.'

Back in the . . . lounge? sitting room? drawing room this time, Terry chimed cut crystal and handed Charlie a pale amber liquid which turned out to be, to his taste, a rather bland Scotch. Nevertheless it mollified him, somewhat.

'So, what's the score? Where do we go from here?'

'I've found a competent bloke. He's done it before. More than once. Anne, my sister, will assist.'

'How much?'

'Thirty guineas.'

'Too much. No. Really. I mean, dash it, might as well go to Harley Street and have it done properly for the extra twenty.'

'It'll be done properly.'

'All the same. I say, this is a bit steep, you know.'

Charlie shrugged, let silence develop around them. He was becoming quite conscious now of how silence can be a useful weapon in trading situations. Let the buggers sweat for a moment.

'Look,' said Terry, 'actually we are both, Lissie and I, a bit strapped at the moment and the Dops, souls of generosity though they are, have been putting their feet down. Don't you think . . . I mean . . . for old times' sake . . .'

Their eyes met, involuntarily flinched away. Shagged each other on Coronation Day.

'There is something you could do for me,' Charlie said at last. 'And it's worth ten guineas to me if you do.'

If Charlie's request put Terry in any sort of spiritual turmoil about the ethics of it, he showed little sign of it. Actually, in his way, he was a moral man – the trouble was his morality insisted family first, then friends, then others like us, and then, at last, professional standards and the rest. After only a moment's hesitation, during which he ran his fingers through his lank hair, he nodded briskly, crossed the hall to what looked like a library or study, and came out with a huge bunch of keys.

'Come on.'

Outside he unpopped the Midget again. On the perspex back-window light he had a sticker. *No to Nationalization. Vote Tory.* Surely it shouldn't be a 'z'?

'I can do better than write you one myself. The Dop's got a case on just now where some poor sod over in Sevenoaks has had just the sort of letter you want. It'll be on the file.'

Ah. The 'z' makes you think of Nazis. Clever stuff. Terry took a pair of heavy gloves from under the dashboard. His fist brushed Charlie's thigh as he put the gear stick into reverse.

It took two keys – one brass, one Yale – to get into Mead and Mead, Woolingham High Street, another to get into Old Man Mead's office, yet another to open the filing cabinet. As papers rustled, Charlie looked around. Caged bookcases full of law books, the leather on the desk top cracked and lifting at the corners, the oriental rugs faded and tatty, three pipes stuck with pencils in a pewter mug.

'Here we are.'

Heart lifting, light at the end of the tunnel, Charlie took the paper.

'You could change the bit about racing pigeons to whatever might fit your case.'

'It looks just about right.'

'We'll have to stat it.'

Side door to secretary's office. A photostat machine.

'Takes fifteen minutes to dry,'

'I'll want some headed paper too.'

'Of course.'

'Two please. In case I mess the first.'

They waited for the copy to dry.

Terry looked at his watch. 'I should make it to the Guild Hall. Cheer up Lissie no end to hear we've got it under way.'

Woolingham Guild Hall. Supermac. Boring.

A thought occurred to him.

'You got a Dickson works here for you?'

'Yes. Articled clerk. Does most of the conveyancing.'

'Could I see his office for a moment?'

'All right. But don't push it. I'm doing a lot for you.'

Silence to that one too.

Dickson's office was tiny, created out of a large space with Essex board, but it was tidy, bright and clean. In the pending tray, ten folders. The next to bottom: *Skerrit's Farm, & c, Sale.* To Belgravia Properties Ltd . . . *pleased to inform you that my client has reconsidered your offer and is now prepared to settle on the basis of eleven thousand pounds for the entire freehold with vacant possession.*

Which, thought Charlie, with a sort of angry glee, means that Giles Marsh has robbed me of three hundred and thirty-three sheets plus six and eightpence.

A hundred yards only, down the High Street, took him to Baird and Skeffington's office. At the other end a small crowd, a lot of police, a huge green BBC outside-broadcast television van filled up the road between the Guild Hall and the Conservative Club. For a moment a glimmer of interest flickered in Charlie's mind, but now he had a job on, a job to get finished.

Again behind the closed Venetian blinds, again at Doris's desk, he took the cover off her typewriter and wound in the first sheet of Mead and Mead headed paper.

Twenty minutes later he gave up. One precious sheet covered in smudges and even worn through where the rough eraser had been used more than once, one precious sheet wasted. Somehow or other he would have to persuade Doris to do it.

She did it all right.

Dear Madam,

As solicitors representing the owners of the property known as Skerrit's Cottage No. 1, hereinafter called the landlord, I write to inform you that as leasehold tenant you are given twenty-eight days to quit the above mentioned premises. This is in strict accordance with the terms and conditions of the tenancy agreement as redrawn and signed by you on the demise of your husband.

You will of course be aware that failure to comply with the requirements of the lease render you liable to eviction as laid down in the Agriculture Act 1947 (as amended). In this respect you are already in breach of covenant under two heads.

1. You have neglected the rules of good husbandry by allowing chickens under your care and control to wander close to a public highway.

2. The landlord's interest had been materially prejudiced by your failure adequately to maintain the roofing and tiling. This has resulted in permanent structural damage.

Any redress or compensation you may wish to seek will have been waived by your acceptance of the sum of two hundred pounds paid to you by the landlord's representative. This generous ex gratia payment is more than adequate to cover any costs you may now incur.

The landlord looks forward to finding the premises vacant before the fifth day of October, nineteen hundred and fifty-nine.

Yours faithfully,

And there followed a scrawl which could, just, be read as *F. Mead.*

On Saturday, 3 October, Charlie took Doris out. They met at the office – she in a Lurex gold dress bought with the fifteen pounds he'd given her, he in his sharpest suit – seventeen-inch bottoms, no turn-ups, jacket cut short, tie, black silk, squared-off ends, hair as dark as he could make it with Brylcreem. She smelt of Tabu, he of Old Spice. Sweating with anxiety, he drove the five-year-old Wolseley that Mr Baird allowed him to use for customers only, and took her in the first place to the Prince of Wales.

She went straight to the powder room, he to the cocktail bar, where he ordered a sweet Babycham with a cherry and a dry Martini for himself with vodka and an olive. It tasted foul and he didn't finish it. At the bar two older men drinking bitter, as he would have liked to have done, discussed the election.

'They're on a hiding to nothing.'

'See that election broadcast the other night?'

'One with Supermac in a rocket? Stupid. They shouldn't use Supermac. They don't realize everyone loves Supermac. It's a joke, a gimmick. Reckon that broadcast did more for the other side than Labour.

'You're too right. And that Wedgwood Benn. Saying the Tories are badly shaken by evidence of a Labour swing everywhere. Why say a thing like that when everyone knows it's a lie?'

'Don't like him. Got a nasty look in his eye.'

'Reckon Mead might do it this time.'

'Reckon he might . . .'

He stopped. Charlie looked up from his scarcely touched drink to see why and there, coming across the long, dark, oak-panelled room, her stilettos silent in the deep carpet, the subdued but careful lighting picking her out as she moved from pool to pool of it, or rather floated . . . Doris. Her hair, more puffed up than it usually was at the office, was white gold. Her lilac eye-shadow glittered with gold dust, her dress, brassy-gold, shimmered and sparkled, its drapes moving across her breasts and thighs fractionally after the young limbs that moved it, her legs long and sheer, her feet high, high shoes gold too, and there was gold thread in the gossamer stole about her shoulders. Only her lips and nails were different, and even they not the bright red she wore at daytime, but a sort of crushed strawberry with glitter in it too.

A goddess for the times, and all three men sensed it with awe. Even the barman looked up from the spotless glass he was polishing.

She slid on to the high bar stool. 'This mine?' she said brightly, and popped the cherry into her mouth before sipping the pale gold liquor through which paler gold bubbles rose. Then she leant forward to Charlie so he could feel her breath on his cheek and see the swelling of her breasts down the top of her startling dress. 'Hey. Know what? They got free squirts of perfume in the toilet. Smell.' And she pushed her wrist under his nose.

After the carvery – grapefruit with another cherry, red beef, peas, baked potatoes, ice cream in two colours with chocolate sauce and grated hazel nut, a bottle of warm chateau wine – she asked him to take her to the Lewisham Mecca.

Charlie couldn't dance, hated dance halls, hated the push, the smells, the gloom swept with bright lights that dazzled and swept on. He quite liked the music, though, British big band with a beat so obvious even he could get his feet to fit it, and of course he liked the feel of Doris's body as it brushed his. The penultimate number of the set was a smooch; the lights went right down, Doris put both arms around his neck and hung there. His hands moved down her bare back on to the Lurex and so to her buttocks. With fierce embarrassment he felt his cock thicken, harden; he tried to pull back, but she pressed closer so her round little tummy rubbed sweetly on it. 'That's nice,' she murmured in his ear, 'that's ever so nice.'

The last number in the set was 'In the Mood', started quietly just the way Glen Miller used to play it, just the way James Stewart did it in the film, but getting louder, the lights coming up all the time, the dancers now jigging up and down to the quickening rhythm; each section of the band, trumpets, trombones, tenor and bass saxophones, stood up in turn to be applauded, their instruments glittering in the light; the drummer took a neat break, the music seemed to die away to nothing. Pause. Then back again for one last rowdy chorus. The band leader in his white tuxedo turned to face the floor and brought it all to a halt, with a neat little gesture, like snapping a thread.

'Thank you, ladies and gentlemen, thank you, thank you. That was our last number tonight, we'll be back here on our own next Wednesday. That was of course Glen Miller's 'In the Mood', and if you'll excuse a topical joke, I'm sure You Never Heard it so Good.'

Wild applause, full lights, the band began to pack up their instruments.

Doris took hold of Charlie's hand and dragged him to the nearest exit, and out into the carpark. For a moment, remembering stories of bicycle chains and razor blades fitted in potatoes, and how he actually once saw a gang of Teds chorusing together the horn theme from *The Vikings* as they went down a side street of terraced houses smashing the empty milk bottles on the steps, Charlie felt a moment of panic. But other couples were heading out into the darkness too. Car doors slammed. One or two cars coughed into life, but most stayed put. He fumbled with keys; Doris reached round the stanchion and lifted the lock of the back door, opened it, tumbled in, and pulled him after her.

They snogged for a long time, which Charlie soon tired of, could see little point in, then she took his hand and guided it up her leg, under her dress. The Bri-Lon went on and on, the texture changed, became silkier – he'd reached the tops of her thighs. Exploring, he got to the lower edge of the knickers. Slowly he began to work his way down inside, pulling down the lingerie as he went, but she stopped him firmly.

'Not first time out,' she murmured. 'Next time perhaps.' And she took the hand and placed it in her faintly moist crotch, moving his fingers to make him massage her through the fabric of her knickers. Then, when she was satisfied he was doing what she wanted, she found his zip and pulled his prick into the chilly air.

'Go on,' she said. 'It's not fair otherwise. Kiss me again too, if you like.'

Sounds from the dance hall, arpeggios, drum breaks, a group warming up. Car doors banged, laughter, squeals, giggles, as more expert couples made their way back in.

Then the music, firm, raucous, quite amazingly loud. A jangling guitar intro, then:

'We-ell, that'll be the day, when you say good-bye
Ye-es, that'll be the day, when you make me cry-y
You said you're going to leave, you know it's a lie,
'Cos, that'll be the da-a-ay, when I die.'

Doris had gone still, cold, like stone.

'Well you give me all your loving and your tu-rtle-doving,
A-all your hugs and kisses and your money too
We-ell you know you love me baby
Still you tell me may be
That some day, well I'll be blue . . . '

Charlie disengaged himself. 'Hey, what's the matter?'

No answer, though he saw her gorgeous spun-gold hair move as she shook her head. Then a headlight swung round the carpark, briefly lit her face. Mascara, make-up, swept away on the tide of tears . . .

'You said you're going to leave, you know it's a lie
'Cos that'll be the da-a-ay when I die.'

He never found out why she wept and wept, and had to be taken home, never connected it with the black-framed postcard in her desk.

Part Three

1

Using his bulk as a substantial and hard weapon to get to the nearest unused strap before the train started, Charlie bulldozed to one side three old ladies with string bags, a man in a macintosh, muffler and bowler hat who was smoking a foul pipe, and a slick black who sported a pork-pie hat above an anti-smog mask.

'Man, you full of shit, you know that?' he hissed through the gauze, and dark eyes glittered up at Charlie.

Charlie's face, already at twenty-three a touch fleshy, reddened up. Nigger, he thought. That Colin Jordan has the right idea. This is the worst sort – not a buck nigger, but a poufter, a pervert, a dope peddler. Crack his head in my elbow like a nut, but I wouldn't want to get myself dirty.

The train jerked forward and fell into its nagging, noisy rhythm. I hate this, thought Charlie. I really hate it. Often he walked the one and half miles from Belgravia Properties to his flat off the Cromwell Road north of Earls Court, but outside, the smog, in its second day, was quite impenetrable; you could get lost in it, and it killed too – freezing sulphurous gases.

As he usually did at times like this, he fell into an obsessive reverie, half fantasy, half a frenetic fumbling of thoughts, ideas, that turned over and over in his mind like so many foreign coins whose value he did not know – a refrain or ground bass that echoed the rhythmic metallic roar of the train: 'How do I get rich, how rich can I get, I must get rich.' He had six hundred and seventy-five pounds seven shillings and sixpence in the Woolingham Building Society – the net profit from the transactions of October 1959 plus three years' accrued interest: he had not used a penny of it, and would not until the veil was lifted and he could see clearly where and how to put it out to make a sure-fire Jack Cotton, twenty-three-carat Charlie Clore, copper-bottomed fortune.

Meanwhile he worked for Belgravia Properties, an opaque institution, difficult to grasp, with personnel constantly changing, the properties themselves hardly ever on the books for more than a month or so. He told people he was in a junior executive position, but he did a variety of things: straightforward rent-collecting; threatening recalcitrant tenants; easing out or pushing out those who would be better off elsewhere; exerting a mixture of blackmail and physical threat, even force, on reluctant sellers, bad debtors, and so on. His superiors, so far as he was able to identify them, valued his services – especially his solid, clean-cut, well-kept appearance; his voice, which had deepened as his chest filled out, which could on occasion shift from a very passable Kensington Posh to something which sounded like a plain-clothes copper who was not about to stand for any nonsense; and not least, his apparent total lack of scruple.

As the train rumbled on, and the almost dead bodies in it swayed and bobbed against each other like so many drowned corpses weighted by the feet, the question nagged on like bacon rind trapped in a rotten tooth. For the most part, from where he stood in the foothills of the financial dung-heap, it seemed to be a matter of constantly moving the stuff about: goods, property, title deeds, stocks, shares, gold, diamonds, coffee, tea, copper, steel, even notional futures in such things – anything, indeed, that you could exchange for something else. And, above all, the simple straightforward lubricating oil of exchange, the loot, the pelf itself, your actual money, moving it about, constantly changing it from one thing to another in the market places of the City, of the World – and if you were lucky, if you were lucky, if you were lucky every time you passed a bit on, a bit of that bit stuck to you, and if you were really lucky, a whole lot stuck to you, a ruddy great steaming cartload of it.

How did you get to be lucky then, really lucky – that was the question. Was there more to it than exchange and taking your bit as it passed by? What was the secret that the Cottons and Clores knew that he didn't, the private secret, the dark, warm, wet, sweet-smelling secret, the very cunt of the bitch goddess herself that would let him into a permanently rented suite at the Dorchester, and out, right out of this . . .

Hell. The train had shuddered to a stop. Somewhere on one of the open stretches of line between Sloane Square and Earls Court, it had run into a thick bank of the yellow muck. You could see it rolling and heaving, reflecting back the dimmed lights of the train, ever so lazily caressing the windows and doors, feeling with its tentacles between the cracks, its freezing chill settling about their heads in advance of the actual smog. Charlie looked about him. How many – a hundred? – jammed tight into this ugly submarine-like tube, and all wretched, fearful of the sudden stillness, of the fog, of the train coming up the line behind them, of the cancers in their bowels, of the strain near the heart, of the green phlegm coughed up in the morning, or urine stained with blood, of skin gone slack, of poverty . . . and the rentman. They stank of it – of fear, and poverty, and fog.

The motors whirred, the lights brightened, the train shuddered into motion again, but awkwardly, as if limping, jolting on down the track towards Gloucester Road. A collective sigh breathed out, one or two offered tiny, secret smiles to themselves or even to a neighbour, and the man with the pipe uttered through brown clenched teeth, 'Never nice when they stop, is it? You always wonder.'

Christ! I've got to be rich.

Up through the tiles of Earls Court, pushing clear at last of the density of packed humanity and into the blanked-out alleys that led up to the Cromwell Road, Charlie went, no chance of getting lost, the whole bit far too familiar – including the pair of drunks touting for sixpences for a cup of coffee only twenty yards from the off-licence, including the launderette he used, though he hated the Aussies who treated it as a club.

Cromwell Road westbound was solid; the traffic looked as if it hadn't moved for days – not that you could see more than three cars and then the lights of the next two, twisted by the fuming exhausts, spewing and spinning their poison into the poison that lay on everything; a poison that was solid now, a grey, freezing slime that lay on the trees, the lamp-posts, the railings, on windscreens save where the wipers sliced through it.

But then a vision.

Something gave a little, each car moved its own length, and then again, and brought up to Charlie, just as he was about to step off the curb, a pale blue, nearly new Roller. The interior lights glowed, made it look like a showcase, a cut-off world moving on its own, untouched by fog or poverty. A large man, florid and fat, with pouchy eyes, thick lips, pale grey suit, bluish-grey silk tie, very large, with pink dots, huge gold watch on a hairy wrist, straightened on Charlie's side from the cocktail cabinet and almost daintily passed the fragile glass which misted with the cold of the booze against the warmth of the cabin, even as Charlie watched, and passed it across to . . .

She was wearing a coat – a solid, three-quarter-length, no messing, the real thing, Russian mink. She was dyed blonde, a distant recollection of Doris, but, like the mink, the real thing, a top-drawer professional, a rich man's whore.

Charlie knew she was dyed blonde, and knew she was a whore, because as she moved to take the drink the coat fell open and revealed a cherry of a nipple and a triangle of neatly edged pubic hair – black, and as glossy as the mink.

She sipped at the drink, holding it in one hand, while with the other she casually pulled the coat around her again. The traffic moved and the Roller purred on, maybe no more than fifteen yards, but gone, into the smog.

A rich man's whore, but the man old as well as rich. Christ! I must be rich young, dear God, not old.

Down the worn, narrow area steps he went, into the tiny tunnel under the main entrance, fidgeting his key into the door, black paint flaking, putty coming loose round the frosted glass, sodding thing always sticks, and so into a tiny kitchen – what had once been the scullery. A shallow, glazed sink, a possibly lethal gas heater that stank of half-burnt fumes, two gas rings, quarry tiles cracked, and a cupboard of plywood from which the once white paint was flaking, and a table covered in scored Contact paper. Tins, old bread, Blend 37, a half-empty pint-bottle of milk. Then a door into what had once been the big house's kitchen, was now a bedsit. A very dirty, very old carpet, a large bed piled with filthy blankets, centrefolds from *Playboy* pinned to the walls, the crotches hazed out into blank sexless triangles, a small gas heater in the large alcove that had once housed a kitchen range, another table, three wooden chairs, a bedside locker (ex-NHS), a low, small, squat armchair with corduroy-covered cushions spilling flocking at the seams, and a hardboard wardrobe varnished, and the varnish streaked to simulate wood-grain.

On the mantel that ran along what had once been the chimney-piece there was a collection of twelve or so books – *Accounting, Business Studies, Company Law, Teach Yourself Book-keeping* – the simpler ones well-thumbed, the larger, weightier ones still pristine: mute tombstones witnessing their owner's continuing inability to concentrate his mind once the going got tough. He was now determined that one day he would employ people who could read, had read, the tough ones – and sack them too.

He threw down Burberry, hat, scarf, leather gloves, pigskin zip-up document case, ran strong fingers through hair cut short but stylishly so the curls lay close to his scalp, took off his jacket and tie and pulled on a white Arran sweater, lit the gas fire. Then he went up the narrow dark stairs that led up from the scullery and through what had once been the green baize door to the dark, gloomy Victorian hall. On a grand, really rather good table the mail for the tenants who now occupied most of the house had been neatly laid out by the landlady – an old gentlewoman, sad, sour, bothered, lost, who lived on the ground floor.

One letter for him. From Aunt Elizabeth. Bad news. He took it down, sat on his bed, opened it.

Dear Charlie,

Your mother tells me you intend not to be with us for Christmas, that you have friends in the country who have asked you to visit them. I think this is a lie. Anyway your place at this time, at Christmas, is with your nearest and dearest.

It is a difficult time, and I know your father wishes to discuss with you things that could well turn out to your advantage. So please be there.

Your affectionate aunt,
Elizabeth

He fought down an irritated nausea spiced with curiosity – what could there possibly be to his advantage at 263 Goldsmith Drive? Unless Grandad was at last about to snuff it and there was a possibility of a legacy. He supposed he had better go. Certainly she was right about one thing – the country friends were a fiction.

Back in the scullery/kitchen he used one gas ring to heat through two tins of baked beans and skinless pork sausages, and the other to boil a kettle for Nescafé. He added a lot of pepper to the enormous dish of beans, and brown sauce as well, three spoonfuls of sugar to his coffee.

When he had finished he put on striped Winceyette pyjamas, poured himself the first whisky of the evening, and got into the bed. He lit a cigarette, and, full-stomached, the whisky beginning its work, the gas fire building up a fug against the chill of the smog outside, entered upon his normal routine of an evening. This was a steady read through all three of the evening papers which made up the entire contents of his briefcase, and as he read he drank more whisky. Usually he consumed a quarter of a bottle of VAT 69 (forty-one shillings a bottle) and was ready to sleep by ten or half past.

Motorway Madness 4 die. Marples repeats warning. Thalidomide parents will sue. SW1 tasteful bedsit with own services £30 per month. Heads you lose, tails I win: Bow Street magistrate castigates Bradford Businessman who stopped the cheques he used when buying chips to play chemin-de-fer.

Charlie read them through, all through, every word – a little more laboriously as the evening wore on and he got into his second and third VAT 69. He chose the brand because it was what Simon Templar drank in the original Saint books, to which Charlie had been addicted from the age of twelve.

New Rover 3 litre, £1662 – don't like it, looks like a Roller made for a grocer. *Mews Cottage, Cadogan Square £4870* – that's cheap, what's wrong with it. That blue Roller with the whore.

Propery King Charlie goes for shipping. Charles Clore, king of the high street and the shoe shops . . .

Professor Carstairs, Reith lecturer for the BBC, yesterday nailed Victorian attitudes to sex which lead ladies to cracking on they don't like it . . . we asked a panel of experts to comment on the Prof's diagnosis of the ills that may befall the marriage bed . . .

The Light of Day *by Eric Ambler, 18s;* Life at the Top *by John Braine . . .* novels. No!

MP's daughter on drug charge. Felicity ('Lissie') Mead, daughter of Freddie Mead, the Member for the London Borough of Woolingham, was today remanded on charges of illegally possessing Indian Hemp. She was granted bail pending further enquiries. In an exclusive interview with our staff reporter she insisted that the drugs had been left in her Fennimore Gardens pent-house by a coloured friend. In spite of the highly emotional state she was now in, she was able to insist that she had no idea what the Indian Hemp was, nor where the police might be able to find her 'friend'.

Christ! Lissie Mead. At Fennimore Gardens, just down the road. Several properties there on Belgravia's books. 'I suppose you won't take a rain check,' she said. 'Till I'm twenty-one. I'll have thousands then.'

MP quizzes Supermac on Vassal Case . . . Charlie read on until he had read them all, but Lissie Mead, the kiss she'd offered him, those thousands of her own, knocked around at the back of his head and were still there when he sank at last into whisky sleep, punctuated towards morning by beany farts.

2

Charlie was not a fool, and he had learnt to distrust impulses, apparent flashes of genius, ever since he had taken out that four hundred pounds from Mr Baird's petty cash without first working out how he could cover the traces. The accountant had spotted the transaction and reported it to his client.

Charlie had not denied that he had done it (though he toyed with the idea of trying to shop Doris), had sullenly insisted he could see nothing wrong in it since Mr Baird had not lost a penny. Mr Baird agreed to keep him on, but very much on probation. Charlie looked for another job. An advertisement in the *Evening Standard* caught his eye – Belgravia Properties wanted young men of firm character and good physique for responsible work, prospects of promotion, and along he went. Two or three times in the first year he had glimpsed Giles Marsh, but after that not at all. Apparently Marsh was now in advertising.

So. Distrusting impulse, Charlie waited to the middle of the following week before doing anything at all, and then all he did was check that Lissie Mead's name was not in the telephone directory: he had not expected that it would be. He thought this over for a day, rehearsed, enacted in his mind again and again how the scene would go before actually carrying it out; and then, on the morning of Friday, the 14th, he went up to Accounts at Belgravia Properties.

Everything at Belgravia was bright. The quite small bedroom near the top of what had been a substantial town house that the firm used at that time had been converted into something that resembled a second-generation coffee-bar rather than an office. There was even a Cona coffee machine.

The girls at Belgravia turned over almost as quickly as the properties they handled, but there was one who recognized Charlie. He visited Accounts quite often, whenever he had actual cash to pay in, and she rather fancied him. Indeed, why not? He was a snazzy dresser, though not loud, had a strong, hard, masculine figure, and if his face looked a little sullen, if his eyes looked a little cold and wary behind the slightly bruised-looking lids, well, so what? Clearly he intended to get on, to make money, and what more can a girl expect from her man?

'Listen,' he asked her. 'I'm trying to trace a bloke who's welshed on us for quite a substantial sum. Three hundred sheets actually. I've got a line or two. He's either changed his name to Mead, or he's shacked up with a girl called Mead, and he's at an address in Fennimore Gardens. Now I know we used to handle quite a bit there, though it's off my track (Charlie handled the downmarket welshers – those in SW1 tended to get solicitors' letter and then a good old-fashioned dunning), so I wonder if you could look it up for me. Mead. Fennimore Gardens.'

'Ooh, yes. We know all about Fennimore Gardens. They cause us more trouble than the rest put together.' She shook bright-red hair, ran carmine nails across her fringe, fingered out reference cards, cross-referenced, slid out a drawer of her filing cabinet and pulled out a folder, and all the time she chattered away, as bright as if she were the first dandelion of spring.

'Lady Kitti Bridge owns one side of it. Remember her? With the Dockers and then Onassis? Jetting about all over the place? Well, she's on the really hard stuff now, you know – *needles.* And broke too. We've handled her rents for five years, then she started borrowing advances off us, and now we're trying to get some settlement out of her which will leave her a bit in hand, and us the properties.

Trouble is, she's in a clinic just now, and what's more she's a cousin of Lord Slaker, you know, the Slaker Group, so we have to go a bit carefully. Here we are. Yes. Mead. Miss F. Flat 6. Number 35. That's the attic, what we call penthouse. And she's no good either, owes us three months, so I wish you luck.'

Smiling brightly she folded, slotted, slid it all away. Talks too much. Too interested in what she's doing, thought Charlie. If I were in charge, she'd be o-u-t, out.

In spite of the thought he gave it all, all the time he spent again creating, rehearsing, re-enacting the scene, he began to feel quite unnerving tremors of unease as he approached Fennimore Gardens. They came from a sense that he was quite definitely and deliberately taking steps into an unknown world, one where, once he was in, if he let himself in, he would have to play it by ear, minute by minute, hour by hour, day by day. There was no charm for him in what little he knew about Lissie Mead, apart from the fact that other men had had her and he didn't see why he shouldn't. He hated her upper-middle-class background, though he still kept a foot in its door through the Old Sydneyans Rugby Club; he hated the way the real plums always fell, went on falling for ever, to such people, how they accepted them easily, naturally as if by right, while he had to graft every inch of the way.

On the other hand: 'I'll have thousands then,' she had said, and just as he felt impelled to put himself in the way of a share of Lissie's body, so he felt far, far more strongly impelled to see if he couldn't get near those thousands.

So, at four o'clock on a cold, dank, wretched Saturday in the middle of December, he set out from Bannington Gardens, dressed as usual for business, though it was the weekend, in Burberry, muffler, gloves and narrow-brimmed trilby with a feather, and carrying his pigskin document holder. As with so many of his decisions, the time he had settled on was largely fortuitous, although it seemed considered. There was no Rugby that Saturday, the pitches were frozen; since the discovery of her address, the right amount of time had elapsed for adrenalin and other hormones to drive him to just that pitch of irritability for him to say to himself, 'Sod it, I'm going.'

He rationalized the decision in a non-verbalized way by sensing within himself that it would be a quiet time of day, an empty, fag-endish part of the day, the year even, a time when nobody would be doing much (in those days, even the big stores closed on a Saturday afternoon and bugger the shopping days left to Christmas), a time when she would be in, bored perhaps, waiting for the short dark day to become night, a time when she would welcome distraction, a novelty, a new, or not too familiar face. Or prick.

He dressed as he did for he needed an excuse to call, and since she was three months in arrears with her rent, why not as a rent collector?

On the way, out of habit, he bought an evening paper, and zipped it into his empty document holder. The headline bold, shock horror: SHOTS FIRED IN KENSINGTON.

Fennimore Gardens turned out much as he had expected: a square of drab lawn with plane trees still clutching about them a few heavy umber leaves like dirty rags; rusty chain-link fencing shutting them off from the large terraced houses, each of which had its Corinthian portico, the stucco so overpainted that the acanthus had lost its edges and looked like over-boiled grey cabbage.

The street door to number 35 was unlocked and pushed open on to a drab, linoed hall, painted cream and brown and furnished only with a table, a mirror and a pay phone. Charlie climbed brass-edged stairs to a first floor, which, since the conversion, now had one landing window, and one modern front door with spy-hole and Chubb locks – clearly Lady Kitti Bridge had kept all of it: a not insubstantial apartment for one person. Somewhere a small dog, shut up and forgotten perhaps, howled and whined.

The stairs went on, narrower now, up past two more landings each of which had three front doors, and finally shrank away to what amounted to little more than a short flight of grubby deal steps to a plain red door set up above the eaves – the roof sloped to below shoulder height on either side of it.

There was no knocker or bell, just a Yale lock and a spy-hole. The unease increased critically towards funk, but again a sort of desperate fatalism which masked a complex of conflicting emotions ranging from boredom to greed drove him on, and he climbed the steps, rapped leather knuckles on the door.

No answer – but in the gloom the spy-hole glowed with the light on the other side, and faintly he could hear music, tinkly stuff, classical.

He knocked again, louder. The music stopped. The stairs, the landing, the whole house, even the small lonely dog, held their breath. The light in the spy-hole went out.

'Who's there?' The voice was high, urgent, nearer than he had expected, and, disconcertingly, was off script: his scenario had been that she should open the door to his knock, and then, after the slightest of pauses, recognize him.

'Me. Charlie Bosham.'

'Don't know you. Are you the police? I'm sure you're the police.'

'No. I'm not the police.'

'Oh, God. Why not?'

There was not, as they say, an answer to that.

'Well, who *are* you then?' Said not with agression but despair.

'Charlie Bosham.'

A dull thud on the other side of the door, silence, then a

sob or two, then: 'I suppose you're one of them.'

Charlie sensed the possibility of advance. 'Come on, Lissie. It's Charlie Bosham, from Woolingham. I met you a couple of times. Let me in.'

'From *Woolingham*? Oh, Christ.' More sobs. 'Oh, who the hell you are, I don't care . . .' At last the click of the latch.

She was falling away from it as the door gave and he had to catch her, haul her back into the flat, the room, hands in her armpits, to plant her on a divan covered with a red tasselled cloth. Not that she was heavy. Not at all.

He looked down a longish space, the length exaggerated by the way the ceiling sloped at the sides because of the roof. The lit lamps, with tasselled shades, hung waist-high in the middle; there were brushed ink drawings of frisky ponies with oriental scribble down the edges; a rug with long tufts of wool or hair, but brightly orange, a low, round black marble table mounted on gilt legs; a Dansette record player on which an eight-inch record revolved, the needle now lifted. Vivaldi. *Virtuosi di Roma. Oboe Concerto.* He read as much off the sleeve that lay on the rug, though not a word of it meant anything to him.

3

He stood up; his shoulder nudged one of the tasselled lights and sent it swinging. The shadows rocked about the angled ceilings, and he looked down at Lissie Mead and her thousands. She was a bag of bones in a bulky jumper and jeans, sobbing on a red bedspread. She had a nice flat, was rich, came from Woolingham upper-middle class, her father was an MP. She was on an Indian Hemp charge, and so what. Her people would see her through.

Charlie looked around. There was class here, he could see that. The fantasy that he would bring her back to his basement (and he saw it for a moment in his mind's eye, Playboy centrefolds, the baked beans, the dirt) collapsed. He decided to bolt.

Perhaps she sensed this, turned on her back – her tear-stained white face, eyes puffy, short black hair all over the place – and flung out a thin white hand, pathetically ludicrous coming from the floppy full sweater. 'I remember, I remember. Charlie. You fixed me up when I . . .' The sobs came again. 'You and . . . your sister.'

'Yes. All right. Well. You're all right.' He spoke grouchily now, almost angrily.

'Please, please, please. Don't go. I'm so frightened. Take me with you. Don't go.'

This was close enough to the fantasy to revive it; he was curious too.

'What are you frightened of?'

'Promise you'll take me. Promise first you'll take me away, hide me.'

Charlie had never had much difficulty giving bribed or blackmailed promises – they were the emotional currency of his childhood – and so had no trouble at all breaking them if need be. He promised. The story tumbled out quickly enough. Three Jamaicans sold her Indian Hemp, which she passed on to the quite wide circle of acquaintances she had – comfortably off middle-class girls who worked in the new boutiques or as receptionists in advertizing agencies until they had bartered their arses for an engagement ring from some guy in stockbroking, insurance, banking or commodities. One of the Jamaicans had been busted a day or two after the police had raided her, and now another of them had apparently gone beserk and emptied a gun into a car carrying two of her acquaintances – Christine and Mandy. She didn't know why. But if they thought she had given their names to the police they might come and shoot her. Or worse. (Worse? thought Charlie. What could be worse?) Or the police might connect her with the shooting and withdraw her bail . . .

'You've got a flat somewhere?'

'Basement. Bannington Gardens.'

'Take me there. Please.'

He hesitated, looked down at her, felt again, just as he had three years before, the appeal of her fragility, the sense of strength her weakness gave him.

'It's a bit of a dump.'

'For Christ's sake.'

'All right.'

In the taxi (he was soon to learn that, if or when she ever went out, she expected a taxi) she asked, 'Anyway – why did you come? What did you come for?'

'To collect your rent arrears.'

She looked at him incredulously, then collapsed across him, laughing hysterically.

It took Charlie less than a week to realize basically he could not stand Lissie, but it also took him about the same length of time to discover that she still had nearly eleven thousand of the thirteen that her maiden aunt had left in trust for her until she was twenty-one. He also found that on the whole he preferred fucking her to wanking on his own, and she let him do it almost whenever he wanted. And he wanted to quite often – with her clothes off, the almost skeletal thinness of her body, her tiny breasts, sloping shoulders, hollow belly, small buttocks like a boy's, filled him with such an exciting sense of his own largeness, hardness, toughness, that for a time he thought this was what being in love was, and even after he admitted to himself how awful she was, it still turned him on.

On arriving at Bannington Gardens she looked around without comment, then spent an hour cleaning the place up, but skimpily, not at all thoroughly or expertly. They drank some Vat 69, then she took off her clothes and lay on the bed.

'You can do it to me if you like.'

He did, coming almost as soon as he had got himself into her, dry as she was, but it was his first time and he came twice more before he rolled off her. She showed no sign at all of having enjoyed the experience, and, such was his ignorance of such matters, he had not expected her to.

The next day, Sunday, she made him hire a van, driven by an Australian, and they collected her things from Fennimore Gardens. The Aussie was boorishly jovial about it all: 'Doing a flit, are we? Well, why not? So long as I get paid. Fact is, sport, most of my work is at weekends, people of your sort doing a flit.'

Certainly the marble table, the orange rug, the pictures and lampshades improved the basement.

Lissie reformed Charlie's diet, but not in any way he could see for the better: she sent him to Italian shops and the new delicatessens for pre-filled pastas, salamis, salads with apples, raisins and nuts in them, bread with strange-tasting seeds, and dried smoked fish. She played tinkly classical music on her Dansette, and sent him out to buy new records three times before Christmas. She nagged and bitched at him about the smell of his socks, about nail-biting, about his grammar, and once she flew off into a raging tirade, sarcastic, taunting, for no real reason – except that probably she disliked him as much as he disliked her. She broke off into those hysterical sobs again when for one moment his eyes blazed and he clenched his heavy fist beneath her nose.

He found the experience of sharing a bed quite impossible – and on the third night he got out, collected all the odd cushions and pillows he could find, and slept in front of the gas fire. The next day he bought a foam mattress and a sleeping bag. She did not comment on this change, and he supposed rightly that she approved it.

Yet, when he told her he was going away for three nights over Christmas, she sobbed again and would not speak to him for a whole day. On the 23rd she went out, for the first time since she had moved in, just as the early dusk was coming down, and did not come back until two o'clock in the morning. From his sleeping bag he heard the taxi, the door slam, then heavy feet on the steps, a fist knocking at the low sash window.

'Wake up, mate. Got a package for you.'

On the freezing pavement, in dressing gown and slippers, he took delivery, hoisting her up on to his shoulders, in an easy fireman's lift. 'Is she drunk?' he asked.

'Not she. Doped.Get a lot like that these days.'

She was awake though, just legless. From the bed she looked up at him with big, black, dilated eyes. 'I'll be all right, Charlie. I'll be all right. Just let me sleep.' Her speech was thick, slow, but not slurred, so he did as she sad. In the morning she was still asleep, but breathing normally and her colour was better. He checked there was food and coffee in the kitchen, and left.

4

Mr Bosham got two pairs of carpet slippers; Mrs Bosham got two aprons, both floral; Anne got three nurses' diaries, Aunt Elizabeth, two; Grandad Bosham, who was senile and now lived in the boxroom over the hall which had once been Anne's bedroom, got nothing at all. Charlie got two boxes of handkerchiefs, one set which was monogrammed CR and the other BC. The excitement of present-giving over, there remained two hours of tedium to be got through before Christmas dinner would be ready. Charlie escaped to his old room – kept just as it was, so he could come back any time – threw himself down on the yellow bedspread and smoked. After a time, he realized he was cold, very cold, and he got off the bed to put on the single-bar electric fire that stood in the boarded-up grate, then paused to look out of the window at the long strip of garden that lay behind the house.

Even allowing for the time of year, it looked drab, neglected. Two broken fence palings had not been replaced; there were dry brown grasses, silvery and stiff with frost, in the flowerbeds, and dead nettles where always before there had been sprouts. One windowpane in the garden shed at the very bottom of the garden was broken.

A knock.

'Come in.'

It was Anne. The bloom she had had at eighteen had gone: already she looked coarser, tougher. She sat on the bed, accepted a cigarette.

'Dad's let the garden go.'

'Yes.'

'Why?'

'Don't you know?'

'No. Should I?'

'He's broke. Going broke.'

'Christ.'

'And he's just given up. Giving up everything. Can't cope. I'd say he was ill too.'

Charlie turned from the window, looked at her. His eyes looked back at him but from a face spotty, pasty, fatter. His eyes, and as warily expressionless as he knew his own to be: both were anxious to find out if they were each other's allies in this crisis, or if either had been enlisted by some other member of the family.

'What happened? I mean, why?'

She shrugged. 'How would I know? I can guess. Lots of factors. Woolies enlarged their premises, put in more hardware. There's a lot of new fads around. New ways of doing things. Do-it-yourself, they call it. New ways of packaging. He wouldn't keep up. Didn't stock the right stuff. I don't know. That sort of thing. I think he got caught on purchase tax too. You know he always fiddled that.'

'Most shopkeepers do.'

'Most don't get caught.'

He let the silence grow between them, but she knew that technique too, so eventually he said, 'What about the shops?'

She stubbed out her cigarette. 'Can I have another?.

He handed it to her. The smoke had taken on the acrid headache-provoking tang it does in cold closed rooms, but neither noticed it.

'Alderson is buying him out of the one in Church Lane, for enough to get him of the hook where the law is concerned, and clear him of most of his debts.'

'And the one in the High Street?'

'The lease has less than four years to run. No one's going to take that off his hands.'

This time the silence extended because Charlie was

thinking and thinking hard. And the last thought was that Anne had really done him something of a good turn. Why? Well. Offer her a token now.

'Thanks, thanks, Anne. Forewarned is forearmed, isn't that what they say?'

She turned to find the ashtray.

'Thought you should know,' she said. 'I mean, on the spot, you're not the world's quickest thinker, are you?'

'I suppose not.'

'Anyway. Next year. Perhaps. You'll remember my birthday.'

Oh, God.

'It's in October. In case you'd forgotten.'

But she was pleased all the same. Pleased that she had been able to bring the master a bone. 'Well,' she went on, suddenly cheery, 'how are things with you up West? The City Slicker. Got a girlfriend?'

Oblivious of her jealousy, he answered glibly, 'Yes, actually.' It was the first time the existence of Lissie had crossed his mind for hours. 'And guess who. Lissie Mead.'

This did not please Anne.

'She's dirt. You know that. Watch out for her. She's no good. No good at all.'

Silence. But this time Anne gave way first. 'Are you . . . well, you know. Living together?'

'You could say that.'

She blazed, 'Don't worry about babies. Don't worry at all. After the sort of abortion Donald Summers gave her, she's as much chance of ever being pregnant again as' – she looked around her – 'as that toy aeroplane.'

We are, as a nation, rightly famed for maintaining standards in adversity: dressing for dinner in the heat and dust of India; maintaining a proper sense of decorum and caste in the mud of the Somme (and shooting the dissenters); business as usual during the blitz: that sort of thing. So, as the Bosham family gathered in the front room towards one o'clock it was no surprise to find Dry Fly Sherry (18/6d a bottle), Watney's Light Ale, and marmite-coated Twiglets laid out on the Sheffield plate tray, just as per usual, with Mr Bosham presiding . . . even though he was virtually up Carey Street without a paddle.

They were six on that Christmas Day, gathered together under the paper chains and the holly, with the everlasting silver-tinsel tree winking in the window, and the cards hung, in the relatively new fashion, from looped strings across the alcoves on either side of the fireplace.

Six – that is: Grandad, who had been carried down from his boxroom and planted in a corner on his commode, but well wrapped round with rugs and blankets so no one would have thought he was sitting on a pot; Aunt Elizabeth, thinner and more starched than ever, who had supervised the arrangement of Grandad with her usual total competence, and scorn for the old man's feelings or pride; Mrs Bosham, May, fatter and more floppy than ever, staving off a nervous breakdown over the fact that she, who had to think twice to remember where the tin-opener was, was now attempting to cook nine different things at once; Anne, fat but not floppy, her aunt's grit in her mother's body; Charlie, looked very sharp in a charcoal suit, Van Heusen shirt with the rounded collar ends, black silk knitted square-ended tie, large gold cuff-links; and finally Mr Bosham himself.

Actually Mr Bosham was not himself; at any rate he was not his old self he had sustained for thirty years, and which now, clearly, he would never be again. In nine years, since Coronation Day, he had aged eighteen. No amount of Brylcreem could conceal the fact that his own hair was white and the toupée was not. His eyes were moist, there were flecks of high colour in his cheeks, his bottom lip drooped a little, the skin beneath his chin, there was cigarette ash on his Rex Harrison cardigan, his trousers hung loosely over shanks much thinner than before. A third of the sherry had already gone and one did not have to get close enough to smell him to guess where.

Nevertheless standards exist to be kept up. Once he had seen that everyone had a drink, he placed himself in front of the simulated-coals electric-fire, and raised his glass. A true pater-familias to the end.

'Here's to us then. And a Merry Christmas everyone.'

A moment of pained silence. Then Aunt Elizabeth said, 'There's something burning,' Mrs Bosham screamed, 'The sprouts, they've boiled dry,' and ran for it, knocking Grandad's glass out of his hand. Anne went for a cloth. Mr Bosham turned to his son. 'Well, Charlie. I see Supermac has done it again.'

'Eh?'

'Ah. You missed the news yesterday? Back from Nassau with our own nuclear deterrent in his pocket. Polaris. Fired from underwater. That's technology for you. Last us two decades or more. Give the Russkies pause for thought, eh? Great man, Supermac. One of the very best.'

Charlie was utterly dumbfounded. Never in his entire life had his father spoken to him thus, at such length, without a hint of criticism, rebuke, reprimand, sarcasm, or put-down of one sort or another. And it went on.

'Nice suit you're wearing, Charlie. Real quality there. Can see it a mile off. Cost a bob or two, I daresay. Doing all right then? Fine. Fine. Care for a drop more? Think I might. Christmas. Marvellous. Once a year, eh? Just as well. Ha! Hear that, Elizabeth? Once a year is enough.'

Not only is he being civil with me, Charlie thought, he's embarrassed about it too. He's up to something.

'I expect you noticed. Had to let the garden go a bit. Truth is. I don't seem to find the energy as well as I used to. Ah well. Anno Domino. Catches up with all of us. Look at poor Grandad. Not much more for him, I daresay. Light at the end of the tunnel from his point of view, I daresay. Be a release when he goes. And not only for him.'

Grandad had clearly heard and understood every word. He glanced up fiery-eyed through unkempt eyebrows, and waved a withered claw at them. Aunt Elizabeth gave him a sip from his refilled sherry glass, and wiped the spittle from the corner of his mouth.

It went on. It was not even condescension, Charlie realized – it was capitulation. For a time he felt heady with the glory of it. This man, this ignorant bully who had been on his tits for almost two and a half decades, who had never done him a favour or a good turn without making it a bribe or coupling it with emotional blackmail, who had annihilated him with sarcasm ever since he had asked to be congratulated at the age of three for drawing a house with a recognizable chimney, and, on six occasions, each remembered with mortifying clarity, had belted him hard enough to draw blood, this fucking tyrant was . . . creeping to him. Straightening, in his fine suit, shooting his cuffs with their chunky modernist real gold links, feeling the solidness of his own chest and thighs, he looked down at the suddenly little, little man at his side and felt, with the sherry in him, that he could blow him away, or break him up into twigs and rags to start a bonfire with.

He was even invited to carve the turkey. But when he stuck the carving fork deep into the breast, pink fluid oozed out round the prongs. He cut in with the knife, lifted out a half-moon of flesh and found it got pinker until it was almost red as the middle.

'That bird is not cooked,' Aunt Elizabeth announced.

'No,' agreed Charlie.'It is not cooked.'

His mother, sobbing again, carried it back into the kitchen with Anne in attendance, who came back a moment later.

'It was a frozen one. She's never cooked a frozen one

before. She thought it would thaw out in the pantry, but this weather the pantry's freezing anyway,'

The pantry was a walk-in cupboard on the outside wall with a vent. A larder really, but pantry sounded grander.

'We'll have some soup. Thick vegetable soup or tomato?'

'Whatever she got a frozen one for?' remarked Mr Bosham all petulance. 'She never done that before.'

Anne, arms akimbo, at the other end of the table, fixed him with her pale, cool eyes.

'Because they cost two thirds of what a proper butcher's one costs, that's why.'

They drank more sherry until the bottle was finished, and then the soup, and a chill irritability settled all over them. It was the coldest Christmas for years, freezing hard outside in spite of quite frequent spells of winter sun. The Boshams had never had central heating put in, had had open fireplaces boarded up, and had always thought it an unwarranted extravagance to put more than one bar of an electric fire on, and then only in one room at a time. And that even when they were very comfortably off. Now . . .

The turkey duly reappeared surrounded, inevitably, by burnt potatoes, rock-hard chipolatas, and sprouts that had been reduced to balls of barely green, heavily soaked cotton-wool encased in burnt outer leaves. It seemed less of a triumph and more of a chore to carve the thing now and Charlie grumbled as he got on with it, swore when some grease spattered on to his cuff. They drank Pomagne with it. Last year there had been Blue Nun Liebfraumilch.

The Christmas pudding was less of a disaster, being a bought one and having had ample time to cook right through, and the custard was scarcely lumpy at all. By the time it had gone (Grandad nearly went with it: he choked on the sixpence which Mother had tried to manoeuvre towards Charlie), a sort of good humour had returned. The dining room, not really a large space at all, had warmed up with people in it and the heat from the kitchen. Condensation formed on the French windows and hid the disaster the garden had become; no one could claim to be hungry; and the men at any rate had had almost enough to drink.

Bit by bit the table was cleared; a small bowl of tangerines and brazil nuts appeared. Mr Bosham sat back at one end of the table and said to his son at the other, 'I've got a drop of port in the sideboard. Like a spot? Be a good chap and fetch it out. And a coupla glasses. And come and sit by me. Take your jacket off, if you like.'

Charlie did as he was told. Through the frosted glazed door to the kitchen sounds of washing up and subdued chat between the three women. Grandad snored.

'Co'burn. Always remember that, my boy. It's Co'burn. You can tell a gent because he knows that. It's ignorant to say Cockburn. Well. Nothing but the best. Leave the bottle out.'

Father stripped a tangerine. With the nutcracker almost hidden in his ample palm, Charlie cracked a nut.

'Remember the Colemans? Mrs, striking lady, used to work for us in the High Street shop. Lovely people, Lovely children.'

The hypocrisy of this did not in the least surprise Charlie. He hardly noticed it.

'Jane, Janet, Jane. That's right. Got married last Saturday. Picture in the *Woolingham Advertiser* . . .

Haze of brownish fair hair between her legs.

'There was talk, wasn't there, she would marry George Alderson.'

Father was annoyed at the interruption.

'That was four, five years ago. When they were still kids.'

What happened to George?'

'Joined the Met. Doing well. Detective Constable.'

'At Woolingham?'

No. Up in town. The Met. Camden. Anyway. Jane

Coleman's done better than that. Bloke's a scientist. Proper little egg-head. Got a job with Esso. So she's done all right for herself. Oops. Pardon Mr Arden. Always find Christmas pudding lies a bit heavy. Drop more! Yes? So'll I!'

Chink gurgle. Chink gurgle. Father went on, 'So that's Jane Coleman settled down. I expect you'll be settling down quite soon. Got anyone in mind?'

Charlie cracked another nut.

'Quite right. Not my business. All the same, you want something solid behind you when you settle down. Permanent. It's what I had, thanks to Dad. It's what I'd like you to have.

'Fact is, Charlie, it's all got a bit much for me. And the quack says I should ease up a bit. Dodgy ticker, that sort of thing. Well. David Alderson is taking the Church Lane shop off my hands, and what I want to say, old man, is this. I'd like you to come in with me on the High Street. No. Don't say anything yet. These things don't need to be rushed. Think it over. Take your time. But let me say this. You'd be in on an equal footing and not a penny of capital do I want down. What the old firm needs now is a younger head than mine, and a younger body too, one that's ready to do some grafting. And I know I can rely on you for both of these – you're no fool and, by golly, I know you can work, work like a nigger if need be. You wouldn't be your father's son if you couldn't.'

Here he looked up from the simulated-cut-crystal glass he had been twirling. The moistness in his eye was far more obvious, his bottom lip trembled. He reached across the corner of the table and gave Charlie a playful little tap with clenched fist on his upper arm.

'What do you say, old son? What do you say? We'll make a go of it together, eh, show the world there's life in us yet.'

Charlie pushed back his chair, let it tip a little – a deliberate gesture, one which his father had always jibed at as slovenly. He let his chin drop, appeared to be deliberating. Up from under his fair eyebrows he could see how the kitchen door had drifted open, how his mother, sitting on a kitchen chair with her back to him, was peering over her shoulder at him, how his aunt was frozen with the meat dish, a large floral oval, in her hands with a dish towel, how Anne at the sink also had her back to him, but was motionless too, head on one side, ears searching for his answer.

It was his moment of triumph and he was high on it. High on glory, two glasses of sherry, the best part of a bottle of Pomagne, and two glasses of port. High, above all, on revenge. No Mafioso closing a vendetta with the last ritual killing of the last Don to hold out against him ever knew an emotion as strong as Charlie's at that moment. And he was going to relish it. Not hurry it. He might be a bit quick at climaxing when it came to sex, but this was going to be a slow, slow burn.

'Dad,' he said, 'you are a businessman. And, as you said, this is not the sort of thing to be entered into lightly. I mean, what I need is some more facts. I have been, 'm, pardon, a bit out of touch recently.'

'Go ahead. Son. Ask anything you like. Anything. If I'd thought you'd not take my word, I'd've brought up the books. But short of, well, the detail like, ask away.'

'Well, Renumeration (sic). In the first year, how much would *I* make? What would my salary be? I mean, actual cash in my pocket.'

'Son, You're not with me. I'm not talking about salaries, hire, wages. We'll be partners. Joint. Taking profit, not salary.'

'Oh sure there'll be profits. But salary too. Salaried director. Paid monthly.' He put an edge to his voice. 'How much?'

There was a long pause.

'You'll have your room, board, heating, light.'

'I've always kept your room for you, Charlie, you know that.' His mother, at last, from the kitchen.

'What do you say to that? I'll bet up West you're paying all of five hundred a year for bed and board. So. Let's say another three on top of that, and when things pick up, as they will with you grafting away down there, well, obviously there'll be more to come. And share of profits, whatever the accountant advises, at the end of the year.'

Pause.

'Accountant, Dad? You never had no accountant before. What accountant is this then?' Deliberate again, the lapse in grammar – one that his father had always been very ready to be sarcastic about in the past. Just let him try it now. 'Well?'

'Only Tom Judd. You know, lending a hand like. For old times' sake. Fellow Leonine Rotationist. You know Tom.'

'I know Tom Judd.' Baird and Skeffington's accountant. 'And I don't suppose he's looking at your books for any other reason than he's been asked to by some wholesaler you owe more than you should to. Or maybe a' – he searched for the word – 'a consortium of such. Now. Listen, Dad. Let's get back to question number one. You're offering me bed and board and three hundred a year. Right?'

'Right, son.' An almost final effort at brightness. 'With prospects.'

'OK.' Another solecism the ageing man had tried to discourage as American. 'OK. The concern I work for as of now pays me fifteen hundred. With prospects.'

'Some flash-in-the-pan firm of crooked shysters. Yids. Oh, I know. How long do you think that'll last?'

Good. It's getting through. He's beginning to realize he's on to a hiding, and sod it, a hiding he's going to get.

'Come on, Dad. We're having a business talk. That's no way for a businessman to carry on. Now. It's the High Street shop you're stuck with. Right?'

'Right, son.' Though wincing at the 'stuck with'.

'Now,' looking first at his chewed fingernails, then up through the kitchen door. Anne had turned now, was facing him. Forewarned is forearmed. He gave her a slow wink. 'The lease on High Street premises has . . . three years to run?'

'Just over. But renegotiable. That's always in the contract. Renegotiable.'

'Sure. A High Street site with a yard behind that could be built over. Fine. Look, Dad, I'm in property. At the moment. And I just do happen to know a bit about the market. Do you know what Charlie Clore is prepared to pay for a good High Street site at this moment in time? Listen. We have a Woolies. We have Timothy White's just opened. And I suppose between them they've mopped up your custom. But no Boots. Do we have a Dolcis or a Manfield? For *fuck's* sake. We don't even have a Marks. And you tell me you're going to renegotiate that lease in three years' time . . .?'

Suddenly, like a bored matador with a bad bull in front of a bad crowd, he'd had enough. Enough of it. Put away the sword, take the *descabello.* Come on, you bastard, drop your head and let me stab you in the back of the neck.

'Piss off, Dad.'

Aunt Elizabeth dropped the meat dish. Charlie ignored the crash.

'In fact, not just piss off over your renegotiable lease, but piss off over the whole sodding business.'

Anne moved in: 'It's gone three. We're missing the Queen.'

All filtered through the dining room into the front room, but Charlie first, planting himself in Father's chair (Did he remember Bambi at the end of the film?), large hands squeezing the worn brown moquette as the screen flickered into life.

Telstar, and her sister satellites, as they arise, can now show the world to the world just as it is in its daily life . . .

Aunt Elizabeth paused by Grandad. 'Either he's had too much to drink,' she said, 'or he's had another stroke. I'll get my stethoscope.'

Some people are uncertain which star to follow, or if any star is worth following at all . . .

I know what star I'm following, thought Charlie, sodding right I know what star.

5

Charlie

Thanks for everything. You've been quite a brick. But I can't be left on my own. Sorry if this causes you trouble.

Lissie

The stupid bitch, thought Charlie, as the euphoria from his recent victories leaked away. She was curled up in the big bed, underneath the orange rug, thumb in her mouth, skin waxy and white, dragging in each breath as if it were a sack of potatoes too heavy to lift. He took her bare shoulder, clammy to touch, and she flopped as if she were lifeless already.

He rang up the nurses' home at St Chad's from the pay phone in the hall. He knew she'd be there - they'd separated on the way from Woolingham only half an hour earlier at Charing Cross. She was free until the night staff came on.

'Get a doctor,' said Anne.

'I haven't got one.'

Pause.

'All right. Listen. Half a bottle of whisky and her sleeping pills? Barbiturates, I suppose. And you say she knew when you were due back? And you weren't late? OK, she's not serious about it then. But don't touch her until I'm there, you might make her vomit and that could be fatal. Get the room as warm as you can and make a lot of very strong black coffee. It'll take me twenty minutes in a taxi, if this blizzard doesn't get worse. If I'm not there in half an hour, then dial 999 and get an ambulance. And Charlie?' Pause. 'This is going to cost you fifty plus the taxi fares.'

He had never seen his sister doing her nurse's bit before. She peeled off a heavy, belted raincoat, unzipped calf-length lined boots, shook snow out of her hair, took her ordinary shoes from a plastic bag.

'Let's look at her.' She folded back the rug, took Lissie's pulse, raised an eyelid, 'OK. No problem. Plenty of time. Warm me a pint of water to hand temperature and dissolve three tablespoonfuls of salt in it. Get a bowl. Where's the toilet? Is it warm? OK! We'll keep it all in here and clean up after. All the towels you've got.' She pushed back sprung clips on a black leather case – inside, rubber tubes, with rubber bulbs. 'We get two or three a week like this, you know. You're right to keep her here if you can. There's someone at St Chad's on a retainer to the newspapers, and you'd have had Lissie Mead all over them again. Wouldn't have done you any good either . . .'

She bustled about, and choosing a moment when her back was turned, Charlie picked up Lissie's note, folded it neatly in half, and put it in the most inside part of the new soft leather black wallet he had bought himself for Christmas.

For the next fortnight Lissie treated him like a sheik. She was docile and meek; kept the basement tidier, almost clean; cooked him sausages, bacon and tomatoes for his supper, and called it mixed grill; brought home quart bottles of light ale.

She taught him ways of fucking he'd hardly even dreamt of, had just guessed at from the hints in the smutty books he got hold of at times. These were still wary of publishing explicit details of anything other than straightforward missionary-position fucking which it was known would get past the courts, since Lady Chatterley, as art. Other ways had to be alluded to in codes for which Charlie and Her Majesty's judges lacked the key.

One night, with new snow falling on frozen snow outside and some cars that passed jingling with chains, he pulled the cord on his winceyette pyjamas at the sight of her sitting naked on the bed, but paused as she held up her hand.

'Stop. Look. This is another way of doing it.'

She twisted round, knelt on the bed, and spread her bottom at him. He was amazed. Revulsion and excitement fought a war and revulsion lost.

'Put it in my bum-hole. But gently. Use the Vaseline.'

Quite often, at least for his first entry into her, she made him use Vaseline, so it was there on the bedside locker.

'You must be gentle. Very slow. At least at first. Once you're past the muscle it gets easier. Ouch. That hurt a bit.' She wriggled, improved the angle, and suddenly something gave and he slid right in, further and further until her buttocks were pressed right into the pit of his stomach.

'Now,' she said, 'put your hands round the front of me. No. Lower down. Come on.'

He had never touched her there before with his fingers – he had always just pushed away until he got in, or she guided him in. Now he was tentatively, darkly afraid he would get her wee-wee on his fingers.

'Oh, come on.' Awkwardly she tipped her weight all on to one arm, to bring her right hand down to guide his. For a moment it seemed as if the whole comic edifice, perched on two levels, his feet on the floor, her knees on the bed, might topple or fall apart.

'That's right. Go on. Up a little. Sort of tickle me just there, please, yes, that's just right.'

As his fingers at last did what she wanted, he began slowly to ease himself up and down, and when, quite soon, she came, he felt the spasms in her sphincter, and, although he had no idea at all of what had happened - he was totally ignorant of female orgasm - it made him come too.

Afterwards they smoked cigarettes, drank whisky, she

under the rug now leaning on one elbow beneath the cracked parchment of the lamp that stood on the locker, he in the armchair, safely back in his pyjamas.

'Where on earth did you get the idea of doing that?' he asked.

'Good, isn't it? Most of my friends do it every now and then. We got the idea, oh, a year ago was it? From that article in *Encounter.*'

He had no idea what *Encounter* was, but since it carried instructions on sodomy, he supposed it was a particularly dirty magazine. The name suggested it.

'You know. That man Sparrow. He showed how Mellors actually buggered Connie, that Lawrence never really said so, but that's what he meant. If the prosecution had realized, they'd have won the case. Anyway, ever since then everyone's been doing it.'

He always hated it when she said 'you know' and 'everyone', and assumed a shared knowledge of things like magazines called *Encounter* or the right name for a squiggly-shaped piece of pasta; but he had learnt to hide it, for he hated it even more when she called him an oick, a philistine, an ignorant yob. It all reminded him of that easy world she came from where no one grafted and the plums fell into your lap if you crooked a finger – you did not even have to shake the trees.

6

Domestic peace and erotic experiment did not last. As January wore on, Lissie became nervous and frenetic again. He found strange pills in her handbag – Preludin, amphetamines – and he began to fear a repetition of her suicide attempt. It was, he surmised, all due to the fact that her case was to come up again in the second week of February. On his side the thought nagged, and became an obsession, that though he had her body Lissie's thousands remained beyond his reach. And it wasn't only that he wasn't getting any of them, but that she was wasting them, throwing them away. She paid a lot for the drugs she bought; she was extravagant over clothes, twirled around in them, chucked them out – literally, into the dustbin. 'What's the use?' she'd say, 'You never take me anywhere.'

Exasperated, one day he did. He took her in a taxi through the frozen streets. There were piles of dirty snow on the corners, ruts of ice in the side streets, grit and salt slush in the gutters. It was amazing how the snow, which, occasionally, you could catch pure and unsmirched in a park or garden, made everything filthy beyond belief . . . He took her in a taxi to Covent Garden.

It was *Falstaff*. He thought she would like it because the music was by a wop, and judging by her record collection she liked music by wops. Once it started, he rather supposed she did like it. At any rate she made a good show of liking it. He hated it.

He hated it first because there was a slip in the programme, that cost all of five bob, saying that the title role would be sung not by Geraint Evans but by a wop called Tito Gobbi. He felt that a fast one had been pulled on him that a refund on the tickets, a guinea each, was in order. He hated the smooth way the audience slid to their places – many of the women in long dresses, most of the men in dinner jackets – their glossy sparkle, their well-fed shine, their easy drawling accents. Everyone seemed to know someone else if not everyone else: they waved nonchalant hands across the gangways: 'Eh seh, Michael. Theyess Susan eover theyer.' 'Which Susan, darlin'?' 'The Thompsons' Susan, darlin', you kneow.'

The performance bored him at first, but the boredom grew into an impacted cold anger sitting in his chest like the piles of dirty snow on the pavements: it was so utterly stupid. People singing instead of talking was stupid, the costumes were stupid, the scenes changing in front of your eyes . . . stupid. And a story that revolved round a fat drunk old man who tried to seduce scarcely less drunk old women, all done in wop although Shakespeare had apparently had a hand in it, was insulting in its stupidity. And all this was meant to happen in *Windsor?*

He quite liked the music on the rare occasions when it was loud and fast and no one was singing.

The intervals were worse. For all his size and strength, for all he could do a very passable Kensington Posh when needed, the barmen had his number. They worked down the counter to the man next to him and then up away from him three times before they served him, by when he was near to apoplexy. And all around him, him and Lissie, the bright easy chatter, the warm smells of expensive perfumes and cigars, the talk of Prunier for supper, do you think? Hev you booked? Yes, ectually. Weel then, eh think it should be Prunier, deon't you? . . . All that added a fine edge to his resolution that one day he'd get even, one day he'd be there, one day he'd show them.

He refused to leave his seat during the second interval. 'Please yourself,' said Lissie. 'I've seen two or three chums who'll probably talk to me if you're not there.'

He was soon even more bored in the two-thirds empty

auditorium. Only aged couples, mostly both of them women, had stayed behind to eat ice cream out of tubs, bored with nothing to look at but the blank wall of red velvet in front of him with its gold E II. Probably cost as much as he earned in a year. Anyway he wanted a slash.

At the doorway into the bar he met Lissie coming out. Her face was ashen, even whiter than usual.

'Oh, Charlie. Oh, Charlie, please take me home, we should never have come.'

It was the last straw. All that money spent on her and she wouldn't even sit the sodding thing out to the end.

In the taxi she tried to explain but it was all confused, carried too many references to things he knew nothing of, but he gathered an outline. In the bar she had met a girl friend who was secretary to an MP who knew her father. And this friend had been, well, almost horrified to see her, but relieved too. She tried to explain why.

People had been looking for her, a private detective employed by her father, the police – even apparently the Special Branch. It was fearfully important. Yes, of course to do with the weed charge. Weed? Indian Hemp, the stuff they found in her flat. But there was more to it. There was a fearful stink on, connected with people she knew, with the people she had taken the weed from, and with some too she had passed it on to. Fearfully important, to do with a cabinet minister. And a Russian. Everyone's talking about it, but nobody knows. And that shooting, the night before she came to Bannington Gardens, and that was another reason why she was so frightened.

'And I don't know what to do, I don't know what to do . . .'

By now they were in the basement, she sobbing on the bed, he pacing up and down wishing she would be more coherent, pull herself together. Shouldn't you slap women when they were hysterical? Certainly, he felt, a thump would seem in order.

'I don't know what to do. If I tell people where I am, they'll come for me. If it's so serious, the police will take away the bail and I'll be locked up. Oh, Charlie, I couldn't bear that, I'll kill myself, I swear I will, I swear I will, Oh, Daddy, poor Daddy . . .'

'What's your sodding father got to do with it?'

'Oh, Charlie, you must see. He'll lose his seat if it all comes out any more. I've already done him enough harm, but if it comes out I'm connected with all that lot, they'll crucify him, he'll have to resign even before the next election, or stand down or something. It'll kill him, it really will . . .'

'Oh, Jesus. For Christ's sake. Shut up. Really, I'll hang one on you if you go on like that. Now belt up.'

'Charlie, Charlie. What'll I do? I'll kill myself. Seriously, I mean properly. Not so you can find me, I'll really kill myself . . .'

He hit her. First almost tentatively, and then, savouring the satisfaction, quite a lot harder.

She looked at him; a bead of blood grew in the corner of her mouth, blossomed and spilled down her chin. Then, to his amazement, she stepped up to him, put her arms round his neck, and her head on his chest, and, by letting the strength go from her legs, forced him to put his arms round her in an embrace that mimicked tenderness.

Like that he sat on the bed and she contrived to curl up to him, weeping for a time, but not the gasping sobs that had maddened him. Eventually she pulled away a little, looked up at him. The blood, not much of it, had smeared across her cheek; the tears, grubby with mascara, streaked into it.

'Charlie. Do something. Twice, three times you've saved me. Do it again.'

'I'll try.'

'I know you'll do it. I know it.' She sniffed, almost a sort of a smile hovered, 'You're really rather awful. Very awful.

But you do fix things. Fix this, and I'll do anything for you.'

For a moment the words 'marry me' hovered in his mouth, but he swallowed them back. He knew her now, knew her well, and that would not be the way. Marriage yes. That was the way to the thousands. But not ask her, no. She would have to ask him – otherwise she would never go through with it. Meanwhile . . .

'I'll think of something.'

In fact he already had. He had remembered that George Alderson was now a detective constable with the Met and based at Camden nick.

Absentmindedly, provoked by the possibilities this suggested, he patted Lissie lightly on the shoulder. She snuggled up closer, and her thumb went to her mouth.

As always, Charlie now moved not *deliberately,* which implies a sequential train of action carefully thought through, but *warily,* testing the ground as he went, taking some trouble to get it right, before actually committing himself. He operated not exactly by instinct, but by feel, sniffing around, finding out, waiting until his nerves had screwed him up to the point where he had to act, waiting for the moment that he sensed would be the one where things would go right. Later in life this hiatus between inspiration and action, filled by more or less relevant 'thought', he called 'doing his homework.'

Charlie bothered with nothing, ever, that was not more or less under his nose – apart, that is, from his obsession 'to get it made.' He had read the evening papers before Lissie moved in, but out of boredom, and, with the whisky, to induce sleep. She had taken their place, though the whisky, shared now, remained a necessity. As a result, he was less aware than almost anyone who lived at that time between, say, Chiswick and St Paul's of the rumours, speculations, gossip that hummed in every bar, at every party, across office desks and shop floors. Perhaps, if we are to believe some of what we read, Supermac knew less than Charlie of what everyone was talking about, but I doubt if anyone else did. Even children in playgrounds were making up skipping songs about it all.

He therefore spent two or three days 'doing his homework'. He went to pubs and eavesdropped. He bought *Private Eye.* He chatted up the girls at Belgravia Properties. And the more he found out about it all, the more he liked the feel of it. There was a very thorough investigation under way into the private life of a senior minister. National security came into it – spies and all that. People mentioned Vassall; some remembered Burgess and Maclean and how Philby had issued a statement saying that he was not the Third Man. Weed, Indian Hemp, came into it too, and that shooting in Kensington, and the name of missing Felicity Mead was mentioned twice. All in all it was a stink. A first-rate scandal. People, big people, top people, people who went to listen to wops singing at Covent Garden, were in the shit and doing their damnedest to get out of it. And somewhere, somehow, Lissie had touched it, Lissie had strayed in and *they* could be looking for her to find out what she knew, how much she knew, whether what she knew should be told or bottled up. In short, she had a marketable asset.

On her behalf, Charlie went to market. He rang up the Camden nick and made contact with George Alderson.

They met in the snug of an unfashionable pub near Archway. To the barmen they looked identical: large young men, well dressed, with a sort of bullying authority about them – both of them, he decided, police officers. But when Charlie came up for a second round, he could see the difference. The one buying the drinks was sharper, much more expensively dressed, not as grey-looking or as tired as the other, not quite so ox-like. Well then, a young businessman on the make, in insurance, perhaps, chatting up the CID . . . possibly plotting how to split a reward.

Which wasn't far from the truth.

'Listen, Charlie, if you know where Felicity Mead is, you should just go straight to her father. He's just offered a thousand sheets to anyone who finds her,'

'Oh yes?'

'True.'

Tempting. A grand on top of what he already had would begin to look like capital. But less like capital than the ten grand still in Lissie's bank account. No. George had never won a game of Monopoly in his life, had always been too ready to take one fast buck rather than ten slow ones, and he'd always be a copper.

'Well. It's not as easy as that. Listen. What have you got on her?'

'Just possession. The West End lot wanted to hang a pusher rap too, but they say they can't put it together. The top drawer are like that' – he linked his little fingers - 'you know? No one was going to stand up in court and say they bought weed off her. I expect one or two of our lot came in the way of a backhander too.'

'What'll she get?'

'Fine. A year on prob. Nothing really to worry about.'

But, thought Charlie, that's not what she thinks.

'Couldn't you just drop the whole thing? If she turns Queen's Evidence?'

'Not really. You see we've got the spade who was flogging it to her, and she won't know any more of it than that. If she did, then there'd be some point. 'Cos, tell no lie, we're not getting anywhere with him. No matter what frighteners we put on him, there's someone behind who's got him a sodding sight more frightened than we can make him.'

Charlie drank, and his small eyes glittered over the rim of the jar. 'What would you think,' he said, 'if I told you the spade you've got was working for another spade called Edgecombe?'

The policeman's reaction was satisfactory. He became almost furtive, as furtive as an ox can be, set down his mug, glanced round the small brown room, checked the barman was out in the saloon, pulled out a large white handkerchief and blew his nose.

'I'd be interested,' he said.

'Yes.' Charlie waited, used the silence.

'Um. Anything else?'

'Come on. Charges dropped?'

'On the cards.'

'Two girls. Lissie mentioned them once. Christine and Mandy.'

Charlie leant back, narrowed eyes, forced his sharkish mouth to keep firm, not to laugh, not even to grin, for George was now in the grip of even more intense emotions, which he, on his side, could not control.

'Yes, Well. I'll be . . .' With hands that shook a little, he pulled a sliver of Wrigley's from his top pocket, unwrapped it, popped it in, and chewed feverishly for about ten seconds. Then, unable to contain himself any longer, almost babbled, 'Um, anything else? I mean, you must know where you're at now, this could be quite big . . .'

Quite big for you, detective constable. Charlie knew enough about the Met to know that a detective is rated by his superiors on the reliability and discretion of his informers, that if George went back to the nick with not only a line on where Lissie was, but also with a lollipop like this, he'd be on his way. Up. The trouble was that Charlie had now shot his bolt, but George was too eager, let him in too easily.

'I mean . . . well, come on, Charlie, what else?'

'She's talked a lot to me. I don't understand it all. Give me a line.'

'A doctor. A bent doctor. Ward.'

'Yes,' lied Charlie, 'she mentioned him.'

She gets her pills from somewhere. Why not from a bent doctor called Ward?

'Your *pater* – that's what you call him isn't it? – has got a grand out for you.'

'I *never* call him *pater,* and you know damn well I don't. Yes. I know. Didn't take you long to find that out, did it? Don't go to him, Charlie. Listen. I'll write you the cheque.'

Which was, again, tempting, but Charlie had used the gambit consciously to prepare the way for what came next.

'Don't bother. 'Listen, Lissie. I can get you off your charge.'

'Charlie!' Wide-eyed, she breathed the word as if it were the secret name of God. 'Charlie. You're not having me on, are you? This isn't one of your games?'

'No. But you've got to do what I say. It's very easy really. You've got to let me bring a couple of guys here. Police. Special Branch. They'll want to talk to you. Question you. And if you let them, then that's it. All charges dropped.'

Tears began to flow, she put her knuckle in her mouth, but couldn't stop the sobs. Between them: 'I can't . . . I can't do it . . . oh, Charlie.'

He shook her, gave her another slap. 'Lissie. You've bloody got to. If you don't they'll hammer you for pushing the stuff too. That's why you got remand. So they could complete their enquiries re the possibility of a pushing charge. But you let them talk to you, here, no need to go out, and tell them all you know, about Edgecombe, the Keeler girl, all that, and they'll drop the lot. Let you off the hook and no more scandal to bother . . . yes, the Dop. The Dear Old Parent. What's more, he'll be able to keep his thousand sheets.'

'But I don't know anything about Edgecombe or Christine.'

Silence.

'Christ. You must know something. You've mentioned them both. You said so. Coming out of that opera and since.'

'Well. Yes. All right. A bit.'

'And what about Ward. Anything about him?'

'Never heard of him.'

Heart beating with chagrin, chewing his nails, Charlie paced round the basement for two minutes, then: 'You'd better start by telling me all you do know about all that. Every last detail. Then, we'll work out how to tart it up a bit, add a bit, you know, amplify it . . .'

It worked, but only just. There were dozens of people on the fringe of the Profumo Affair who knew as much or more than Lissie, that is, very little indeed – just enough to swell the roar of gossip that swept through the town. Charlie realized he should have known that Lissie's psychosis (not his word) demanded that she should wholeheartedly exaggerate her role in it all, even invent a role.

When the Special Branch men came, Charlie was invited to leave. He spent a very anxious two hours in the Aussie launderette and returned to find that they had got from her as much as they could get, that they would keep their word and drop the charge, for a couple of addresses and a telephone number she had been able to come up with.

George Alderson remained well pleased. After all, he found Felicity Mead – although his superiors advised that it would not be appropriate to claim the reward, since Lissie had insisted that her father should not be told her address, only that she was alive and well and that the charges had been dropped. However, they accepted on George's behalf five hundred pounds for the Police Benevolent Fund. And they gave him a firm pat on the back.

7

Charlie now put in motion step number three, or was it four or five, in the process of getting his hands on Lissie's ten thousand. After his success in getting her off the hook, she became again, as he had expected she would, the dutiful concubine. Sausages returned to the menu, and bum-hole, and, as an extra, sucking. But he was cool, off-hand, dismissive, sarcastic, deliberately riled her in order to provoke a row. One evening, she rose to the bait and bit him.

In spite of the thump he gave her, he sensed the possibility of laughter. Never in his life had he exercised so much control over his own body, except once or twice in a Rugby scrum when the opposition had equalled his own savagery and cynicism. He really was in quite nasty pain, worse than she was suffering with a ringing ear, yet he showed no sign of it as he got his clothes on, not his pyjamas but his outdoor clothes.

'What are you doing?'

'I'm going.'

Silence.

'Where?'

Silence.

'Oh, come on, Charlie. You started it. Don't throw a moody.'

As he tied up his shoelaces, she began to whimper. When he got his suitcase off the top of the hardboard wardrobe, she began to cry. He took his unpressed underwear from the plastic bag he took to the Aussie launderette and rammed it into the case, then the laundry-done shirts.

'Charlie . . . don't go . . . I'm sorry. Charlie, I really

need you. You've been so good to me . . . and, Charlie, I really have tried to be good to you. But nothing I do seems to please you any more.'

He waited.

'Charlie, I'll do anything you say. Anything.'

This was the point, or near enough, when, according to the scenario he had worked out, she would say, I'll marry you if that's what you want.

But she didn't. She pleaded all right. Offered to suck him again if that's what he wanted. Offered, with a touch of sarcasm that he could not help noticing, to cook him spotted dick as well as sausages if *that* was what he wanted.

'OK then. You just tell me. You tell me what I have to do to make you stay.'

He was aware of too much: mainly that this was a scene that could not be repeated. The next time he got down his suitcase she would probably help him pack. With a sinking feeling, the sure certainty that he'd blown it, but that this was the last chance, he said:

'Marry me.'

She froze, naked as she was, half sprawled, half kneeling across the orange rug to which she had scuttled when he hit her.

'Why?'

Silence.

'Charlie? For Christ's sake, why?'

A longer silence. One which for once he was forced to break.

'Why not? I mean . . . it's the decent thing to do, isn't it? We've been fucking for seven weeks.'

'Eight.'

'Eight. People are meant to marry when they fuck. That's decency. That's what people of my sort do.'

'Charlie, please don't hit me again. Please don't. But I think I've got to laugh. No. No. It's all right. I'm under control. I won't laugh, I promise you. Right. Charlie, we've got to talk this through haven't we?'

'Yes.' Sullen, knowing he'd suffered a major reverse, but sensing terms in the air.

'Right. But we must be honest. Tolerably honest. And I want you absolutely, cross your heart and hope to die, to promise not to hit me again.'

'Promise.'

'Cross your heart.'

Sheepishly he did.

'And hope to die?'

'And hope to die.'

'Charlie, it's my money you're after, isn't it? Always, has been. Right?.

This time it was not the tactical silence he placed in front of his opponents so they would put their feet in it, but an involuntary one as his mind wrestled with an exceedingly unpleasant situation. But she had shown the way: honesty was the name of the game, tolerably honesty.

'Ten grand is an added attraction, an *added* attraction.'

'And what happens when it's all gone, all spent. Then, married or not, you'll throw me aside like a worn-out glove.'

'But that's just the point, Lissie.' He stood up, began to pace about again, gnawing nails. 'That's just the point. Two points, in point of fact. A. Number one. I don't want you to spend it all. I don't want you to spend it at all.'

'But it's not worth keeping. It's not enough. It fetches seven hundred a year after tax. What's the point in that? But spent for fun it'll last three, four years, and at the end of the day I'll have had fun.'

'Doesn't seem much like fun to me.

'What doesn't?'

'The way you've been going on.'

Silence. Then: 'Point taken.'

'And another thing. What do *you* do when it's all gone?'

She shrugged. She was sitting now, still naked, legs pulled up clasped in her arms, chin on her knees, pubic hair just showing between clamped thighs. The gas fire popped and breathed – in spite of the cold outside, it was very warm in that basement, 'By then an unmarried aunt might have gone to join our forefathers. Even the Dop himself. He's quite old. I could work. I *can* work, you know. But most probably I'll marry. And not you, Charlie Bosham, but someone stinking rich, really inexhaustibly rich.'

It went on for a further half-hour: his exasperation at the idea of her throwing away a capital asset, her insistence that it wasn't capital, it wasn't enough to be capital . . .

'No, not capital like in a bank, or insurance, or shares or something, but . . . in a business, or something that makes money fast.'

'A popular music group? A film? You're joking.'

'Of course not. Something with much less risk. You could buy a row of terraced houses in Willesden or Islington or Battersea for ten grand.'

'Yes. And I'm sure you're right; there'd be a very handsome profit in what . . . Two, five, ten years' time. But what do we do in the meantime? I'm not going to live on the measly pittance you earn.'

What came very clear as this honest confrontation went on was that, in spite of her apparently very severe mental defects, her emotional instability, her reliance on drugs, her acceptance of, even appetite for, sexual humiliation, she was very keenly aware indeed of just whose her money was. It was quite an education for Charlie, who was still mystified and angered by the upper classes and their plum trees, to find how properly proprietorial she was about hers. She might be spendthrift, a conspicuous consumer, a waster, but, by God, *she* was going to be the consumer, not anyone else. In all the eight weeks, he had never known her so serious, so coherent, so determined.

Yet, at the end of it all, he won some ground. She

conceded that it might be possible to get really rich out of ten grand, and quite quickly too, conceded that many great people had done just that. But was Charlie great? Well, they'd see. If, or when, he came up with an idea, a really sound, foolproof, copper-bottomed way of converting ten grand into twenty, forty, sixty in a reasonably quick time, then she'd go along with it. 'Mind you, I'll need a lot of convincing.' In the meantime, she'd try to spend less, keep within her income and his, not waste the capital any more. At least not for, what? Three months?

'And will you . . . shall we . . . get married?'

She looked at him over her knees for a long time. Then said, 'Charlie. Perhaps.'

They went to bed – he in his sleeping bag, she in the big bed, under the orange rug. She turned out the light and he turned out the gas fire. Street lights glowed through the hessian curtains some seamstress employed by Heals had made up for her. Footsteps on the pavements. Tyres purred through the slush.

Out of the darkness her voice came. There was a note of glee in it Charlie had never heard before.

'Charlie.'

'Yes.'

'You know something I've never told you before?'

'What?'

'I hate my father. Some of the time I feel all cuddly about him, but mostly I hate him. I hate Terry too. I hate what they've done to my mother and what they are doing to me. I know this because they sent me to a trick cyclist after that abortion, and that's what he told me was wrong with me. Of course I didn't believe him then, but since I've realized how right he was. Especially since I got my hands on Great Aunt Mead's loot. Anyway, he, the trick cyclist, said all these awful things I do are to hurt the male Dop and the male sibling. And the female Dop too, since she is a collaborator.'

Charlie was totally at a loss, said nothing.

'So, Charlie. It's dawned on me the very best thing I can do to really upset them. Apart from splitting infinitives, which they abhor. Better than anything I have done before.' Pause, then, with venom: 'The ultimate ball-crusher.'

Silence.

'Don't you want to know what I have in mind, Charlie?'

He mumbled assent.

'Charlie, I will marry you.' She sighed with very deep satisfaction at the thought, then added more briskly, 'But mind you. Don't get any ideas. The deal stands. The loot is mine and stays mine. You come up with that copper-bottomed scheme and I'll consider it. All right? Now, Charlie. Just for once, get into bed with me.'

Heart laden with awe and angst rather than triumph, he did as he was told. On his back, she put her head on his shoulder and her knee across his stomach, and, sodium amytol doing its bit at last, was almost instantly asleep.

He lay there for an hour, listening to the drip of melting snow, before easing himself out of the bed and back to his sleeping bag. He fingered his torn and bruised prick and thought that yes, he and Lissie shared one thing – this hate of Meads, father and son, and yes, the day he confronted them with his marriage would be a good one.

8

The thaw came and Rugby started again. Commuting back to Woolingham to play for the Old Sydneyans was a chore Charlie felt he should keep up . . . not least because he was curious to see how it would feel to be with Terry Mead, to swap banal commonplaces with old-chap-slap-you-on-the-back-who's-in-the-chair-I'll-have-a-pint bonhommie, and know all the time that the wet fart was his brother-in-law. There would be glee in that, enhanced rather than otherwise by the sworn promise he'd made to his wife (his wife! by a special licence in a registry office) that he would not let on, that the secret would be kept until she was good and ready to let it out.

In the event the match, against a team of bank clerks, did not turn out just as he had hoped. He met Terry briefly before the game, found him as affable, as *gentlemanly* as ever, but of course no more than that. Still, it was enough to make him wonder why Lissie hated him, even to make him wonder why he, Charlie, hated him. That was the trouble with UC and UMC shits – they screwed you rotten with their faces turned away, but when they confronted you they were as smooth as glass, as sweet as honey, as affable as oil. But the trouble came with the game itself.

Charlie was badly out of condition. For several years he had played Rugby in winter and some cricket and tennis in the summer. He was young, and the young burn off fat and alcohol just by being young. But nearly eight weeks of frostbound grounds, nearly eight weeks of Lissie's mixed grills, of light ale at supper and whisky after, and no exercise apart from fucking, had left their mark. Moreover, the opposing prop forward, who was built on much the same lines as Charlie, had somehow managed to keep in training, and, worst of all, had an almost equal share of downright bastardly in his make-up.

The consequence was that Charlie arrived at the scrums a couple of yards behind the rest, and arrived out of puff. Out of puff, he lacked push. His opposite number had push, and not only push. Ten minutes into the second half, as Charlie's feet slipped and the packed wheeled for the fifteenth time, his opponent, only a sodding bank clerk after all, skilfully hacked his feet from under him.

Next scrum and Charlie bit half his ear off, and the jumped-up bank clerk withdrew, squealing with pain, and threatening, between squeals, civil action for assault. Charlie was sent off, spent the rest of the game on the touchline.

In the showers afterwards the Old Sydneyans, who had lost by 21 to 3, were subdued, and no one said a word to Charlie. As he left the ground, through the tarmacked playground, used as a carpark at weekends, he suspected that he had played his last game of Rugby. On Monday (in those days there was still a collection on Sunday afternoons) a polite note informed him that for the foreseeable future he would not be asked to turn out for the Old Sydneyans. Many thanks for all your past gallant efforts. We'll miss you. Best wishes. Terry.

Charlie said to Lissie, 'Lissie, just why do you hate Terry so much?'

'Because he's a boy and older than me.'

'What's wrong with that?'

'Because he is going to be a solicitor. He's going to make a lot of money. Perhaps, he'll be an MP like the male Dop. Or a barrister. Or a judge. Do you know what the Dop offered me when I left school?'

'No.'

'A secretarial course. Oh yes, a very good one. Half the House of Commons have secretaries who have been on it.

They service the best law firms, the smartest agencies. I expect your boss's personal secretary at Belgravia went there. Great. But they didn't suggest I should go to University College and then to Lincoln's Inn. So that's partly why I hate them and Terry. But it's more than that, Charlie. It's what lies behind it all. They didn't even *think* about it . . . oh shit. I'm not going on about it all now. How did the game go? I expected you home much later and beerily pissed. Terry always is. In the nicest way, of course. And the only time the Dops saw me a mite under the influence they gave me an awful jawing . . .'

Charlie thought she was talking cock, but knew better than to say so. But it was nice to know that, when it came to the crunch with her family, she'd still be on his side.

Of course there was no crunch. One day she rang up Mums and told her she was married. To Charlie Bosham. Ask Terry, he knows him. Darling, how lovely. Why didn't you tell us? But of course you must bring him over. Let me see. How about next . . . oh dear, we do seem to be terribly booked up, all the way to Friday week. No, darling, don't dress, not even for such a lovely occasion. No one does now, do they?

They had a perfectly awful meal in the green and white room, sitting at the oval mahogany table round a centrepiece of daffodils and forsythia, in front of the marble fireplace, and everybody was terribly sweet, even absolutely darling. Terry didn't say a word about the footer game; Mrs Mead assured Charlie that he was just what Lissie needed, a steadying influence; Freddie Mead, MP, looking shinier than before, with a permanent flush in his cheeks and his hair no longer off-white and lank but hallmarked silver, briefly quizzed him about his position and prospects. 'Belgravia, eh? Jolly good firm. I believe Mead and Mead have done some work for them once or twice. Though of course I'm too busy at the House to poke my nose in there much these days,' Before they sat down, he showed Charlie the flint arrowheads and the old coins, including the Kruger half-crown.

Mums managed to ask Lissie the two important questions which were on everyone's minds and offered the one piece of advice she thought was necessary. Since the ladies did not withdraw, she had to do this at a point when conversation between the men reached a level of self-absorption that precluded them from overhearing.

The Member for Woolingham said, 'I was in the House. I heard him. He was very positive, very clear. Very straight. He said, quite frankly, "I admit knowing her. But I deny impropriety. Miss Keeler and I were on friendly terms. There was no impropriety whatsoever in my relationship with Miss Keeler."' Charlie said, and indeed was echoing the wisdom of many, 'Well, he would say that, wouldn't he?' And Terry, dropping the bonhomie for once, said, 'Come on, Charlie, that's not really fair. Not cricket. The man was on the carpet in the House and he did the straight thing. He knew her. He admitted that. No impropriety. He stated that. Case closed. Eh, Dad? Case closed.' While all this went on, Mrs Mead asked her daughter, 'Are you pregnant? No? Good. Have you let him touch your money? No? Good. Don't. And darling. Please do realize. If you ever regret this, then please don't worry. Daddy will get you out of it.'

On the way home Lissie was gleeful. 'They are *mad'* she exclaimed, 'They really are in a rage.' Charlie couldn't see it but took her word for it.

All of which was peripheral. The main thing was that, during this time, with ten grand in his reach, Charlie cracked the code, discovered the secret, unravelled just how it is you convert capital into wealth, income, and more capital, in a never-ending cycle of gain.

The relevation came in three stages.

9

For days, weeks, he kicked round the old question. How do I get rich? Really rich. How do I convert the assured income from eleven grand – which is about one grand – into eleven grand a year? What makes money make money? What is at the bottom of the heap?

He answered these questions on his own, without any help at all from books, education, newspapers, teach yourself, the BBC, ITV, anything at all. It was not surprising that he had to do it on his own, since the culture he was a part of, however disparate, contradictory, conflicting, competitive, greedy and grasping, was unified at one point: it would conceal from itself, from all its disparate heterogeneous parts the one great secret of all – the source of capital. Perhaps one in ten thousand knew, but they weren't going to tell Charlie. Why not? If you had the secret of untold riches, would you tell the rest of the world? Of course not. So he had to find out for himself.

Here is how he did it.

First he obsessed himself with products that sold nothing for something. Particularly he doted on those firms that sold air. Aero chocolate. J cloths. Polo mints. Corrugated cardboard. All ways of packaging air and selling it. The one he liked best was aerated water. To package air in water, chuck in a squeeze of lemon and a drop of quinine, and get a man with a cut-glass accent and a funny beard to advertise it – and make . . . MILLIONS.

So, for a week or two he was obsessed with this idea – or rather lack of a new idea, a new way of selling air. He thought of, or stumbled on, many more ways of doing it.

Foam rubber in all its forms from mattresses to shoe-liners. Mousses, lemon or chocolate flavoured. Bubbles – yes! those little pots of liquid detergent with a plastic ring you dipped in and blew through . . . Christ! In that version you even conned the punter into providing his own air. But, they were all thought of already, patented, tied up, shares quoted on the Stock Exchange, no chance now of getting in on the ground floor.

'Why was I misguided
I wish I had decided
to buy elastic-sided
. . . bootees.'

So carolled Bernard Cribbins all through the winter, mocking winklepicker shoes, the last fad of the Teds before Mods and Rockers took over the scene. And Charlie had done just that: bought a pair of very expensive Italian, elastic-sided bootees. By March the appalling winter had torn a neat little hole in each sole, and he took them to a tiny cobbler's shop in one of the alleys between Earls Court and Cromwell Road.

A day later, on his way to pick them up, he had an odd but total recall of very early childhood, sitting on Aunt Elizabeth's knee while she read him *The Elves and the Shoemaker:*

'The same morning a lady came into the shop to buy a pair of shoes. The Shoemaker showed her the pair he had found on his bench. She said, "I have never seen such well-made shoes." The lady tried on the shoes, and they fitted her perfectly. She was so pleased with them that she paid the Shoemaker twice the usual price. With the money the Shoemaker was able to buy leather for two pairs of shoes . . . That morning, a man came into the shop to buy some shoes. The Shoemaker showed him the two pairs of shoes he had found on his bench. The man said, "I have never seen such well-made shoes." He was so pleased with them that he bought both pairs of shoes. He paid the Shoemaker twice the usual price . . . And so it went on. Many rich customers came to his shop to buy these perfect shoes. So, in time the Shoemaker and his wife became very rich indeed . . . '

And where did the wealth come from? The story had a surprisingly convincing, not to say honest, if you could read the code, explanation.

'In came two tiny elves. They were dressed in old clothes and their feet were bare. They began to stitch and sew and hammer. They did not stop for a moment until all the cut shoes were finished.'

'That'll be ten and sixpence please. Sir. Ten and six.'

Charlie snapped out of his dream, looked around, took in the tiny dark shop with its single unshaded light over the workbench, its grinding wheel, heavy sewing machine with thick bent needle, the lasts, hammers, pliers, the stack of skin-shaped leather, the smell.

'Ten and six?'

'Yes, sir. It sounds a lot, the price of leather these days is something chronic. But see. We done a good job.' He pulled one of Charlie's shoes out of the bag he had already put them in, and went on with perky cockney obsequiousness. 'Good as new they are now. Lovely pair of shoes. Italian. Lovely craftsmanship there, pleasure to work on them. Cost you a bob or two, I expect.'

'Five guineas.'

'There. I thought so. And they'll last you another twelve months at least.'

This man, thought Charlie, is an idiot. I have spent ten and six and saved myself the cost of buying a new pair of shoes. I have made a profit of four pounds, fourteen shillings and sixpence.

He picked up the bag and began to walk very slowly back to Bannington Gardens, but he was still thinking it all out when he got there, so he went on, walked in circles for another half-hour until he was certain he had it worked out.

What had he bought for his ten and sixpence? A pair of shoes worth five guineas. No. That's not it. That's the way his bankrupt father thought, the way most people thought. They see an article, a product, a commodity at one price and they buy it, and then they try to sell it at a higher price. But what have I *really* bought? Two small pieces of leather. What else? How long did that idiot work on my shoes? Twenty minutes. So for twenty minutes I bought his shop, or rented it, paid for his electric light, the power of his machines, the machines themselves in a way (he wasn't too clear about this, but sensed that the machines had cost, were perhaps still costing, the cobbler whatever he had had to lay out or borrow to provide himself with them), his rates, and even the stale steak pie which his breath demonstrated had kept him going since lunchtime, his taxes, the rent on his house . . . What else? His skill, and a portion of what it had cost to give him that skill. Not only his skill. Everything he is. Everything he will be. Even his obsequious, dull, idiot mind that was happy to charge ten and six for something worth five times as much, and then apologize.

For twenty minutes I bought all that. But none of that put two new soles on my shoes. Those were all static, preconditions for the process, the activity, the . . . work.

I bought his labour.

Not treasure to be found, which is dead, but a transforming agent, the thing that actually changes one thing worth so much into another thing that's worth a fucking sight more, that secret little grub . . . is labour. Other men's work. Not a thing you can touch or feel, but an action; not an abstraction even though you can't get hold of it, because it is movement, energy, something after all real, concrete, something you can buy as easily as the electricity through the meter.

What I need, thought Charlie, is a load of elves. Preferably in old clothes and bare feet: they come cheaper like that.

But what should his elves do, what form should their labour take? At least this second insight had given a sharper logic to the first one, the one about packaging air. The reason why he had been obsessed with that was now clear: it was the simplicity that attracted him. Labour was the source of wealth, but most of the time there was a whole heap of complications on top of it, obscuring the simple fact that, by and large, the elves who provided the magic ingredient were screwed rotten by everyone else.

His mind felt the presence of these complications, secondary worlds he named them as, like dark, impenetrable mountains – for few of the perceptions that were now blossoming in his mind were fully articulated – many felt like physical presences bumping around in his mind. A larger part of the heap he sensed sat almost literally on top of the secret, obscuring it, making it into a mystery, above all controlling it: governments, police, armies, school-teachers, vicars. Another lot controlled and regulated it in an entirely different way: banks, accountants, insurance, building societies, laws, regulations, customs. Yet another consisted of those systems like the one he belonged to, that lived off old labour, the centuries-old labour that had built houses like the one he lived in, on land that had not belonged to the elves, with tools and bricks that had not belonged to the makers of those tools and bricks, and now it was all sold, and resold, and sold again, to be bought and bought again, and rebought by people who had gathered in to themselves the profit to be made from someone else's, some other elves', labour somewhere else . . .

Charlie felt all this like a sickening weight in his mind; he realized it was far beyond his capacity to manipulate it on his own, to cream the profits of labour at seven or eight removes from source. You needed to be a Cotton or a Clore, a Rockefeller or a Getty or a Gulbenkian, to do that. And if you couldn't do that, then you were just stuck somewhere in those black lumps, the secondary worlds, as a cog, an employee, albeit well paid, salaried, but in someone else's bank, insurance company or property firm. And Charlie, a loner, did not want that. He would rather make a meagre ten grand a year out of directly employing his own elves, rather than the same sums or even more servicing the employment of someone else's.

But he knew his limitations. It would have to be simple, dead simple, for him to manage it on his own. What he wanted was a way of owning *air*, of hiring a few elves to package it, make it saleable, and then he would sit back and let nature take its course in the very simplest way possible.

Summer came. A bad summer after an appalling winter. The West Indians set about thrashing the daylights out of everything that came their way. But what was worse than a load of niggers playing cricket better than anyone else was that Lissie had started spending money again – on clothes, on a Centre Court ticket, on a share of a box at Ascot, and, what was worse, he found himself excluded from both. When he remonstrated, she declared that his three months were just about up. If he was going to make a fortune out of her ten grand, he'd better get a move on.

On one of the first days of June, he got another letter from Aunt Elizabeth.

Dear Charlie,

I think you should know that your Father has finally gone bankrupt. Also he is not very well. Alderson has agreed to take over the stock that's left – about five hundred pounds' worth, I understand – at cost, which is a very fair offer. However, he has nowhere to put it, so it must be stored for a few weeks at least.

I have found a place which will look after it for a not unreasonable fee – Williams's Storage in Mottingham – but it must be moved there quickly and at as little expense as possible. The bank has agreed to let us keep the van until next Monday. I calculate three trips will be sufficient. I should like you to come over and help us to move the stock, as above, to the warehouse, since it is out of the question your Father should do any lifting or carrying. On completion of this small service, I will give you five pounds.

Your affectionate aunt,

Elizabeth

Which must be at least two pounds less than any quote she's got from anywhere else, thought Charlie.

His first instinct was to refuse, but then he thought about it, thought about how he would be assisting in the final toppling of his father's empire, the end of all the pretension, the bullying, the self-congratulation, the self-righteousness, that had been built on his father's apparent ownership of a rotten little business with a shop on the High Street. So he went, having first squared it with Aunt Elizabeth, by phone, that he would not actually have to see either of his parents.

Williams's Storage was a bomb-damaged cinema – not a large one, but the sort that used to be called a flea-pit; now the seats had gone, it was nothing more than a large shell, with corrugated-iron roof, a dais at one end, and an upstairs office in what had once been the projection room. It was three-quarters filled with a miscellany of furniture and packing cases, with here and there a real absurdity sticking out from the rest: an invalid chair made out of basketry, a stuffed tiger and thirty-six *black* lavatories.

When Charlie dropped the first load – six tea-chests filled with nails, screws, broom-heads, paint, brushes and gallon tins of turps – two men, one old, one a negro, helped him carry them in on trolleys, while a little Welshman – your actual Williams, Charlie presumed – told them where to stack them.

'Short term, is it? Less than one month? Right, boy, we'll keep it all up front, then, all right?'

As he drove back to Woolingham for the second load, the significance of all this dawned on Charlie with organic slowness. It was all so simple. Williams – who wore a good lightweight tweed suit, had a gold watch on a chain, and smelled of whisky – owned *air, air* enclosed in a shell. To make it pay not just a little but a lot, he bought the labour of two elves. No doubt he could have managed without them, but, if he had, eighty per cent of the air would have remained unsold. To maximize the profitability of the air he owned, it was necessary to have elves to stack the objects people displaced his air with in the most efficient, the most profitable way possible. The long-term stuff at the back and at the bottom, the shorter-term stuff in the middle, the three-, four-week stuff in the front and on the top.

And so these two elves converted the air into wealth by their labour. It was better than Aero chocolate. It was better than Ssssch . . . you know who? There were no materials to be bought once you had the shell that enclosed the space, the very minimum of overheads and upkeep; it was the divine reduction to its absolutely barest essentials of the process of wealth creation. Two elves, for whom you did not even have to provide shoe leather, whose skills did not have to be paid for since no skill was involved, provided, for absolutely the lowest wage that one could get away with paying able-bodied men, the labour that coverted air into wealth, and Williams – at least until

Charlie bought him out – took the profit, the loot, the riches.

The elation grew like a lovely crimson flower in his chest, in his throat, in his head, all through the afternoon – a prize won by a knight for his lady, a gift brought by a small boy for his mother – and was just about unfurling its velvet petals, releasing its gorgeous perfume, as he trotted up from Earls Court tube, along the alleys and ringing pavements, past the newsstands (MINISTER RESIGNS), through the warm lovely air of a June evening, down the steps and into the basement flat.

'Lissie, I've cracked it. We can do it. We're made.'

'With love from me to you' came bouncing off the Dansette, instead of the usual Vivaldi or Telemann.

'Have you?' she said. 'If you could buy a piece of that sound, I'd believe you.'

Considering how he had come in, with the whole sweet secret of success buttoned in his mouth, and ready to spill it out before her, it's a wonder he didn't brain her on the spot, not surprising the fathomlessly deep disappointment he felt.

10

There's not much more to be said about Lissie and her ten thousand. She continued to spend it, driving Charlie crazy as it dribbled away, and absolutely refused to have anything at all to do with his plans to buy air and labour and thus, by the alchemy of putting them together, create wealth. She was not, she said, about to become the spouse of a warehouseman. Not on her money, anyway.

She insisted on moving. In early summer the basement was gloomy and drab – its cosy virtues no longer significant. They went to St John's Wood for a week, but it did not suit, and then to a two-roomed apartment at the top of a Regent's Park terrace with one roof window actually giving a glimpse of the zoo. It was horrendously expensive. She installed a telly and spent a fortnight drinking expensive Scotch and watching Wimbledon. She even left it on when Charlie came home from Belgravia and fucked her, and she watched on over his heaving shoulder. And all the time she had a booked seat on the Centre Court she never used.

There was a telephone and soon old friends of hers dropped in, drank more of the Scotch and smoked weed. They gossiped about Stephen Ward, and left. All, all ignored Charlie. He might just as well have not been there. And so what had been a crimson flower turned into a crab, a cancer, gnawing and scrabbling inside his skull as her money drifted away, as, and he could see now that it was inevitable, she too was cutting loose.

On the morning of Finals days he found the ticket. While she was still in bed he crushed up her sodium amytol and barbiturates and dissolved them in her Cutty Sark and went off to watch Margaret Smith play Billy Jean Moffat. It rained. For several hours he watched the rain fall on the covers, and waited for it to stop, and it never did.

When he got back she was in the bath and a very deep coma. On the telly David Jacobs invited a panel to push buttons to decide whether or not Dave Clark and his Five were a hit or a miss.

She had left a note:

Charlie

You're a fucking bastard and I know you laced the Scotch. OK. If that's the way you want it, that's OK by me. But I think actually you've murdered me.

He burnt this, and taking the earlier version from the soft black wallet where it had nestled for six months, substituted it:

Charlie

Thanks for everything, You've been quite a brick. But I can't be left on my own. Sorry if this causes you trouble.

Lissie

and dialled 999. She was taken away and he never saw her again.

After a fortnight in hospital she discharged herself, went to her bank and drew out two thousand pounds. Two days later she drove a Lotus Elan into a lamp-post and died almost instantly.

Intestate.

There was enough left.

Enough. Charlie continued to work for Belgravia Properties until it dissoved like the Cheshire Cat into the network of companies that it was part of. That was in 1966.

By then, the six warehouses he had leased, using Lissie's money and the profit from the Skerrit's Farm transaction, were turning over twenty-five thousand a year and putting a clear three thousand into his own pocket. He took a small office in Woolingham High Street and was glad to leave the West End, where he had never felt at home. He hired a secretary, didn't like her, hired another. He used a High Street accountant – not Tom Judd – who did most of the purely financial work, and who, in 1967, advised him to go to the bank and borrow.

With the extra capital he bought a lease from the Ministry of Defence on a disused hangar out in Kent – it was understood that the MoD would be one of his principal customers. It was an arrangement that worked well.

Publicly he dressed well, used new cars, ate and drank out. Privately he remained stingy, lived rent-free with his widowed mother in Goldsmith Drive, did not take holidays, bought few consumer durables, and kept clear of the craze for things on the never-never. Above all, he screwed his elves and sacked them when they objected or tried to unionize. By 1968, he was doing well, was known in the business circles of the borough as a sharp man, but one of us.

Part Four

1

A large hangar on a disused airfield, five miles out into the countryside from the last of the posh suburbs. Nevertheless the Garden of England was a touch run-down here, with docks and nettles sprouting round the broken huts, and a small herd of rather mucky cows grazing in the angle between the runways. The sky above blue, save where a brisk spring breeze, warm enough to promise summer, cool enough to have showers in its wake, trundled white clouds across it.

A Renault 17, almost new, F registration, plum-coloured, one of the first of the hatchbacks, though no one called them that yet, nosed down the lane and came to a standstill outside the large gate made of tubular steel filled in with chain-link. A hawthorn tree, white buds just bursting, dipped to caress the roof as the wind blew a breath quicker. Inside, Charlie, heavier now, in a good-quality half-length tweed top-coat, shook out a Chesterfield and snapped a gold gas-lighter at it. His fingernails, still chewed, exaggerated the heavy, prize-fighter look of his hands. He inhaled, smoked for a moment or two, allowing his anger at what he could see in front of him to build up a charge before getting out to face it.

Four long-haired youngsters in donkey jackets and jeans leant against the posts of the gate, to which they had attached a piece of cardboard on which was painted: *International Socialists and Local Workers against the War in Viet Nam.*

Charlie got out of the car, chucked his cigarette into the ditch.

'What the hell's going on here?'

The tallest of them took a step towards him. He was dark, had long black hair that rested on the PVC reinforcements on his shoulders. His skin was dark too, dark enough to be Indian or Eurasian. He spread his hands, palms out below waist level, and smiled.

'Peace, brother,' he said.

He wore beads. Charlie's anger began to throb, you could see a pulse in his thickening bull-like neck.

'Just tell me what the fuck's going on here.'

Another of them moved. A girl this time, Charlie thought, difficult to tell these days when they're in jeans.

'"Fuck" should not be an aggressive word,' she said, in an even voice which had a sort of irritating whine at the back of it. 'Fucking is loving and giving.' She handed him a Gestetnered handout and a tulip. As soon as Charlie saw the bereted, bearded ikon of the dead Che, he crumpled it up and chucked it. More deliberatly he pulled the petals off the flower.

'Tell. Me.'

'Brother,' said the tall youth, 'there are in there crated components made in a Camden Town factory for a government contract. These components will eventually be shipped to Belgium, where they will be incorporated in a radar-scanning device, which in turn ends up in American helicopter gunships. These are used to massacre defenceless villagers in the Mekong delta and . . .'

'Do any of you work here?'

'No. That is . . .'

'Then you have no right to be here.'

Here, brother, is the public highway.'

'You are impeding access, and if you don't get out of the way I'll run over you. And just in case you think I might not be aware of my rights, let me tell you I own that.'

Across the giant hangar in sans-serif letters, white on blue, WOOLINGHAM STORAGE CO. LTD, and a Woolingham telephone number.

He moved towards the gate, but the girl and one of the others who hadn't spoken yet got there first, he thought to bar his way. But they pushed back the huge gates for him and held them open. The girl offered him another tulip. He got back in the car and drove through – to four VC salutes.

'What the hell's going on here?' Charlie repeated, up on a gantry now, overlooking the vast, cool, echoing hall, filled with packing cases, chemical drums, vast bobbins of industrial textiles. Down below, a small workforce, five men only, manoeuvred fork-lift trucks and a travelling hoist, displacing and manipulating air, space, the commodity Charlie owned enclosed in this giant asbestos and corrugated-iron shell, thereby adding to its value a hundredfold.

His foreman, Tomkins, who managed the place on a day-to-day basis, taking his orders by phone from head office in Woolingham, looked up at him. He was small, round, fat; at fifty years old, a good twenty years older than his boss. He was frightened. The five men below, two of them black, worked for a wage which was as far below the going rate as Charlie could push it, but his foremen were quite well paid, and while the actual workers turned over three or four times a year, the foremen were more or less permanent – for as long as Charlie thought they were doing their jobs properly.

'Well, sir, they know we handle MoD stuff and . . .'

'They know about some of it.' Charlie was thinking of shipments consisting of twenty unlabelled black cyclinders that occasionally came through, full one way, empty the other, with the docks at Gravesend as one destination, Porton Down the other. With demonstrations planned at Porton Down that weekend, and the newspapers already reporting that the army would be called in to ring the place, he reckoned to himself there would be more than just four of rent-a-crowd on his back if that got out. He went on,

'The point is how?'

Tomkins shrugged. 'They may have a mole in Edgar and Stevens' – the light-engineering factory in Camden Town – 'but if it's any of our lot, it's Manly White or Bill Gould.'

'Give them their cards. Both of them. Two weeks' wages in lieu.' He pronounced it *lee-yuh.*

'I'm not sure, sir, it would be . . .' Tomkins's voice tailed off.

'What's the matter?'

'Manley White'll be no trouble, but that Bill Gould is in the T and GW.'

Charlie turned on him, blazing. The little round man, ash-faced now, babbled, 'He wasn't when he come here, sir, I swear it, but he is now, and what's more he's been trying to get the others . . .'

Charlie wanted to hit the man. Very badly he needed to hit him. Instead, he banged his leather-gloved hand on the rail beside him until the need receded enough to be coped with.

'Right,' he said at last, 'which is Gould?'

'Over at the back there, operating the Climax.'

'Christ. He's as old as I am. Older. And look at the way he's handling that thing. He knows what he's doing. Tomkins, you are a fucking idiot. That man's been warehousing all his working life. Of course he's in the bloody union.' He thought on. 'And they probably put him in here to get the place unionized. Jesus. It's probably the whole firm they're after,'

He turned on his heel, strode off the gantry and into the tiny office, placed above the main entrance, where Tomkins did most of his work, stood at the window and looked down at the flower people outside. They were all on the other side of the road now, moving about on the grassy bank, playing with large flint cores picked up from the edge of the wheat field beyond. The field was hazed with green shoots; cloud shadow and breeze slipped across it like a shoal of fish below the surface of a green sea.

Charlie felt hedged in, betrayed, caught, boxed up . . . very bad indeed. If he'd had a great heavy machine gun in his hands just then, he would have slaughtered everything in sight, the cows too.

The flower people had to go – he'd lose his MoD contracts if they stayed. Gould had to go. If Woolingham Storage was unionized it would cost him a couple of grand a year at least. He gnawed on the knuckles of his glove until he felt pain. And Tomkins, well certainly he'd be out, on his ear. I'd like to get him by the scruff and punt him down the stairs, down that concrete path and out through the gate right now.

Hope glimmered. Perhaps Gould would take the job. He certainly looked a capable enough sort of bloke . . . and no doubt had his price. Perhaps one Charlie would feel justified in affording. Well. That could be looked into.

Meanwhile . . . the flower people. What are they doing? It had became clearer. They were spelling something out in chalk rocks and flint cores, laying them out on the grassy bank.

F A S C I S T C U N

But then the girl who thought there was nothing aggressive about fucking (what sort of screwing had she been having then?) appeared to remonstrate. C U N became S C U

Charlie grinned, slapped his gloves together, and trotted quickly down the ringing stairs from the gantry to the floor, and so to his car. He drove it hard and fast at the four hippies, stamped on the brake just in time as they scattered . . . yes, he'd given them a real fright, shit-scared they were, no spunk in them at all.

He was out in a second, picked up the nearest of the flint cores and smashed it hard into the back window of his hatchback Renault. The shattering glass was a release – an orgasm come with the swiftness of lightning.

Then he picked up two more and tossed them less savagely, but with enough force to mark the metalwork between the starburst window and the fender.

He turned and faced them.

'Now. I am going back into my office.' He pointed up at the window where the round, white face of Tomkins could just be seen, 'and I am going to ring up the nearest nick. And I am going to say that you have caused my car serious damage, by maliciously throwing stones at it, that you have used insulting behaviour.' He strode across to the girl, who was staring at him with wide, incredulous eyes, and snatched away the bundle of handouts. 'And with these for evidence, and that' – he pointed to F A S C I S T S C U – 'there's not an Old Bill in the land won't believe me, and not a beak neither. So. On your bikes. Quick. Piss off. It's your only chance.'

He got back into the car, reversed it, engine roaring, back up to the hangar, and ran up the steps, back to Tomkins's office.

They didn't have bikes, but an old unconverted VW van, split windscreen, painted psychedelically, and it moved off up the lane before he had his breath back enough to use the phone.

He was not bothered about the damage to the car. Insurance would pay, and he had no no-claims bonus to lose. No-claims bonuses are for cissies.

2

Leaning back on a big, black, leather-covered, chrome-framed chair which he spun about in as if he were Lew Grade, he smoked and talked.

'To the Legal and General. Policy number whatever it is. Renault vandalized. Police at Sevenoaks have been informed. Garage estimate follows. OK, Valerie, you know what to do about all that.'

Valerie nodded, recrossed her bare thighs. Her mini skirt was just about round her navel, but she kept twisted away from him most of the time. Fanny pelmets, they call them.

'Get George Alderson, you know, at the Woolingham nick, on the blower, and if he's out get him to ring back. Don't do that now, when we've finished.'

She tossed her blonde head, hair still long, backcombed and heavily lacquered (though the really up-to-date chicks had just gone short, in Charleston-twenties style) and scribbled a note. Valerie was a big girl – heavily built, big-bosomed, strong-thighed, played tennis, and swam. She was very, very efficient. Her only apparent weakness was a pebble called Dylan. It sat on her desk in a nest of straw inside a small cardboard box. Occasionally she talked to it.

'Right, has there been any trouble anywhere else?'

She flipped back her pad. 'Lee Green and Orpington all right. And Skerrit's Industrial Estate. But Mottingham had a picket. Same as you saw at Stoney Cross. But Nailer called the police and they went quietly.'

Good man, Nailer, got some nous, unlike Tomkins. Charlie chewed on his thumb – that glorious pillar of thigh, sort of golden creamy, not white and lardy as most were, so smooth yet so strong. It fascinated him, put a heck on him, whatever that was, made his prick swell a little; but at the same time a core of anxiety swelled in his diaphragm. Valerie frightened him too.

'Ring up Hertz, or whatever the nearest place is, and have them send round a Cortina. For four days. A new one, mind. Anything else?'

'Your mother rang.'

'Shit.'

'Said there's a pool of water under the freezer, what should she do?'

'Tell her to mop it up. Then ring the Electricity Board and tell them to get it fixed pronto. I mean *you* ring the Electricity – no use asking her to.'

A short smile dimpled in Valerie's cheeks. She liked it when he asked her to look after the domestic side of things. 'Right, let's get on with the real stuff.'

She went through the mail with him, then the day's shipments in and out of his eight storage warehouse facilities. Two ex-cinemas including Williams's at Mottingham, a factory shell on Skerrit's Industrial Estate that had never been let as a factory, an open tarmacked space at Lee Green that had once been an elementary school but a bombed one, the hangar out in Kent, and three purpose-built warehouses near Tilbury.

He now phoned each in turn and set in motion the day's operations, a little late after his trip out to Stoney Cross; how space should be filled and emptied and filled again by the labour of his elves and thus converted into a saleable commodity. Very saleable: he and Valerie (who in fact suggested most of what was done, and always had her eyes on what was coming in or going out up to three weeks in advance) ran a smallish, tight, competitive business that was really doing very well indeed.

He kept his ear close to the ground in Woolingham

through the country sports club, where he played squash two or three times a week, through the pubs and a drinking club he went to, but most especially through a small caucus of businessmen, local merchants in touch with the commodity markets in the City, who bought in bulk when the price was right and needed cheap discreet storage until it was time to go to market again. They valued his services and put other business in his way: thus he often stored 'fire-damaged' carpets, 'flood-damaged' furniture, goods that had been bought by East End fences from manufacturers shifting outmoded lines at knock-down prices, having fiddled some insurance on the side.

He never knowingly handled stolen goods, and had fired a foreman whom he had caught storing a lorry-load of whisky and cigarettes.

One thing nagged at him though, and that was that he actually owned none of his sites. They were all leased. He used an accountant who proved in ways Charlie could never quite follow that this was a profitable way of carrying on, especially with the Labour government's proposed land register, and the possibility of a land tax. Well, Charlie had promised himself that he would pay people to make this sort of calculation for him, and now he did it was stupid to worry about the advice they gave. But he felt insecure without a real base, no firm footing, no really solid asset against a rainy day. The memory of his father's bankruptcy, followed by terminal cancer of the rectum, haunted him. Still, he was doing very well indeed and the bank was making encouraging noises. Time perhaps to push on to the next step.

As Valerie typed away in the next room, he began to turn over the pages of a glossy brochure which had arrived, apparently unsolicited, on his desk. It was from a firm that made hoists, trolleys, loaders, giant fork-lifts for the new containers, which, the foreword said, were the thing of the future in freight and storage. There was an IBM printed slip at the front – *See you at the Container Exhibition, Earls Court, 27th May to 31st. We are on Stand 183.*

He buzzed Valerie.

'Yes, Mr Bosham?'

'Have we got much on tomorrow?'

'Just a moment, Mr Bosham. No. Nothing that's not routine.'

'Well, I'm going up to town for most of the day. After I've called in in the morning. Right?'

'Right, Mr Bosham.'

A click, and the typing resumed. In the next room Valerie blew a kiss at Dylan; she too felt that the firm was ready for expansion, and had ordered the brochure herself.

In the evening he went back to 263 Goldsmith Drive, where his mother, fatter, duller, more stupid than ever – at least he thought that was what was wrong with her – pretended to housekeep for him. In fact, she had a daily for the cleaning, and they ate out of the freezer: steak and kidney pies; sea-food platters in cheesy béchamel; sliced pork in wine-enriched gravy with apple sauce, all in the same container; elaborate ice creams in grapefruit or orange shells topped off with glacé cherries, chopped hazelnuts and real cream: all of which was ordered by Valerie and delivered to the door. It was also Valerie's last chore of the day to ring up Mrs Bosham and remind her to get something out and pop it in the oven, so it would be ready when Charlie got in from whatever oasis he had called in at on the way home.

There was one flaw in this system. It still occasionally happened that the frozen dessert – Black Forest Gateau it was in one case – got into the oven, while the chicken breasts with stuffing remained in the fridge.

Since Charlie had a fair bit to drink on the way home, he did not realize that his mother had been drinking all day.

He couldn't smell it, and her heavy, clumsy movements, her slightly slurred speech, the awful messes like baked Black Forest Gateau were, well, just Mother. She'd been like that for as long as he could remember.

Which was accurate. She had started keeping gin bottles in the hatbox on top of her wardrobe when he was eight years old, the year she discovered his father spent the afternoons of early closing day with what she called a whore. Bloodstains across the bottoms of his long johns were the clue. It was almost impossible to catch a glimpse of his actual bottom – apart from the century of prudery behind them, there was also a century of thrift: the house was too cold for most of the year.

She knew nothing about such things, but did know that men are beasts. For the last time in her life she followed a well-thought-out chain of action which led her to a terraced house with shocking-pink lace curtains off Tooting Broadway. What to do? Divorce! Impossible. She'd never get a proper settlement and she knew she could not work. Have it out with him? And get thumped. Take a lover? The thought was like a large black spider that scuttles across a corner of a room, hides under the sofa. A huge shudder, a nervous glance for days at the crack where it finally disappeared, and then the idea rejected and suppressed, only to return in dreams.

Yet she felt cheated, rejected, even deprived. Never again did she grant him what she called her favours, he his marital rights. In the end she discovered that the remedy for the whole awful business that marriage to Edward Bosham had become lay at the bottom of a bottle of Gordon's.

So, that evening, Charlie went home to Duck à l'Orange followed by Baked Alaska that had not been baked, merely thawed, and desultory conversation with his three-quarters cut mother until it was time for the news.

Benn asserts 'we shall have to find a new popular democracy to replace Parliamentary democracy'. The row continues . . .

In Viet Nam the war once again comes to the suburbs of Saigon . . .

The Thalidomide trial in West Germany opened today with a brief statement . . .

Preparations for Wednesday's European Cup Final took a new turn today when Matt Busby declared that . . .

Student action in support of their counterparts in France . . .

He drank some more whisky, watched some rubbish, was dimly aware that his mother had attempted to peck him on the cheek. Finally he went upstairs to his old room.

The Spitfire continued to hunt the Messerschmidt over the dirty yellow bedspread. He smoked a last Chesterfield in bed and idly turned the pages of a glossy coffee-table book he had recently bought – *Small Arms and Side Arms Since 1850.* He loved the finely engraved and coloured plates; the 'historical' notes describing important occasions on which the arms had been used: the assassinations of Abraham Lincoln through to JFK.

3

'Charlie. George here. Sorry I couldn't reach you yesterday. I was in court all day.'

'George. Info I need on a chappie called William Gould, lives at 36 Primrose Crescent in the Flowers. Works for me as of now, might be a troublemaker, might turn out to be NCO material. Could go either way. Are you with me?'

'Certainly am.'

'That's it, George. OK?'

'Can do, squire, can do.'

He replaced the phone.

'Anything else then, Val?'

'I don't think so, Mr Bosham. Have a good day.'

He kept away from the parts of Earls Court he connected with Lissie, had a pub lunch of Cornish pastie, two pints and a large Scotch, and then made his way to the Containerization Exhibition. There, with his stomach heavy and his breath foul with rancid lamb fat and burnt onion, his head thick with alcohol and nicotine fumes, a sort of euphoria set in.

Most of the men there (there were no women amongst the visitors) fell into one of two groups. Either they were about his age, but looked poorer, more tired, more harassed, nervous; or they were quite a lot older, in which case they were bald or had lank grey hair, dandruff on their shoulders, blackheads on the rolls of flesh that hung over their coat collars, and tobacco ash on their admittedly very expensive suits. Those unwise enough to ape the new fashion for lightweight, light-coloured suits often showed embarrassing damp patches where inadequately controlled sphincters had let a dribble of pee drip on. Whereas he, Charlie, was well dressed, was his own boss, took orders from no one, had a bob or two of his own, and was still young enough to enjoy it.

These shabbinesses contrasted extraordinarily with the glamorous new world of containerization. Neat toy trains slid along gleaming tracks, brightly painted hoists lifted the unfamiliar boxes from the decks of ships directly on to freight trucks and lorries. There were huge grainy photographs of Rotterdam and Yokohama, where experimental container ports already existed, displaying quays in sharp perspectives idyllically devoid of anything as nasty as a docker. There were film displays in tiny curtained-off halls which smelled of Chanel and put Charlie in mind of Soho clip joints, films which showed wide hoists trundling on huge wheels, strange cranes that looked like ladders with rungs missing, and huge ships piled high with thousands and thousands of boxes.

And best of all there were the dolly-birds. Blonde, white blonde, gold blonde, lilac blonde, silver blonde, but all blonde with giant gleaming bee-hives made out of spun glass instead of hair, in dresses with plunging necklines, with gilt chains above their fanny pelmets, with faces painted into dehumanized perfection, and the brisk, tirelessly welcoming good manners of angels at heaven's gate. It was, after all, not a bad exhibition: things of that sort were done in style in those days, under the influence of the brave new radical chic of the Royal College of Art.

The messages got across and at four o'clock Charlie took them away with him in his hired Cortina – beating the rush hour, wanting to get back to his office for unfinished business. The overt message was rationalization. The real message was screw the dockers, screw the seamen, screw the truckers, screw the freight-yard worker, screw the warehousemen.

Not a bad scenario, but caution in business, moderate

caution, had always been the name of the game with Charlie, and he'd looked into it a bit further before committing whatever loan facility he could screw out of the bank.

Back at the office.

'George. Any joy?'

'Not a lot, Charlie. He's in the IS. International Socialists, and if you haven't come across them before, let me tell you they are bad news. He's also a T and GWU activist. I wouldn't touch him with a bargepole, though I might with my truncheon.'

'Buy him?'

'Not likely, Charlie. That sort doesn't want money. Get shot of him, but go carefully. He's probably got a bit of clout behind him.'

'Thanks, George.'

'Any time, Charlie.'

'Valerie.'

'Yes, Mr Bosham.'

'A case, no, half a dozen, good Scotch to Mr Alderson, OK? Get Unwins to send it round and charge it.'

'Yes. Mr Bosham. Anything else?'

'Get me Councillor Duxbury, if you can.'

'Charlie. Good to hear you. What can I do for you?'

'I'd like to give you lunch, Councillor. And maybe ask your advice. Quite urgent.'

'Let's see, Charlie. I'm booked up the rest of this week, but the Leonine Rotationists meet on Thursday. You've been my guest there before, haven't you? Twelve thirty at the Wellington then, all right? Fine, Charlie.'

If it was absolutely necessary to be old – fifty-five, sixty even – then Charlie hoped he would be old like Councillor

Duxbury. He was a big man, with a big stomach, which you wouldn't quite describe as a gut, though that might have been because of the skill of his tailor – for the same reason you wouldn't quite call him fat-arsed. He was bald and appeared to be proud of it; you'd think he polished his dome with the finest of oils, and maybe he did. He had a face which age and mild though chronic dissipation had not ruined – it had a long sloping look, leaning always towards his nose, which was large, predatory, a beak. What most impressed Charlie, what almost he would have liked to have had even at twenty-nine, was the deep voice that resonated out of a barrel chest, a voice that crackled throatily too, for the vocal chords had been smoked for a lifetime in good cigars and marinated in cognac.

Councillor Duxbury was a builder's merchant, but on a big scale: he could afford to play the market, which was why he knew Charlie and valued his services. From his council connections, he always knew which building projects would get off the ground; he also had links with County Hall and across the river at Westminster, knew how building regs were to be changed even before a Green Paper appeared, and so could buy, say, glass-fibre insulation or double-glazed windows months before they became commodities in short supply – and what he bought ahead of the market he stored with Charlie.

4

The saloon bar at the Wellington in Woolingham High Street was a large room with a long, curved counter of polished wood, brass footrail always immaculately polished, deep good carpets, and original oil paintings of Highland cattle, Spanish gypsies selling silvery sardines, Parisian mignonettes with blue umbrellas, all in gilt frames, and each with its separate overhead light. Even the Gents was plushy for those days – one of the first outside the West End to have coloured tiles and stainless-steel urinals, above which hung wittily drawn pictures of mongrels straining passionately after a poodle bitch in heat. Charlie was there on the stroke of half twelve, but Councillor Duxbury, of course, was not.

The Leonine Rotationists foregathered – Woolingham's elite: the top GP, the top dentist, the six most successful businessmen, the deputy headmaster of Philip Sydney, the Chief Inspector from the nick, an estate agent (not Baird), and a solicitor (not Mead). Also their guests – Charlie, and across the room he saw Peter Coleman, also a man who was identified as Head of English at Woolingham Comprehensive, and, even more extraordinary, two youngsters, a youth and a girl. The youth, in spite of the suit he was wearing, was hippyish with shoulder-length hair; the girl neater, more conventional.

The conversation became general.

'What a great game last night, what a great game. A night to make us proud again to be British. The best since the World Cup.'

'The way young Kidd flicked in that cross.'

'And Nobby afterwards. Did you ever see such a great toothless grin?'

'Mind you, the Portuguese manager reckoned his lads took a beating in the first half, and he could have a point.'

'Balls, You see, what these continentals don't understand, it's a game of physical contact. Can't be played any other way.'

'What's yours, squire? Time for another, eh?'

'Quack, told me to lay off the hard stuff, so I'll stick to the bitter. Just a half.'

'But that is the name of the game when the chips are down, thanks, squire, a Scotch with a splash, and the problems in my neck of the woods are legion . . .'

'But seriously now. What is de Gaulle up to? One hundred thousand on the streets of Paris and the old bugger potters off into the country . . .'

'And they gave them a ten per cent rise. Ten per cent! Every sodding workman in France got ten per cent.'

'Mind you, your average Frog still seems to know the meaning of a fair day's work . . .'

'I take your point. Whereas our lot . . .'

'Shirkers, malingerers, time-wasters, every rotten sodding one of them.'

'The nig-nogs – oops, pardon my French, have the Race Relations on me – our lovely friends from further climes, the folks with a touch of sun-tan, are the worst of all.'

'I don't know about that. Unfortunately, it's the cross I have to bear. I have four or five Micks amongst my lot . . .'

'Aha. Did you hear the one about the announcer at Paddington. It goes like this. Hang on, let me get it right . . .'

'Your call, I think.'

'You're dead right.'

'The train to Cardiff will leave at five fifteen . . .'

'Scotch with a splash.'

'A half of bitter.'

'The train for Bristol will leave at five twenty-five . . .'

'Bloody marvellous. It really was. He just lifted his arse and away he went. Just let him see the whip, know it was there and be-e-r-r-r-o-o-o-o-m. I don't mind admitting I had a fiver on Sir Ivor. Hark at me, poet and don't know it. I'm not a betting man, but I had a fiver on Sir Ivor.'

'The train . . . for where is it? That place up in Wales where all the Micks take the boat for Dublin? Holyhead. That's it. The train for Holyhead will leave when the big hand, no I tell a lie, when the *little* hand is pointing to the five, or just after the five, if you take my point, and the big hand . . .'

'No. It won't happen here. The students yes. They're feeling their oats. They want to be heard. Why not. But not your English workmen. Not he. He knows which side his bread is buttered . . .'

'Ah, Councillor. What'll yours be? And a large Courvoissier for Councillor Duxbury.'

The voice. The presence. Around them, if not in the further flung corners of the bar, a respectful hush. 'About the British workman, my friends, there is no dispute.' A rasp of intaken breath across those golden chords. 'What is true of Woolingham is true of the country at large. Thank you, Ted. Very nice. As I say. We've had a Labour council here for as long as anyone can remember, and most of the time a Labour MP. Apart from poor old Fred Mead's brief encumbrance. But we on the council, just the same as all of us in business, have always got on well with the other side . . . and for why? I'll tell you. Because the British Working Man, and his Party. Know where their best interests lie. They know. Prosperous business means good wages. And acceptable levels of unemployment . . .'

Shortly, this merry band, urged by the solicitor, a thin officious man called Swivel, began to mount the heavily balustrated staircase to the genuine oak-panelled function room upstairs. There they seated themselves – not, alas, at a round table, but at three long ones set out in a squared horseshoe, laid with tolerably shiny SPCN cutlery and cruets, with tolerably white napery folded into mitres. There followed a few minutes of genteel shuffling: 'Over here, old boy, if you don't mind,' 'That's right, guests all on the top table,' 'There we are then,' 'Everybody set.'

A hush settled over all. Indeed, Councillor Duxbury made sure there was no noise at all before he picked up the tiny felt-headed stick in front of the central place, and tapped the miniature gong with it.

With one voice, to the tune of 'Tannenbaum', they sang:

'May God the Master bless our fare
And give those here the Lion's share,
As gathered here in friendly glee
We share it round quite easily.'

which ended on an enormous unison shout from each and every Leonine Rotationist: HURRAH!

This pleasant little ritual completed, all sat down in a flurry of unfolded napkins. Four waitresses dressed properly in black with white aprons served oxtail soup, lamb chops with Jersey Royals and cabbage, followed by spotted dick with custard. Two barmen went the rounds taking orders for beer and light ale, and all fell to with gusto.

Charlie had been placed between the long-haired youth and Peter Coleman, and found this situation embarrassing. Coleman was now a tall thin, young man with brown hair, NHS spectacles, and a High Street tailor's suit that did not fit too well. He had a row of ballpoints in the top pocket, and an incompetently knitted pullover underneath. With that old memory suddenly before his eyes – Jane Coleman's fur-edged fanny offered to his view because he had let this beanpole beat him at Monopoly on Coronation Day – Charlie turned quite brusquely to the long-haired youth on his other side.

'Hello, then. My name's Ken. Ken Langley.'

'Yes? I'm Bosham.'

'Great to meet you, Bosham. Mr. Bosham. Hey, you know,' said this Ken Langley, tilting his bowl of soup towards him and drinking out of the front of his spoon, 'I just can't get over that hymn or whatever.'

'You mean the grace at the beginning?'

'That's it. I mean, you know what the tune was?'

'"Tannenbaum".'

'It's what I sing 'The Red Flag' to. Come dungeons dark, or gallows grim . . . What do you do for a living?'

'I own a warehousing and storage business.'

'Ah. You have others who earn your living for you.'

This was so precisely the way Charlie saw it that there didn't seem to be any comment to make. He attempted a sort of reciprocal politeness.

'What do you do?'

'I'm a sixth former at Woolingham Comp. Shortly I shall be a student at Lancaster. If I get a B and two Cs. Which will be a dolly. There I shall study political science and revolution. And the taxes you don't quite avoid paying will pay for me. Ve-rr-y inter-rest-ing. But is it socialism? Not quite. But it's a step in the right direction . . .'

Charlie found himself forced to talk to Coleman.

'Well, Cole – Peter. Long time no see.'

'That's right, Charlie.'

'What are you up to these days?'

'Well, I've been in Accounts at Town Hall. Housing Accounts. But I've just passed my last exams, says he with becoming modesty. By correspondence. And Mr Barton here is taking me on . . .'

Barton. Owns three garages in the area. Has the Renault and Simca franchises, and is reputedly talking to the Japs, who are testing the temperature with their little yellow toes. Charlie didn't like that, talking to Japs. It was bad enough the Huns doing so well, but the Japs were a bit over the top. He'd seen *The Bridge Over the River Kwai,* knew what they were really like.

'That'll be a step-up for you then.'

'I'd say. A fifty per cent rise for me.'

Charlie thought: one day I'll have my own accountant on the payroll instead of creeping to some guy who runs his own business charging fees to punters like me.

'And . . . Jane. She all right?'

'Well, yes. Depends what you mean.' Coleman speared a new potato, and looked at it.

'Well. Is she all right?'

'Oh, fine really.' Popped the potato in. 'Got two sprouts, boy three, girl one. Pigeon pair.'

This news pissed Charlie off a bit since presumably these sprouts had not materialized through Virgin Birth or the intervention of the Angel Gabriel. He turned back to Ken Langley, thought for a moment, trying to dig out something that might needle the lad.

'Too bad Robert Kennedy lost that primary.'

'Too bad? You're joking. That Eugene McCarthy is the greatest thing since sliced bread. You'll see. All the kids are rooting for him. He'll get in. You'll see, come the California primary next week. And that'll be it for the Kennedys, their come-uppance at last. Good riddance.'

This shocked Charlie for conflicting reasons. But Charlie never really noticed contradictions in his thought processes which were based on sensation, feel, prejudice. Shocked because on one side he felt sure this Langley would be a Kennedyite. All lefties were. Hadn't JF called businessmen sons of bitches? Hadn't Bobbie had a poke at the Mafia? On the other side, though, he himself liked the Kennedys, admired their style, their glamour and even sensed, and liked, the taste of the rottenness underneath, the sweet corruption you get on your tongue from a bad tooth. And as for Jackie, well!

'Gentlemen, Leonine Rotationists. Pray silence for your secretary.'

Swivel, the thin, shifty-looking solicitor, stood up. With brisk unintelligibility he ran through the minutes, apologies, plans for Woolingham's Summer Fayre, welcome guests, hand you back to Councillor Duxbury.

'As you all know, for ten years now we have awarded a cup to the best public speaker in the sixth form at Philip Sydney. We entertain the two finalists here, and award the cup, the Duxbury Cup.' Hear, hear, cheers. 'But this year repre– representations were made to me. From the Head of English at Woolingham Comprehensive School. What you and me used to call the Alma Street Elementary. Where me, and some of you, got our educations. And a fine school it was, and no doubt still is – must be, for Woolingham Comp now has a sixth form too, it seems, and they asked me to include them in this competition. So there we are. Today you hear their speeches and you vote for the one you like. Then you hear the Philip Sydney team next week. And the week after, the play-off. All of which, I must say, the hon. sec. is very pleased about since it means I provided three events to round off our meetings, and he was running out of ideas. So. Gentlemen. Leonine Rotationists. I give you Miss Christine Gratwick of Woolingham Comprehensive School, lately known as the Alma Street Sec Mod.'

She was a nice girl, spoke well, confidently, about how she'd spent her last summer holidays as a filing clerk in the Architects' Department of the Town Hall, and she had a lot of good jokes about it all, which pleased them very much. Good fun at the expense of the local bureaucracy. Solid applause when she sat down.

'And now Mr Kenneth Langley.'

'Mr Chairman. Leonine Rotationists. The subject of my talk is *Hair*. Not a lot about here, so perhaps I can fill you in about what appears to be a gap in many of your lives . . .'

He was very good. A brief history of hair revealed that it signified strength and lustiness – Samson had hair, Attila the Hun had hair, the more decadent Roman Emperors either had none or cut it short. Why connect it with softness, effeminancy? There had even been times when men who were short on hair actually wore wigs. Charles II, the most heterosexual monarch in history, wore a wig. The Duke of Marlborough saw off every army in Europe in a wig . . . and so on.

He needled them, even insulted them, but they took to this Kenneth Langley. He was a big lad, had good solid hands, strong wrists, a face, which, though not ugly, was certainly not weak or girlish. Most of all, they liked him because he clearly came from a solid background most of them shared, or at any rate had sprung from – lower-middle class or upper-working. There was nothing toffee-nosed about him like there often was about the Philip Sydney lot. He came to his peroration: 'I hope, gentlemen, that in the last ten minutes or so I have managed to rearrange a little your prejudices about hair. If anyone has a doubt left, then I challenge them.' He looked slowly over the whole room as if weighing them up, then nodded slowly, shook his long locks. 'Race you to the bar and the loser pays.'

Laughter, applause. Then a busy little fuss, taken very seriously, during which each Leonine Rotationist marked his paper and Duxbury counted the votes. Langley was the winner by a narrow margin; they had liked both speeches. A Parker ballpoint for each . . . Gentlemen, that concludes the business of the Woolingham Leonine Rotationists for this week.

Well, not quite. They split up into small groups, ordered more drinks, and with an 'Ah, Bob, a word in your shell-like' and a 'Re that little matter you mentioned last week . . .' and an 'I spoke to the Super about that, and he thinks he might see his way . . .' many of the little knots, stoppages and wrinkles that might otherwise have blemished the even flow of Woolingham politics, business and industry were smoothed away.

'Well, young Bosham. What can I do for you? Mother well, is she? And that sister of yours, Anne? Fine.'

'Thank you, Councillor. Actually the thing is I've got a spot of potential trouble, an actual known troublemaker, on my work-force. Bill Gould his name is. Lives in the Flowers. Now, how my foreman took him on, God only knows. But he's an activist, an International Socialist. Shop steward in his previous job up in Greenwich and had them all out after only three weeks.'

'What union?'

'Transport and General.'

Councillor Duxbury put a heavy arm round Charlie, who had to resist showing the revulsion he always felt at all but sporting physical contact with a male. Worse still, his shoulder was patted by the plumb but hairy hand.

'No sweat, young Bosham. No sweat at all. Councillor Welsh, the Chairman of the Highways Committee, owes me a favour or two, and he'll see you straight on that. He has the local T and G in his pocket. Anything else, son?'

'Advice.'

'Advice costs nothing. The other matter will. I'll let you know what and when. But advice is free.'

'Containerization.'

Councillor Duxbury removed his arm, put one elbow on the other wrist, and slowly tapped his huge beak with a podgy finger.

'You're thinking of buying hardware to shift them.'

'Yes.'

'Cost.'

'A lift to shift a twenty-five-ton container costs twenty grand. Smaller, cheaper, obviously.'

'Don't touch it. I'll tell you for why. It'll come. But the big unions will have to fight it every inch. They'll have to.

Their rank and file will make them. So it may take years. Oh, I know what the bright lads say: buy now while it's cheap. But it never works like that. Once the ice breaks, unit costs will drop. Until then, stay out. Right, son?'

'Right, Councillor.'

The big man moved on. Others claimed his attention, had dues to pay or favours to ask.

5

‘There’s a bill from Unwins I think you should look at.’

Friday. Tanks ringed Paris – not for nothing those Haussmann Boulevards. At Hull, Hornsea and Frankfurt, students sat in and on. Timothy White’s, who had bought up Alderson Senior (he now lived in the Algarve), were in turn bought up by Boots. A Kray twin was charged with murder. Valerie was going through the invoices and bills, writing cheques for Charlie to sign. Occasionally she hummed, *sotto voce,* ‘Lovely Rita, Meter Maid’, but now she paused to pass the slip across to him.

Fifty-six pounds, seventeen and sixpence. It was itemized.

‘When did we last pay them?’

‘Four weeks ago.’

‘I haven’t had all that. Gin? I never drink gin. I never even give the stuff away. What the hell’s going on?’

‘I didn’t think so, that’s why . . .’

‘Give them a bell. Now.’

She stood up, used the phone on the corner of his desk. She certainly was an eyeful, so tall, so well built. Yet soft too, as she cradled the phone between cheek and shoulder, shook out a long Peter Stuyvesant and lit it.

‘Could I speak to the manager, please? Woolingham Storage. Your invoice number A stroke 4032161B. I’d like to query some of the items, since Mr Bosham feels there has been some mistake.’

‘Fucking cock-up,’ muttered Charlie, then hitting on the mode phrase just then current: ‘Got their knickers in a twist.’

‘Yes, yes. I see. All the gin? For six months? I see. Yes, of course we’ll settle.’ She put down the receiver, stubbed out the cigarette, looked down at him through double eyelashes, eyes serious now, but an almost tender seriousness.

'Mr Bosham, you're not going to like this.'

'Well?'

'It's your mother, Mrs Bosham. She's been buying two or three bottles of gin a week on that . . .'

Two huge fists hammered the desk. Then silence. Then he looked up at her. She was terrified. His face had gone white, his knuckles showed white, his mouth was pulled down into a shark-like grimace.

'I'll tear her fucking head off.'

He stood up, shot up; the desk tipped so she had to steady it. He stormed out of his office, through hers, then back again, kicking in one of the panels of the connecting door.

'I swear it. Where are my keys? I'll go right up there now and beat the shit out of her, so help me, I swear I will.'

'Mr Bosham. Don't. Please don't go on like this.'

'Get out of my way or I'll hang one on you.'

'Please . . . Charlie.'

Charlie.

He glared at her but the rich mist of rage began to fade just a little. There she was, straight as a young tree, with the gold chain just above her fanny pelmet and that look of serious tenderness still in her pale brown eyes, a touch of pallor beneath her golden skin, a hint of a pout in her full moist lips. Then she stooped very slightly to the side, lifted one leg up under her and slipped off one long, shocking-pink, T-strapped, sharply pointed, stiletto-heeled shoe; with the other hand she groped for Dylan.

The stiletto was almost just that, ended in a tiny disc of hard metal. Charlie had read of a would-be rapist getting one stuck a quarter of an inch in his temple. Perhaps she had.

'Don't go there now, Mr Bosham. Charlie. I don't think you should go there for a day or two.'

He subsided on to the edge of the desk.

'What the fuck am I to do?'

'Listen. You play squash? I'll give you a game. Help you to work off your feelings. Then we'll think of what you should do. OK?'

He nodded.

'Then you can drive me round to my place and I'll pick up my things.'

His were where he always kept them – in the Renault, just that day back from Barton's garage.

He took her to the country club he used about four miles away, not far from the Stoney Cross hangar, and at half past three on a Friday afternoon found no difficulty in getting a court.

He changed quickly. She did not – encumbered as she was by the necessity of maintaining a feminine appearance, and a deodorized one at that. He had worked off some of his aggression before she arrived, belting the pill about the echoing pit – sometimes, just for the hell of the noise, deliberately thumping it into the tin.

His vanity began to reassert itself, and deeper emotions too carried exhilaration. He knew that he still cut a good figure: bulky, yes – but trim and hard in his Lacoste Aertex shirt, his thin cotton shorts which left the outline of his jock-strap very clear. The deeper emotions were to do with his mother. No longer need he feel guilty about her. She'd put herself in the shit. Thwack. She was a drunk. Bang. She'd been asking for it for a long time. Bang. Drunken old slag. Thwack. She was . . . *rubbish*. Thwack. Always had been. Thwack. And poor old Dad. What had he suffered? Thwack. Poor old Dad. No wonder he went under. Bang. With an alcoholic wife . . .

'OK, Charlie. Here I am.'

Wow. She had a green crocodile too – just above her left nipple. And a tiny pleated skirt above white towelling knickers. And white socks halfway up her tight strong calves. Oh, dear me.

'Can I knock up?'

'Of course.'

They pushed the ball about for a bit, and he realized he had a game on his hands. She might not hit the ball as hard as he could, and she lacked his reach, though only by an inch or so, but she was wristy, intelligent, and had a hell of a dropshot. She was, on the other hand, innocent: no one shows they can do a drop shot like that in the knock-up. Unless it was a fluke.

'OK, you serve.'

She got to five before she hit him. He claimed hand-in. She claimed a let. They reversed their claims.

'No, no, you were quite right. You were well back.'

'I absolutely insist. A let.'

She took the first game off him 9-3.

He began to play more ruthlessly, body-checking her by half a pace, so it didn't look too deliberate; holding up her service by dropping to one knee to retie a shoe-lace; switching from backhand and bellowing *'turn'* as he scooped up a forehand out of the corner and over her head as she scuttled back from the advantageous and correct position she'd taken up to kill the backhand. They went to 8 all. He won 10-9, but felt flaked. Smells – of sweat, of deodorants gone sour, of urine, and of something more sexual – began to blossom in the pit.

'Call it a day now?' he asked. 'I feel better. I'm not just about to tear my mother apart as soon as I get home. And you look pretty whacked.'

'I'm all right. Come on, Charlie. Let's play it out.'

'OK. But I need a piss.'

In the changing room he swapped the medium-slow ball they'd been playing with for a medium fast. She noticed the deception – of course. But she was a woman. Knew her place. And took a licking in the final game. Thwack, thwack, bang. Her drop shots no longer dropped, but bounced back in. Scarcely had time to get out of the way before thwack, thwack, she was wrong-footed by the speed of his return.

He noticed her desperation and the old elation crept back, the triumph, the knowing that he was boss.

'It's always the same,' he said, 'the ball gets faster the longer you play.'

'Oh yeah?' she answered. And then threw her racket into the corner as yet another dropshot came out a foot further than it should have done and he slammed it in an angle round her before she'd even had time to get back. 'You're a bastard, Charlie.' And she leant up against the wall, head on her arm, gasping for air.

He came up behind her, put his strong forearm round her waist and pressed her tight bottom into his groin. Then he turned her round, forced her back up against the plaster wall, holding her wrists out away from her and drove his body against hers until she had to plead for breath. He let go of her wrists, ran his hands inside the top of her tiny skirt, inside the towelling pants, and, holding her buttocks, began to grind her against his now very tumescent prick, chewing with his lips and teeth into her neck and ear, grinding himself against her stomach while his fingers delved.

'Charlie. Not here.'

'Eh?'

'Come on, Charlie. Take me out. Take me to bed. And sock it to me.'

They drove down the new motorway towards Canterbury, found a brand-new motel near Maidstone. In an ambience made intimate by the assorted cartwheels, wheelbarrow wheels and carriage wheels made out of glass fibre and hung over the lights in the ceiling, they had prawn cocktails, rare steak cooked over charcoal briquettes and served with coleslaw and jacket potatoes, and drank two bottles of warm Côtes du Rhône. In bed he came almost as soon as he entered her. He began to pull away, but it was now she who clasped his buttocks. She was a strong woman and she held him there, slowly circling herself against him, feeling into him with her fingers and nails, finding his balls from behind until at last he began to grow big again. She drove him on now, but against his will, her excitement alienating him with every thrust she forced him to give her, the effort of trying to achieve the second orgasm and tearing at him, though machismo demanded on the other side that he felt pleased he could manage it, until suddenly, it took him quite by surprise, her bottom arched up off the bed, her nails, long as they were, sank into his backside, her mouth opened into a large, round, audible 'O', her eyes turned up so he could see the whites between fluttering eyelids, a mottled flush spread over her neck and across her breastbone and then she let out a long, long shuddering moan, and so subsided.

He did not know what had happened to her. He knew he did not like it. He knew nothing like that had ever happened to him. He realized, with icy despair, that if the relationship was to continue, she would expect it to happen again. And again.

She slept. He lay awake, cold with a numb feeling that was beyond anxiety, was not quite fear, was something he had not felt since he was a very small child, the recent recipient of a sibling (Anne) and terribly alone in a world where no one had any time for him at all.

Part Five

6

Charlie sat on a low, stone-topped balustrade and watched the lithe figure of his eight-year old stepson. The little lad fished with solemn concentration. He was using a brand-new fishing rod, small but functional, which Charlie had bought at the hotel shop ten minutes earlier. Slowly Jason wound the clicking reel and rebaited with food scraps provided by one of the waiters.

'Charlie,' he said, in a calling voice, 'I'm going to put less bait on this time. Smaller pieces, I mean. Because I can see them nibbling, but they don't eat a whole piece at once.'

'Good idea, son.'

Charlie, on a belated honeymoon, after a very good lunch from the hotel buffet, and three large Cuba Libres before it, beer with it, and coffee and Soberano brandy after it, was beginning to feel calmer, more relaxed – satisfied, which, with Charlie, meant self-satisfied.

He looked around him. The hotel, the Sol y Sombre, which he called Solly Somber and joked that it was the name of the Jew-boy who built it, belonged now to Trust Houses Forte: the discovery of this had been cause for a grumble. Charlie was always ready to keep his wife in place by grumbling at anything she had arranged. 'We needn't have travelled this far to stay in a Trust House.' he'd said. But really he had been relieved. If the management was British, his good sense said, then there was unlikely to be any of the hassles you heard about from fellow Leonine Rotationists: workmen still laying concrete at the end of the corridor, sewage rising in the toilets.

And, he had to admit it, it was a nice situation. Built into the side of what had once been a tiny rocky inlet or cove, from the deck above the sea where he was now sitting, it rose seven storeys (only four from the main entrance at the front, which was that much higher up the hill) in a long uniform rectangle of identical triangular balconies with blue tessellation rising in columns between.

The deck itself was spacious, on three levels, with a marble dance floor up by the hotel shop, then tables, then those reclining couches for dedicated sunbathers, and little tables with thatched roofs round a swimming pool shaped like a figure eight, the smaller circle shallow for the kiddies, the larger one deeper. The opposite shore of the cove was still unspoilt, at least from a distance: a headland stuck a finger of brown rock into the sea, then rose a little to a ridge crowned with umbrella pines. It pointed up the coast to Palma, ten miles away, a brown haze on the horizon to and from which big container ships, and occasionally even bigger oil tankers, would push their way through the indigo sea. Charlie liked to watch them – too much undiluted nature made him anxious.

'Charlie, Charlie, I've got one, I've got one, come and see.' On the end of the line a silver doubloon threshed in a tiny paroxysm of fear and rage. The small boy, white blond, was ecstatic almost equally with joy and doubt – for he did not know what to do about it, or rather he did, but couldn't bring himself to touch the thing.

Charlie had no doubts. He trapped the fish in the cave of his big freckled fists, where it beat against palms like a wet but spiny bird, then he felt out its head with the finger and thumb of his right hand and squeezed. A slight resistance, then a sort of pop as from a flat and brittle grape. The mad fluttering ceased. He tore the hook out and spread his hand.

'There, son.'

It was oval-shaped, flattish, but not a flat fish, spiny, less than three inches long. The silveriness was already fading, one glazed eye had been displaced and Charlie discovered a smear of dark crimson blood on his thumb.

The boy looked from the fish, then up into Charlie's face. He reddened, turned away, wiped his eye on the back of his wrist.

'Thanks, Charlie.'

'Here, I'll put it in your bucket for you.'

'Thanks.'

He watched the boy bait up again. What was wrong? Jason sometimes seemed a bit nervy, a bit difficult, though open enough, on the whole did as he was told without too much fuss, and accepted Charlie, on the face of it, without reserve, even if he had not actually shown any overt enthusiasm. But he won't call me Dad. Why should he? his new wife had said. He already has a Dad. Yes, Charlie thought, but not every Tom, Dick and Harry knows that, and I'll be a nuisance trying to explain it every time he calls me Charlie. Sharon, two years younger, slipped into calling him Daddy sometimes by accident, not meaning to. To her, her real father was less real than he was to Jason.

Charlie, back on his low wall, fiddled in the pocket of the beach wrap he'd left there for the packet of JPS, bought on the plane. Plenty left in their room. Should last out the fortnight.

He had not liked the plane one bit. He had never flown before, never been out of England – in fact, tell the truth, had never been further north than Woburn Abbey, further south than Brighton, further east than Maidstone, further west than Hampton Court. The Hampton Court and Woburn Abbey trips had been years ago – fourth-form coach outings from Philip Sydney.

He had not liked the way the wings shook as the plane taxied, in spite of the reassuring RR on the engines; he had not liked the noise, the shocking acceleration, the lurch of the earth as it fell away below them, though he was glad to see that the wings stopped shaking as they got airborne. He had looked down once when Sharon, excited as anything, insisted he should – at the Isle of Wight, just like a map, and that had been enough. Then, as the whiskies and brandies, and even half-bots of champers flowed (Once a year, old sport, got to make the most of it) and conversation with the people across the gangway or a little up and down became general, he had begun to pick up what people then called bad vibes.

'Bad business those two chaps caught in their midget sub.'

'No way are they going to get them out.'

'So he cut a corner or two to stay in the White House. Well, I've cut a corner or two in my time to get where I am. You have to these days – inflation being what it is, business a bit slack, pound . . .'

'What is the peseta?'

Rustle of newspaper.

'One four one.'

Jesus, thought Charlie, it was one four six when we first planned this trip.

'I've been watching it. Had my eye on it, I can tell you. First Naples. Then Rome. Now Sardinia. Cholera . . .'

Jesus *wept,* thought Charlie and dug out the booklet the airline had left on the seat, it had a map of the route . . . Sardinia was virtually next door!

'Of course it's boiling up in the Middle East again. You see, I reckon it's just dawning on those Sheiks of Araby that they've got us by the short and curlies, where oil is concerned . . .'

'Did you see where the United Nations chappie said Jerusalem was the capital of Israel . . . I'm surprised Hussein and Sadat didn't go to war on the spot.'

'Oh they will. No doubt of it. Unless the Jews put in a pre-emptive strike.'

'Could spread. Ghaddafi in Libya seems ready enough to take on the Yanks. Could spread like a forest fire.'

No. Charlie had not liked the plane. And he hadn't much

liked what he saw first of the island. They dropped out of the cold clear terrifying sunlight into and through a low coppery haze; the captain announced ETA five minutes away and the temperature was twenty-two degrees, seventy fahrenheit, only two degrees higher than Woolingham two days before, and there it had been sunny.

The airport was frayed and dark after the glamour of Gatwick. The town looked crowded and raucous, the cathedral didn't have a spire or tower.The long narrow road was bumpy and often interrupted by roadworks, threaded through resort after resort, each looking tatty and half finished, and one smelling of sewage . . . it all confirmed his worst fears. He had had a headache, a sour stomach; Sharon slept on her mother's chest, Jason shifted irritably, nervously trying to conceal the fact that he was clutching his winkle . . . poor lad hadn't been able to get to the toilet before the plane touched down.

And then, and then to find that after all it was all right. That Jane had been so right to insist they spend a hundred quid each more than they might have done for what was really a rather good hotel – four star – with comfy beds, grand bathroom with gentle lighting or spotlights, whichever you preferred and a . . . what did Jane call it, a bidet, which, she had said, he could wash his feet in if he liked, but was really there for her to wash her fanny . . .

He grinned, tossed the cigarette over the parapet and into the sea. Here they came, from the shop, Jane née Coleman, ex-Crathorne, now Bosham, and Sharon, her six-year-old daughter, both wearing gaudy ponchos.

'Good God. What do you want those for?'

'Keep the sun off when we begin to burn.'

'Some chance.' He gestured at the still-coppery sky.

'You'd be surprised. If you can tell where the sun is, and you can, you can burn . . .'

'Mummy, Mummy, I caught a fish.'

'Darling, did you? Let me see.'

She sank on to her haunches and dipped towards the yellow plastic bucket, showing deep cleavage between her long warm breasts, and Charlie felt that kick in his diaphragm that told him she was a snip, a right smashing bit of crumpet, just what he'd always wanted, knew he really deserved.

'But Charlie killed it. I wanted him to put it back.'

'Never mind, darling. Anyway, you've got it now, got it for ever.'

'Can I put it on the balcony to dry? Like a kipper?'

Next morning the coppery haze lifted. A waiter brought them flaky pastries shaped like horns, good coffee, warm milk for the kids, and sponge fingers, which they adored. Looking out from the balcony, Charlie saw sun bright and hot, the terrace with sun-loungers by the pool practically deserted, the umbrella pines across the water, which heaved now with a bit of breeze that had chased off the haze, and a jet's wings winking silver in the morning light as it dropped towards Palma: and he felt good.

'I'll go and bag a couple of those couch things by the pool.'

'OK,' Jane looked up at him from her trayed breakfast.

'I might even have a swim.'

'Fine.' She dunked her second croissant in her coffee, something Charlie knew his mother or Aunt Elizabeth would have rejected as continental and filthy, but which he guessed was probably all right since Jane did it. He pulled off his pyjamas, pulled on a pair of trunks, and picked up a towel.

When he got down to the pool every sun-lounger had a towel on it – and not hotel towels either, but personal, private ones. He assumed that they had been left from the afternoon before.

'Bloody careless,' he thought.

He shifted two towels from two of the loungers near the edge of the pool, sat on one of them, lit a JPS and watched a fishing boat, high-prowed with a little cabin at the back, standing up like a matchbox, roughing its way through the deeper water beyond the headland.

'Hey. What do you think you're doing?'

He looked up and his whole psyche, mind and body, lurched. For a moment it was Lissie in front of him.

She had dark hair cut short, creamy skin but with mild eczema on cheekbones and shoulders, was not more than twenty-five, anyway quite a bit younger than he or Jane, dressed in a black shiny bikini with a flame-red bath wrap.

'I'm sitting here.'

'Those are our sun-loungers.'

'Why?'

'They've got our towels on.'

'Not now they haven't.'

'Shit. Don't you know the rules?'

Rules.

Charlie respected rules – not as things to be kept or obeyed, but as obstacles to be treated with respect, not ridden over, what was the word? roughshod.

'What rules?'

She was sturdier than Lissie had been, tougher, more . . . whole. And not ready to stand any nonsense.

'Oh well. There's a first time for everybody. The rules are . . .' She had a high voice, a bit plaintive like Lissie's had often been, but not the posh accent. 'Early in the morning a little man comes out and swabs down the deck, and fetches away any muck floating on the pool and he even, twice a week, sort of hoovers the bottom of the pool. Anyway, if you get up early enough, about seven o'clock, you'll see. And he tips each sun-lounger on its side. The rule is you can reserve a lounger or two for the day if you get down when he's finished, by putting your towel on it. OK?'

'And those are your towels?'

'Right.'

'OK.' He was about to toss his JPS in the pool, sensed a reaction, and chose the now slightly spumy sea instead. 'I'll remember.'

With elaborate ceremony, he picked up the towels he had chucked on one side, and respread them over the sun-loungers.

The third day they took a coach trip. It was a big coach, a luxury one. Charlie, anxious to demonstrate to his new family that he was a fixer, got on first and put them in the front seat behind the door with a chrome rail separating them from the little stairwell down to the folding door. He took the single seat, the only one in the coach apart from the driver's, in front of the stairwell, the one often used by the courier, but today, he had checked, the driver himself would do any talking necessary. Thus he was on his own while they were moving, and this may have been the underlying motive. Charlie was a loner after all, and had been perhaps too much unrelenting in the company of other people over the last few days.

There he sat then, in this single front seat with the instrument panels and heavy gear lever, its foot shrouded in rubber between him and the driver, placed absurdly on his left, and behind him first this new wife and her kids, then forty or fifty people. The coach pulled out of the forecourt of the Sol y Sombre on to the narrow main road and off they went to a factory where glass ornaments were made, then to a lunch of grilled meat.

Behind him songs were sung, 'My Old Man Said Follow the Van, 'When Irish Eyes are Smiling', and 'We All Live in a Yellow Submarine'. In front the narrow road unwound. Other coaches, as huge and chromy as the one they were in, lurched past going the other way, chorded horns blaring. The tatty palms and tattier hotels slipped by, the stink of sewage, a brief glimpse of the marina and banked flowers by the cathedral and then out into the country again, or shanty towns, it was a bit of each, and then suddenly.

A man stepped off the curb at a controlled junction and the driver stood on the brakes hard. Charlie tumbled into the toughened windscreen, took a nasty knock on the forehead and felt horrors of electric pain down his forearm to his fingertips from hitting his elbow on the low ledge below. Angrily he brushed off the concern of his wife and the nearer of his fellow passengers; however, unpleasant recall had been triggered, that lasted him all the way to the glass factory.

Driving home? Anyway from a pub or club to the room he rented, driving in his newish Rover 2000, he had run over a bundle of old clothes that leaked blood and had lost its dentures, which lay broken in the gutter.

'You were driving on your parking lights. Why?'

Because I was drunk.

'I was tired.'

'You've been on a drunk-driving charge before.'

'And I got . . . was acquitted. Charge dropped.'

'Because the constable made an error in the procedure. You were lucky that time.' Cold emphasis on *that*. Not this time, mate. This time we have you by the short and curlies and we're not letting go.

It dragged on, became messy rather than complicated, went to the crown court. One of the worst things was that a young bloke from Mead and Mead was solicitor for the other side, for the dead man's widow, and in the early proceedings in front of the magistrates had cross-examined with what seemed to Charlie to be excessive zeal. He rang up Terry.

'Listen, Bosham. This is most improper of you. I am *not* your brother-in-law. Now listen. I am going to hang up. If you ring me back or try to get in touch with me in any way while this thing is on, you'll lay yourself open to a charge of contempt on top of everything else. All right?'

Fuck you, Terry Mead. I'll get you for this.

In the end the widow cracked, went down with severe depression and settled out of court for two hundred and fifty pounds damages, which Charlie's insurance company paid a good six months later. This had been enough to sway the jury and Charlie got off with careless driving (side lights instead of dipped headlights) and the drink – the causing death being dropped. One hundred and twenty sheets, banned for a year, five hundred costs.

But it had cost him a lot more than that. A hell of a lot more.

'Nasty, very.'

'Eh?'

'That bump you took. I say, are you all right? Not got a concussion or anything?'

Charlie came to, took in the man at his side – a large bloke, greying hair, handsome face going a bit to seed, jowly. Wasn't he with the girl that looked like Lissie? Dirty old man – old enough to be her father.

'No. I'm OK. Silly bastard stepping off the curb like that.'

'Yes. Thought our driver did well. Dear Lord. God knows what they're spending.'

He nodded back into the shop where most of the coach party were milling around buying the coloured glass animals they'd just seen genuine craftsmen make by hand. Charlie had quite enjoyed the operation – as always, he admired the simple approach. Glass was cheap, the tools hardly more than a set of pincers, a couple of blow-lamps, and the labour, for all the guide had gone on about the marvellous and ancient skills involved, very straightforward. You heated the rods, bent them about a bit, let the glass melt into blobs, sheered off the ends, and there you were. A bob's worth of glass into a fish with spines not unlike the one Jason had caught, selling for over a quid in just under five minutes. Well done the elves.

'In business on your own, are you?'

Charlie, surprised, agreed.

'Thought so. Always tell. The independent sorts, loners, we like to be our own bosses, eh?'

This pleased Charlie.

'Mind if I ask what?'

'Warehousing. Storage.'

'Computerized, of course.'

'Er . . . not fully.'

'Ah well. Maybe we'll have a chat about that some time. Here come the ladies. By the way. My name's Dobson. Bob Dobson.'

'Bosham. Charlie.'

They shook hands. It was indeed the girl like Lissie who came up. 'Connie. This is Charlie, Charlie Bosham. I was just commiserating with him over the bump he took when the bus pulled up.'

'Hi, Charlie. Sun-lounger snatcher. Ratfink.' She made a shape like a gun with her hand, pointed her index finger and waggled her thumb.

'Daddy, Daddy, look, I've got a swan. Mummy bought me a swan.'

'What a cute little girl – I've seen her by the pool, no idea she was yours.'

'And here's her mother,' said Jane coming up after Sharon. Introductions all round. She slipped an arm through Charlie's and he let his hand slip, took a handful of her trousered bottom, squeezed it, gave it a slap. He was proud of her. Handsome woman. All his. He felt a glow coming on, the blues he'd gone through in the coach slipping away.

'Well, son. What did you get?'

Jason looked up at him. 'I'm not your son,' he said. 'And Sharon shouldn't call you Daddy.'

For a moment they all thought Charlie was going to hit him.

'Whoopsie,' cried Connie. 'Never mind if he isn't, I'm sure he tries damn hard.'

Lunch was out in the country, eaten off wooden picnic tables with benches, the rustic approach, brings you closer to nature, what you need on a holiday. And the food was in keeping. Huge pork chops with garlic broiled over vine prunings scented with wild herbs, served with giant mixed salads and powdery bread, as white as warm snow inside, teeth-shattering crusts outside, and jugs of sangría, stuffed with ice and orange slices, but heady stuff nevertheless and as much of it as you could drink, all in. Not everyone liked this. One couple were disgusted with the meat and tried to complain: it's burnt on the outside and raw on the bone. *Señora,* in *Mallorca* is how we eat *chuletas de cerdo,* would like an *empanada* instead? It is your Cornish pastie . . .

But the Boshams and the Dobsons enjoyed it, were fast becoming mates – and not least because of Jason's awful clanger. It had, as it were, let loose the floodgates: Bob Dobson was indeed on the merry-go-round for the third time, had two families elsewhere, one almost grown-up . . . Jane, high on sangría and relief that Charlie had not, after all, belted Jason, told all:

'Honestly, I tell no lie, my first husband was a real shit. Pardon my French but he was.' She tossed back her long, waved hair, chestnut with just that hint of red that makes chestnut so attractive. And Charlie looked across the table at her with warmth, even affection – certainly pride that she was such a good looker even after two children – and, of course, possessively. She was wearing a cotton tee-shirt – *Mallorca La Bella* above a map of the island – and one of those new natural bras so you could really see her tits, in her case a bit low-slung and wide-spaced, but so what. Variety is the spice of life. Already she seemed to have picked up that coppery tan Majorcan holidays give us all: though, perhaps the lotions lined up on the bathroom shelf helped a bit. 'Worked for Esso.' Waved a fork in the air. 'Bloody good job. Pardon my French, but that's the way it comes and I don't expect to say pardon again. Yes, Sharon, you may go and play. Yes, Jason, I am talking about your father and if you don't want to listen you go and play too.

'Where was I? A shit. Pardon my . . . no, don't bother. We've done that bit. Worked for Esso. Research chemist. Made a bomb. Charlie, what *is* this? Bob, do you know? Artichoke heart? Well, I'm blessed. It went very well for four or five years. Nice house out in Kent, well Orpington, but in the end it turned out that industry was not for James Clever-Clogs Crathorne, Ph.D. A fellowship. You know what that is? I'll tell you. A fellowship is . . . At Cambridge. Oxford too, I believe, but Crathorne had been at college at Cambridge, so that's the one I know about, a fellowship is where the college pay you, say, five thousand pounds a year. And the university another five thousand . . . I tell no lie. And give you endless perks too – like booze dead cheap because some crud in the eighteenth century left a will saying that should be the way it is. And there they teach people, say, five or six hours a week. Give a couple of lectures or demonstrations in science for twenty-four weeks a year, that's all, and live like pigs in shit.

'Seemed like a good bet, so I said go ahead, James. He liked to be called James, not Jimmie, shows what a shit he was, though he started in Alma Street Sec Mod, Woolingham before transferring on a schol . . . schol-arship to Philip Sydney, just like Charlie here, but there's the difference, no side on Charlie at all, he's not toffee-nosed whatever else his faults, whereas our James was all side and precious little else.

'So he went ahead. But it seems Cambridge is not a suitable place for the likes of I. Not according to him, anyway. I was to stay in Orpington and mind the kids and he'd be back weekends, hols, what they call *vacs,* yes they do, Connie – *vacs*. I ask you . . .' Then, brilliantly mimicking the stiff-upper-lip class of posh: "Ah we awl heving very jolly vecks in Medjawkuh? Jolly good." And he'd have a bachelor room in the old coll. Bachelor room, my arse. And it's a fat one too, Bob, in case you haven't noticed.' (He has, thought Charlie.) 'And next thing I know is: Dear Jane, I think you should know I have been living with . . .'

Here she burst into floods of tears which could only be stemmed by Kleenex, a lot more sangría, and promises of ice creams for afters. Through sniffs and hankies, and swigs of the stuff, she got to the end of her story. 'Do you know, the bastard actually tried to get the kids off me on the grounds the bitch he'd gone off with had more class than I? The next two years were hell. Orpington. Two kids on an inadequate allowance, paid irregularly, with all the neighbours clackety-clacking for two miles around if you open the door when the milkman calls . . .' Bob Dobson drummed fingers on the table and looked off into the wide blue yonder. He'd done just that to his second wife, who lived in Camberley. 'But at the end of the day it all worked out, for who should come along but my very own, my very first flame of all time, Charlie Bosham, like a knight in shining armour to carry me off to Mallorca La Bella. Olé!'

They all cried 'Olé!' and banged their glasses together. Out on the tatty grass Jason and Sharon looked back and wondered and then returned to disputing the possession of the rusty swings and slide and climbing frame with the other kids who were there.

Jane pulled Connie's head down to her mouth and whispered in her ear, and Connie shrieked with laughter. What Jane said was: I gave him a flash of my fanny on Coronation Day, would you believe it.

Wending their way back to the coach Bob Dobson said, 'Got travellers' cheques then?'

'Yes,' said Charlie.

'Cash 'm in. Pound's down to one three eight.'

'One three eight!'

'I tell no lie. Cash 'm in.'

'I will,' said Charlie, with fervour.

That night the foursome danced on the composition marble floor by the swimming pool. Some early Beatles numbers, 'Tweesht and Jout', to begin with, then 'Yellow River', 'Guantanamera', 'Arriverderci Roma'. They got quite drunk. Between numbers a cricket, like the ringing tone on a telephone, echoed over the deck from somewhere near their table.

The closing smooches were a relief for Charlie, who never knew what to do in the faster numbers. Jane in her ethnically printed kaftan, Connie in a straight black number shot through longitudinally with silver threads, twisted and swayed, waved their arms like Indian goddesses, while he and Bob bobbed up and down, first on one leg, then on them other, and, occasionally did a movement with their arms that suggested a three-year-old playing steam engines. He knew what to do in the smooches, all right.

First with Connie. She hung herself round his neck, he put his hands low on her bottom and rubbed her tummy against his prick. Then with Jane, who was bigger than

Connie, and whose head came up to rest on his shoulder and nuzzled wet kisses in his neck, he let himself go a bit slack, breathed in the perfumed luxury of her hair, and tried not to feel too dizzy and sick.

He was sick though. All over the bathroom floor. Jane rang the desk.

'Perhaps you had too much to drink.'

'Not I,'

'I don't mean too much alcohol,' aware that to question that capacity was to cast doubt on his machismo, 'I mean too much *variety.*'

'Maybe. But I think it was those fried round fishy things we had in the bar before dinner. Bloody chewy they were.'

'Yes, well. I didn't like to tell you. They were squid.'

'*Squid!!* No fucking wonder I was sick then.'

A small fat lady in a long black dress with black stockings that ended just above her knees came and mopped up without a word. She was pleased though when Jane gave her *cién pesetas.*

'How much was that?'

'Oh, about fifty p.'

'Ten bob!' But he felt pleased. There was warmth to be discovered in big tipping.

In bed – they had twin beds which had seemed wrong at first, but you discovered how hot it could be, and how sunburn didn't like heat, and while a fuck is over in five minutes a long hot night can last for ever – he dwelt with pleasure too on the thought of having someone there to mop up your sick.

He'd vomited on the tatty carpet, in front of the gas fire when he got home after the accident. Home! A crummy bedsit in the north of Woolingham almost in what had been dockland, was now wog-land, and he had not had the slightest idea of how he should set about cleaning it up.

It was Anne's fault. Traitress. He still felt hot rage at the thought of what she had done to him. Bloody dike. And his fucking mother too.

The bad times started when he unloaded Valerie (his way of putting it) on to an acquaintance who managed, ripped off, three local pop groups. She had to go. More and more she had crowded him where the business was concerned, and he could not stand the way she insisted on 'coming' when they fucked. When she did, she was on a vastly different cloud. It was so clearly so much more of an experience than the squirt of relief he was enjoying.

Meanwhile he had already realized that he could not go on living with his mother, and he called in Anne. She was now nurse-in-charge at an old people's home about a mile from Goldsmith Drive, down towards where the Meads still lived. 'Balmoral' was a large, many-roomed Edwardian villa owned by a bonhomous and very fat lady called Billy Blakely. She too was a nurse but now mainly occupied herself with the administration of her 'home', though she still maintained her reputation for being a marvel at deathbeds. 'Poor darlings,' she used to say, 'it's the least I can do. Hold their hands and help them over.' She was good for Anne, they worked well together, had a laugh, were more than a little in love – though so far this had gone no further than very warm, protracted hugs at moments of emotional relief: when some old biddy who'd been a pain in the arse snuffed it at last, or the new freezer centre in Eltham agreed to give a ten per cent discount on the vast supplies of breaded cod, soya beefburgers, frozen chips and ice cream that she fed her 'guests' with.

Anne agreed to move into Goldsmith Drive – it released another room at Balmoral – but only on condition Charlie moved out: she was not going back to the boxroom over the stairs; she'd have Charlie's room overlooking the now totally overgrown back garden, or nothing. After three days making up his mind to this, Charlie gave in. The trouble was that his mother, apart from being a drunk, had steadily recovered some sense of her own personality. When Charlie bullied her, she shouted back; when he banged the table in rage, she banged it too, and then shrieked with laughter at her parody of his behaviour. And once, four weeks earlier, he had been driven to thump her – not hard, but definitely a thump, and was then horrified out of his mind when she took a swipe at him with an empty gin bottle. Clearly this could not go on.

At last the Spitfire and Messerschmidt came down, were dropped in the dustbin along with his girlie magazines and the box-pleated yellow bedspread. What now was a small collection of books about small arms went into storage – the Mottingham facility.

He stayed in small private hotels for six months, grudged the expense, finally settled on the bedsit where he had heaved up on the night of the accident. But that wasn't the root of his hatred for Anne, oh dear me no. Her betrayal had gone much deeper than merely kicking him out of his old room.

Four months later he was in trouble. Without Valerie the business fell off; without a car, following his conviction, he lost his grip on many of his sites; it became clear that if he were to remain in the big time he would have to equip at least one of them with hoists and loaders to handle containers. The capital outlay was enormous; the bank would not touch it, the finance company he went to insisted he should find ten thousand of it himself.

Swivel, the solicitor who was secretary of the Leonine Rotationists, drew up the documents for a mortgage on 263 Goldsmith Drive with separate sets for Mother and Anne to sign. The point was, Mr Bosham's will had left the house to be shared between Charles and Anne, but only after his wife's decease. Until then, she had the right to remain in it, or do as she liked with it, even let it, but not sell it.

He went up to the house with Swivel, now a grey sick

man who chainsmoked and coughed and wheezed continuously. Swivel set out the papers and began to explain.

'Hang about,' said Anne, after twenty minutes of carefully pitched sales talk. 'Lets see if I've got this right. The bank will accept this house as collateral worth five thousand, even though the house is now worth seven and a half, if Mother and I sign acceptances, as stipulated in these papers.'

'Right.'

'And provided there is no other lien or claim against the property.'

'Right.'

There was a long moment of silence. Each looked at each: Mother, fat still, doughy, but with a glint of triumph in her eye; Anne, fat but not doughy, a wee bit worried, especially in the presence of Solicitor Swivel, but knowing really she was on solid ground; Swivel, always competent where the issues were clear, but at that moment sensing that they were not as straightforward as he had thought, and so sat drumming with the thin grey fingers of his left hand while his right went up and down, to and from his mouth, much like a fairground automaton, puffing out smoke with each jerk.

And Charlie, waiting. The teak-cased clock on the mantelpiece ticked.

Anne drew in a deep breath and said, 'Charlie, three weeks ago Mother signed a document. It said in effect that while she was alive she was happy that she should live at Balmoral, or here, whichever suited her best, and be given, free of charge, the same treatment as the other guests at Balmoral. Free of charge. In return we will use this house as an annexe for the less severely handicapped of our clients . . . guests. We reckon to get seven in here. Three doubles, using this front room as one, and the two larger bedrooms, and one single. The dining room will be the common room. Also we are asking for planning permission . . .'

Charlie slammed the table.

'You can't do this. You . . .'

'I'm not doing it. Mummy already did it.'

'But. . .'

'Listen, Charlie. Dad's will was quite clear. Mummy can do what she likes with it in her lifetime except sell it.

'Mother?'

The fat doughy lady looked up. 'That's it, Charlie. You should never have struck your mother. You should never have struck me.'

The clock ticked on. Swivel cleared his throat.

'Miss Bosham?'

'Ms. Or Sister.'

Swivel was not going even to comprehend that sort of nonsense, let alone go along with it. 'Do you have the relevant documents here?'

'Yes,'

For another twenty minutes Charlie paced about the house and garden. Did he relive memories of a happy childhood? Hardly! What he did feel was a terribly strong sense of property. Even of the sacredness of property. How dare she! He was older than her. He was male. Every crumb in the pebbledash, every slate on the gabled roofs (and one or two needed replacing), even the now woodwormed, tumbledown wreck of a garden shed dwarfed by six-foot-high rhubarb gone woody, belonged rightfully to him. Not these . . . women. And he needed the money. Really needed it. Might go under without it. He chewed on his nails and thumped fences with his fists. What they didn't realize was that he was in business. Whereas, what was Anne? A nurse. Then she should stick to nursing, not fart around with things she knew nothing about. Lots of women like her would give their eye-teeth to be nurses instead of supermarket cashiers . . .

He went back to the front room.

Swivel said, 'I must say, Bosham, these documents do appear to be in order. Miss . . . your sister, has, however, made a suggestion: that you should give up your rights in this property, in perpetuity, for a sum of two and a half thousand pounds. I shall have to look into it, see that this does not go against the terms of your father's will . . .'

Charlie thumped the table. 'Four.'

Anne looked up at him, and smiled almost tenderly.

'Three, and not a penny more.'

As they left the house, Charlie paused at the gate and said, for he was feeling bereft, 'I thought we were friends.'

She looked at him with blank bewilderment, and then laughed. 'Not likely. Allies sometimes. Sometimes our interests have coincided, sometimes not. But not friends. Charlie, I now know what a friend is, and you were never one. Just a brother.'

Fucking dike, said Charlie to himself in Mallorca La Bella. And slept. At last.

At Jane's suggestion Charlie made more of an effort with the children. The next coach party was to George Sand's house up in the hills. Jane wanted to go, she liked Chopin, she said, and she took Sharon with her. Charlie took Jason on a boat trip.

The sailors, three of them, were jolly, and determined to make everyone as jolly as they. They had a big ice box packed with litres of gin and rum and tonic and colas, which they served ad lib to anyone who wanted them, slopping the spirit into tall plastic glasses, a third or more full, then the tonic or cola on top. Charlie loved this, the raffishness of it, the prodigality, he had never thought of G and T as a long drink before. He also understood why the tickets had cost nearly a fiver, which he had thought more than a little steep, and the nag at the back of his mind that it was a rip-off dissolved. Charlie hated a rip-off almost more than anything else in the world.

Just when it seemed they had come to the end of Majorca, were about to zoom off into the wide, empty, black sea with only the seagulls who pursued them for company, the boat swung in towards the land. Then the engine cut back, eventually died, and in the sudden balm of the silence glided past a pine-tree-clad headland into a little rocky bay, not a hotel, or block or café in sight, Majorca as it used to be. One of the jolly sailors went to the bow and swung an anchor out into the crystal water. 'Twenty minutes, we stop,' he announced. 'You can sweem. But,' he raised a waggish but admonitory forefinger, 'you don't go so far.'

Jason, who now lived in his swimming trunks, was the first in, in an almost perfect racing dive that sent the shoals of tiny fishes wheeling and swinging away from his point of impact. His head broke the surface, he shook it, scattering a brief aureole of stars.

'Come on, Charlie. Come on.'

Christ, thought Charlie. The little bastard. He'd have to follow. He had his trunks on under his Bermudas. Clinging to the rail until the last moment, he let himself slip over the side.

The water was colder out here than at the hotel; there was a slight swell that caused his G and T-soaked vision to lurch when it first came under him; and where was Jason?

'Come *on,* Charlie.' A thin brown arm about a mile away it seemed, the cry as remote as the call of a distant seabird. Charlie struck out bravely, and to his relief the boy turned and came skimming back to him, a greyhound in the water to his overweight spaniel. The boy was eager, cheery, and quite untroubled by the distance he had swum; Charlie was heaving in air as if with a shovel.

'Isn't this great, Charlie? Isn't it fun? I *love* this boat trip.'

'We . . . should . . . go . . . back . . . The man said . . . not . . . go . . . too . . . far,'

They turned and Charlie felt despair. He abandoned dignity and began to breast-stroke, holding his large head as high out of the water as he could

'You should drop your face into the water at the beginning of every stroke,' said Jason, earnestly. He too reverted to breast-stroke, demonstrated, and slipped ahead of Charlie as if the water were a different element for him, something that went with him, carried him along, while for Charlie it was a Sisyphean obstacle; the more he clawed and pushed it around him, struggled to keep on top of it, the more it surged back, and with every stroke it became heavier than it had been before.

One of the sailors hooked a strong brown hand under his arm. 'You not go so far next time, *sẽnor,* OK?'

For two years, after Valerie and the accident, his life had been like that battle with the sea, he thought, as the boat chugged off again, and the coast of bays and headlands slipped by and the hotels began to reappear. Without a car, without a ménage behind him, without Valerie to prompt him, offer covert advice, prod him in the right direction at the right time, he had lost more than he was making. He had borrowed too much, and, at the lowest point, could see no way out of the mess other than selling his franchise on the Stoney Cross hangar, now equipped at last to handle containers, to a rival company. He knew that if he did that he'd be on the skids.

While all this built up, he let himself go in other ways. He drank too much, mainly for the sake of saloon-bar company, ate badly, his tummy was on the brink of becoming a gut, his face was pasty, his hair seemed to recede and lost its coarse vigorous look – and all this with him barely in his thirties. He even began to take less interest in his clothes.

Then at last his luck changed. Well, not entirely. Charlie was wont to say he had the nous to spot the right opportunity at the right time, see how the right man could be fitted into the right hole. One evening he was in the Wellington, drinking Wadworths 6X and eating salted peanuts and wondering how the hell he was going to cope with VAT, when . . .

'Long time no see. Buy you a drink?'

'Peter Coleman! Yes, sure, I'll have another pint,'

Charlie looked Coleman over. Yes. Doing well. Quite lost the clerk at the Town Hall look he used to have. Good suit. Nice tie – Hardy Amies, I shouldn't wonder, good haircut. And those gold-rim specs aren't National Health.

'Here we are then.'

'Cheers.'

'Bottoms up, that's how I like them.'

'Well. How's tricks? As Pat says to Dicky each morning over the orange juice.'

'Fine, fine. And you?'

'Can't grumble.'

'Still with Barton Garages?'

Coleman cradled his straight glass – the barman knew how these new-fangled CAMRA fans like it in a straight glass – and peered thoughtfully into the amber brew.

'Yes. And no,' He took off the specs, gave them a polish and put them back on. 'Today, actually I am. Next week, no.'

'Mind if I ask why not?'

'Not at all. Old Barty has been just fine. But old is the *mot juste,* if you catch my drift. The old bugger's retiring. He's made a deal with the little yellow folk which does him a lot of good, and them too, since it closes down the Renault and General Motors outlets in the neighbourhood, but leaves me out in the cold. This particular lots of Nips put in managers and work the accounts and so on, finance, through head office, and since basically I'm an accountant, not a motor-trade man, I'm out.'

'Tough.'

'Hairy, yes.'

Silence.

'Like another!'

'Why not?'

Then: 'Seem to have a fistful of dollars, ha ha,' said Charlie, spreading ten pence pieces in his big palm. 'Might as well lose them, they only spoil the hang of the suit.'

They went over to the fruit machines – still one-armed bandits – and slotted in their florins, yanked on the black plastic, moulded to fit your grip, penis substitutes. Was this more fun than pressing buttons? Not necessarily. Perhaps it appealed more to the auto-erotic, homosexual side of men's natures, whereas pressing buttons, as we do nowadays, may appeal more to . . .

'Jackpot. Wowee!'

That marvellous clatter of cupro-nickel, some spilling on the floor, with even a couple of newish fifty-pence pieces amongst them.

'Crackerjack! Well, I'm blessed. Time to get out. While you're ahead of the game.'

'Too true. My erstwhile employer would go along with that.'

'Have this one on me. Barman. *Barman*. Thank you. Two large Scotches and a couple of those panatellas. Fact is, Peter . . . I'm not sure I couldn't use a chappie like you at this point in time. Point of fact, I really think I could.'

'Oh, really?' Coleman gave his specs another polish, put them back on again, squirted soda into his Scotch.

'I'm thinking of expanding. Taking on more facilities. And I'm just not too sure I can cope with the extra work on my own, if you take my point.'

'Oh, I catch your drift.' Their eyes met, Charlie's pale blue, the lids beginning to droop ever so slightly to the outside, Coleman's a light brown, serious, even calculating. Just so had Jane's looked when she suggested Charlie should quit cheating at Monopoly.

'I think I take your point.' And with a sudden chill of awareness, Charlie realized Peter probably had.

'I tell you what,' Coleman went on, brisk now, knocking back the Scotch, snatching up cigarettes, lighter, car keys, 'I'll come round to your office tomorrow and have a look at your books. OK? Now I must dash. But if from what I see there, I think we can work out a deal, well then, we'll go on from there, Right?'

Charlie was dismayed . . . look at his *books*! Christ, he couldn't understand them himself. But any port in a storm, grasp the floating straw.

'Fine, Peter. I look forward to that.'

'Charlie, I'm *so* bored.'

Well yes, thought Charlie, so am I.

An hour yet before the coach got back.

'Charlie, why isn't there children's telly here?'

'There's a set in the lounge, and another in the playroom.'

'But it's all in Spanish, and I hate the playroom.'

They were sitting under one of the thatched umbrellas not far from the swimming pool. Jason no longer wanted to swim, he had swum enough. He did not want to play with the other children – there were very few about, and the nearest were girls, five or six years old, skipping: 'Thatcher, Thatcher, mi-i-i-lk snatcher.' He didn't want to fish because he knew Charlie would kill whatever he caught.

'Tell you what,' said Charlie. 'You go to the shop, see what there is there you might like, and I'll go to our room and get some money.'

'OK, Charlie.'

On the way back down he went to the ever-open bar. He

bought a Cuba Libre, again admired the marvellous way the barman tipped the rum bottle over the tall glass till, with ice, it was more than half full, before topping it up with Coke, lemon and a tiny parasol. It all made something that had seemed a bit of a rip-off at thirty-five pesetas when you thought of the price of a bottle of spirits in the shops seem quite worthwhile.

There was a terrace outside the bar that ran the length of the hotel, and at the far end ten rooms that had no balconies of their own but doors on to it. He knew Connie and Bob had one of these, and though he had every reason to believe they had gone on the coach trip too . . .

And yes. There she was. On her front, on a blow-up mattress, bra undone, red hankie round her head so you could see the vulnerable nape of her neck, tiny black bikini bottom showing plenty of cleavage. Reading *The Betsy* by Harold Robbins.

'Charlie, mean sod, didn't bring me one.' She pushed her huge cheaters down on to the tip of her nose and peeped up at him.

'I'll get you one.'

'No. Just give us a swig.'

He did, coming down on to his haunches. She reached up and momentarily he caught a glimpse of almost all of one breast, and the brown nipple unsquashing itself from the pressure of her body on the towel.

The ice chimed in the clear brown fluid as she passed it back

'Bob not here then?'

'Nope. Gone to see the Chopin house in the mountains.'

'Jane too.'

'Culture vultures.'

He straightened, moved to the rail. 'Nice up here. You can see further than down by the pool.'

'But not as far as from your balcony three more floors up.'

The palms of his hands moistened. Was this a come-on?

Should he now say, why don't we go up and see? How much longer before the coach got back?

'Do you want to come and see?'

'See what?'

The reddened skin of his face deepened. 'Just how much further we can see.'

'You want to see further?'

His eyes ran compulsively from her lean, brown, still rather spotty shoulders, down the groove of her backbone into the darker shadow of the cleft between her buttocks, cut off by the edge of the black bikini.

She ran a tip of tongue across her top lip and said quite softly, 'Naughty boy, Charlie. Naughty. We're only halfway through the holiday, you know. Start something now and it'll make a mess of everything. But I do fancy you, Charlie, I do. You're a bum man, aren't you?'

'I suppose so.'

'I can always tell. And I've got a nice bum. Bob, really, is a boob man, and Jane, she really is a lovely person, has lovely boobs. So maybe at the end of the fortnight we'll . . .'

A sudden burst of screaming from almost directly below them, then his name coming as part of the screams: 'Charlie, Charlie, Charlie.'

He looked over the edge, and saw Jason being dragged across the deck by a paunchy security guard who wore a heavy automatic on one side of his belt and a riot stick on the other.

'Oh, Jesus,' said Charlie.'What the hell's gone wrong now?'

He went down one lift, while the guard and Jason came up the other, realized what had happened and went chasing back up two flights of stairs after them. The foyer was almost empty, but somewhere over the gasp of his breath and the pounding of his heart he could still hear Jason's screams. The receptionist smiled up at him: You want key? Number plis.'

'No, I don't . . . want key. I want son . . . boy. Pretty damned quick.'

'Boy?'

'Little boy. Screaming. Guard took him.'

'Ah,' Understanding dawned. 'You come this way plis.'

It all took some sorting out since there was no one around who could properly interpret, all the couriers being out on coach trips, but, as Charlie understood it, the shopkeeper and the guard had decided that Jason was shoplifting.

In the end everyone was more or less happy. Charlie bought the transistor radio Jason had been presumed to be stealing, but was shocked to discover it cost almost twice what he could have got it for in England, nearly twenty pounds and no Green Shield Stamps. The manager, with a gesture suggesting the magnanimity of an Oriental satrap giving freedom to a favourite concubine, knocked off two hundred pesetas. He was happy: it seemed Mr Forte would not be told that one of his idiot employees had arrested a guest. Jason of course was now very happy. The guard and the shopkeeper were happy too – they'd sold a radio and got away with being beastly to a gringo kid.

And Jane too was happy.

'Really, Charlie. You shouldn't have. But I'm so pleased, I really am, and Jason loves it.'

They were sitting in the kids' room, next to their own, trying to get them to go to sleep. It was difficult. Just about half the hotel was on the last night of its hols. Glasses dropped – one even from almost the top floor, exploding like a bomb not by the pool but on the terrace where Charlie had flirted with Connie; further down they conga-ed and did the hokey-cokey with style and grace, and every now and then someone fell in.

Jane read to Sharon from her *Lindy-Lou Annual*. 'Jeremy was given a smart red pedal car for Christmas. Sarah was given two lovely dolls. Daddy Jeremy drove the dolls to school in his lovely new car. Mummy Sarah waved goodbye to them . . .'

Outside the noise level rose: *My ding-a-ling, my ding-a-ling . . .*

'At school Sarah changed from being a mummy into a teacher. Jeremy was the headmaster.'

I want you to play with my ding-a-ling . . .

Through it all Jason dozed, thumb in mouth, earplug from his radio in one ear, a smile of beatification on his face as he listened to Spanish-flavoured muzak on Radio Popular de Palma de Mallorca.

'Why,' said Sharon, rubbing her eyes, 'was Jeremy playing at head teacher, and Sarah just teacher?'

'I expect because he was older,' said Jane.

'Because,' said Charlie, earnestly, seriously, for he knew if he was to be a proper father to these children he should be earnest and serious about earnest and serious things, 'because he's a boy, will one day be a man.'

My ding-a-ling, my ding-a-ling . . .

Jane smiled across the darkened room at him, only the strip-light over Sharon's bed was on. She was pleased that after all Charlie was taking a real and loving interest in her kids – for a time she had thought that he would not, that he resented the fact they were part of the bargain they had struck. But clearly he had given Jason a good day, culminating with the radio, and here he was seeing them to bed instead of joining the other dads boozing at the bar. Involuntarily he half smiled back.

I want you to play with my ding-a-ling.

The foursome, sixsome if you count the kids, took the coach trip to the bullfight on the Sunday. There had been much agonizing about this. Was it cruel? Should the children see it? *What about the horses?*

On the coach a brochure was handed out which explained the whole thing is risible English. After they had glanced through it, Bob began to explain to Charlie just how computerized automation would help his business – expecially in container storage.

'You see, my son, with full automation it becomes a press-button job. One man on the floor to check the hoists have fastened themselves properly, and a girl who can choose the right software for each consignment or whatever and read off the printouts. Then all she has to do is press the buttons that activate the hoists. You get scientifically calculated optimum use of space, enormous savings in labour costs, you can even expand on the same site without adding to your workforce . . .'

It sounded like good news to Charlie . . . the labour becoming more elf-like and distanced, pay girls a bob or two an hour more than Woolies, bound to be better than skilled fork-lift operators. And girls did what you told them and didn't join unions.

The bullfight excited him almost out of his mind, although for five sixths of the way it was bad. On 9 September most of Spain is *en fiesta* for the birthday of the BVM, and all the best matadors are in the big places, and the best bulls too. So in Palma that day there were two valetudinarians of no distinction whatsoever at the top of the bill and a promising youngster styled *El Nĩno de la Capea,* the little boy of the cape, at the bottom.

Charlie understood none of this. While the Spaniards went berserk with rage when one of the elderly gents squeezed with difficulty behind the *burladero* whenever his bull turned a little too quickly for him, he laughed with glee and clapped his hands for the bull. When the second bull, a *perdido manso,* proved a total coward, kept returning to the *toril*, the gate by which it had come in, with blood dropping in gouts from its nose, he laughed again while the Spaniards were nearly rioting for another bull or their money back.

'Look,' he crowed, 'he wants to go home.'

At which Sharon, who had been sucking her thumb and cuddling up to Jane, turned her face into her mother's armpit and sobbed uncontrollably all the way through to the interval.

Yet it really got to Charlie: the colour, the costumes, the music, the parade, the swirling cerise and yellow capes, the sprightly *banderilleros* with their fluttering darts . . . the whole thing, but especially the way the bull, given a clumsy *descabello* after the matador had failed five times to make the kill with the sword, tossed its tired head and backed off until its nose was pricked down to submission again between its feet and its neck exposed. Then the moment, the nervy spasm, the pause, and the crumpling away of life in the blink of an eye that turned to meat flesh that had been as alive as mine as I write this and as yours as you read it.

'And how do you fit into all this?' Charlie asked Bob during the interval. They were drinking lagers from bottles, the kids had Cokes, and Bob was still pushing computerized automation as the answer to all Charlie's problems. Not that I have any now, he thought, not since Peter came in. Coleman had known what to do – had stripped unproductive assets, put the money where it would work, shifted the loans to houses that gave better terms, cut overheads by, for instance, employing a security firm that offered guarantees and so reduced the enormous insurance premiums Charlie had been paying, and so on. Oh yes, Peter had known what to do.

'How do I fit in? That's simple enough. You pay me a down payment of a ton. No more, that's all you'll ever have to pay me. Then my team come and look over your whole operation from top to bottom, and with our inside knowledge of the whole ball-game, we put together a kit from all the available hardware and software, even advise you where you should get trained programmers and operators, and if you like the look of it you buy. The point is this. It's a highly specialized field. No one can be expected to run a business and know where and what is available in the hi-tech field and how it could help his particular operation. But that *is* our business, if you go to just one firm, instead of through us, you will get the best *and the worst* of what that firm has to offer. Through us you get a kit that's nothing but the best that's on the market. Can't be bad, can it, my son?'

'And you get your commission from the manufacturers whose products I buy.'

'That's right. And I know what you're thinking. I'll flog to you what they want to shift. There, my son, you are mistaken. You see. My reputation depends on the service I give my customers. I keep alive in a very competitive field by word of mouth. I mean, you can look at my books. Pick out any past client you like, and if you find one who feels he's had a rough deal from me then, my son, you are absolutely entitled to tell me to piss off. Right?'

Bob Dobson grinned a grin of utterly uncomplicated openness and smoothed down the lines of his Zapata moustache, finger and thumb on each side of his tired, thin mouth.

Niño de la Capea, a tall, dark, unprepossessing youth, managed to make something of the last bull, and in the warmth of the gathering evening the whole ring resounded to the rising swell of rhythmically repeated O-O-O-O-L-a-ays. The bull fell to his sword on the third attempt, and relief swept the ring that at last the thing had been done if not properly then not disgracefully. Hankerchiefs fluttered from the Spaniards, were wildly waved by Jane and Connie; flowers flew, hats, purses even, an ear was awarded. Niño took a turn round the ring on the shoulders of his *péons*, and then everyone, in flagrant opposition to the repeated warnings on the loudspeakers, from notices, and in the programme, hurled their flat square cushions spinning into the ring.

As they left, Charlie asked Jane, 'What do you think?'

'Wait till we get home. Ask Peter.'

He was happy to accept that.

Another day, the last coach trip – Thursday, 13 September: the fag-end of the holiday, the fag-end of the season, the fag-end of the world. The coppery haze was back: flat, right across the sky it seemed to hold down beneath it the stale, nicotine-laden, exhaust-heavy, fart-filled air. An afternoon trip, depart after lunch, the usual buffet down by the pool: eight salads, prawns in mayonnaise, rings of fried squid, sliced roast of beef (guaranteed *toro bravo* and tough as old boots), cold paellas with langoustines and mussels, gateaux piled with cream but oddly unsweet to the British tooth, bunches of giant grapes, water melons and honeydew, and as much sangría as you could drink.

Really, thought Charlie, I'd as soon as not go on a coach after that lot, but it was the last trip, musn't miss the caves, and the *barbacoa* on the way back.

'What the fuck is a *barbacoa?*'

'Barbecue, silly.'

A slight delay waiting for the coach to leave, Charlie and Bob in one seat together, Jane and Connie in front of them, the children in front of that.

'You've got to hand it to them, my son.' said Bob.

'Hand what to who?' asked Charlie nervously.

'The dagos. Look at that.'

They looked. A block of flats going up on the other side of the narrow pot-holed road, a shell of empty boxes without ends, the concrete floor/ceilings supported on wooden poles, ladders between the floors, and men shovelling concrete up in steady rhythm from floor to floor, stoop–scoop–heave and a twist of the shovel at the top of the movement and then down again, stoop–scoop–heave–twist and hardly a handful of cement dropped or spattered. A small concern, no cranes, no swung buckets or hoists, but every shovelful shovelled from the mixer on the ground floor to the sixth floor above. The men were naked to the waist, had backs like polished leather, and as tough.

'A floor a day over the last week. You don't see blokes working like that back in Blighty.'

'No. Indeed not. Oops. Pardon.'

'Must have done once. Think of all the building done in Victorian times. Canals, railways. The navvies. They worked like that then. Made us great. Not now, no more Victorian virtues, see. It all depends on the system. Strong government. No to socialism and that. I reckon Franco has it about right.'

If what Bob Dobson was on about was clobbering the elves then I'm right with him, thought Charlie, but Connie had intervened before he could make the point. She was having a good old giggle in front of them. Laughing. At him? Perish the thought.

'What's the joke, Connie?'

'Not for your ears, sweetie.'

'Come on. Share the joke. What you say, Charlie? Can't let the girls keep all the fun to themselves.'

'No, indeed not.' Poor Charlie had begun to sweat, sweat olive oil it felt like. Why didn't the coach move? They were frying in their own juices, waiting.

'OK, sweetie. Jane and I were just wondering which of those backs we'd like to get our nails into. She fancies the one on the third floor, I fancy the one on the top. He looks better hung.'

'Bloody women,' said Bob.

The doors hissed. The diesel engines coughed, settled,

and at last the air conditioning began to work. 'When Irish Eyes are Smiling', 'My Old Man', 'I Say Hello, You Say Goodbye', 'Tambourine Man', 'Blowing in the Wind'.

A long hot drive across the yellow burnt plain, stubble burning, a glimpse of the airport, wind pumps, fields of sunflowers, heads old, brown, dropped on their chests like geriatrics waiting for the grim reaper.

Charlie found he had the *English Language Daily,* where from he had no idea, but he was glad to have his mind taken off the dreary drive.

Dr Salvador Allende suicides in Santiago, Chile. Seventeen bombs dropped on Presidential Palace as Army take control. Salvador Allende was reported to have killed himself with the heavy automatic machine gun his friend Fidel Castro gave him . . .

'This is out of order,' said Charlie.

'Eh?' said Bob.

'This is plain out of order. It says this dictator in South America shot himself with a heavy automatic weapon. Well, that's not on. You'd have to be a contortionist to bring that off,' Charlie knew it all from the glossy books he took such pride in.

'Which dictator was that then?'

'Allende.'

'Got his come-uppance at last then. Commie bastard.'

Charlie read on. A report from the legislative branch of the Chilean Constitution had recently arraigned Allende for stealing farms and industry, for setting up a programme of indoctrination.

'You're right. He was stealing farms and industries.'

'They're all the same. Cut them how you like they taste the same.'

'Nevertheless, he couldn't have suicided with that gun. Not possible.' He'd been assassinated with it. He speculated – probably it was an M60 Castro gave Allende. Even the IRA had M60s.

He read on. Egypt, Syria, Jordan hold talks to

co-ordinate the war effort against Israel. War, a war that could spread, seemed inevitable. Charlie felt a hot tightness in a circle round his head, above his eyes, and could feel the turbulence in his upper gut. Things were falling apart, nothing was secure, safe, not like it used to be twenty years ago. 1953. Jane. She'd been thin then, a stomach like a smooth china plate, dropping and gathering to that haze of fine curly hair. And here she was now, the same person in front of him, her hair, darker now on the anti-whatsit on the seat in front, with a tummy that sagged to a swatch . . .

'Nothing about the cholera, then?'

Christ. I'd forgotten about the cholera. Naples. Rome. Sardinia.

'Two years back we were in Torremolinos. It was admitted to be in Cadiz and we knew it was in Malaga. Just eight miles away. Their sewage on our beach.'

Las Cuevas del Drach. The Caves of the Dragon. A seedy, bunker-like entrance, concrete, dust, tatty gift shops, dying cacti. Abandon hope. Oh, it was extraordinary enough, the fluted columns of greyish stone, the greasy sheen on everything, the strange shapes weirdly brought to life and a sort of prettiness by the cunning use of coloured lights. A stalagmite dripping on to a stalactite, or the other way about? 'In eight millennia they will be united.' In eight millennia I will be blowing in the wind.

Charlie hated to be herded, and to be herded with however many thousands of tons of rock and earth above his head was terrifying, herded down steep, twisting, wet steps, along narrow galleries above spaces which might well be bottomless, across pools and rivers that looked black as ink, and try as he might he really could not make out the likeness in the formations that the guide claimed were there – the Penitent, the Column of the Dragon, Charon's Skiff and Shrouds.

They were put into boats. The seats were too narrow, the

level of the water horrifyingly close to the gunnels, and then when they were well out into the middle the fucking lights went out.

A moment of the worst panic he had ever felt, and of the pitchiest darkness he had ever experienced, the after-images and the swimming cells of his own plasma garishly spread across the darkness wherever he looked, then just as he was sure he was dying of speleophobia and cholera he knew he was dead and ushered into the underworld with music and a dim light.

De dum, de dum, de-dum, de-dum de-*dum*. De dum, de dum, de-dum-de-dum-de-*dum*. Dum dum, da-da-da-dum dum . . .

The light grew stronger, began at last to illuminate some of the rock ceiling above it . . . a barge, much like the one he sat in, propelled as if by magic, moved across their front, and on it five men with stringed instruments and candles that barely flickered in the motionless air.

'The Arriaga Quartet are playing for you the acknowledged masterpiece of Wolfgang Amadeus Mozart – *Eine Kleine Nachtmusik*. The acoustics of this cave are acknowledged to rival those of La Scala, the Royal Festival Hall . . .'

Connie murmured, 'I've never known anything so beautiful . . .'

Next stop a bodega. A barn-like place that tried with roughcast plaster, fancy brickwork and wormy beams to disguise the fact that it had been built out of breeze blocks and steel girders. All round the walls there were hundreds of barrels, some huge and standing upright, other big-bellied on their sides, most tiny, the size you could tuck under your arm like a piglet and carry off. These had taps, drip-catchers, and everywhere there were trays of disposable drinking vessels, each about the size of a petit-suisse container.

'You taste everything.' the couriers insisted, 'and you buy what you like. Do remember your duty-free allowances, and please take my word you will buy nothing cheaper on the island, nor on the plane home.'

'I'd like a nice sherry, like an oloroso, you know?'

'Try this peppermint, not that it really seems great to me.'

'Oooh, they do have Benedictine.'

'This white rum is not bad at all, I mean it may not be Bacardi . . .'

'But it is Bacardi.'

'Golly, so it is.'

'I wouldn't mind taking home a bottle of sangría mixture . . .'

'I wouldn't old love. It never tastes the same back home. Remember the Robinsons tried it at their Guy Fawkes party, and you were sick . . .'

All aboard. Back in the coach. That's better. That settled the old tum and chased away the blues. Maybe I don't have cholera after all.

'I was right about the peseta.'

'You were?'

'One three four. Saved you a bob or two there.'

'You did indeed.' But he felt queasy. Still over a hundred quid stuffed in the toe of his shoe, in the wardrobe back at the Sol y Sombre, and even if they didn't get stolen there was now only a day and bit to spend them in. Mind you, there'd be a bit on the top at the hotel . . . he had signed for a few things and breakfasts in their rooms were an extra. Dear God, perhaps he wouldn't have enough!

Bob now had the paper. Charlie tried to peer round his arm. Bombs. At Euston. Kings Cross. Thirteen injured. Bang! That's an eye gone. Or a hand. Or your balls. Ship the Micks and Paddies back. Tell the Prods they can come over. We let in those Indians from Africa, surely we can find room for our sort. Then those that stay can get on with blowing each other up, and leave us alone.

George Brown. Seventy-five pounds, banned for a year, two hundred and fifty pounds. Lucky bastard didn't kill anyone. Charlie's stomach heaved again, burping back the caramelly odours of cheap brandy, and he saw again the blood on the road, the broken dentures . . .

Bob leaned forward, tapped Connie's elbow.

'It's to be on 14 November.'

'What is, sweetie?'

'Anne's wedding. To that Mark Phillips.'

'How nice! But November. Odd time for a Royal Wedding, I should have thought.' She giggled. 'I hope she's not in a hurry.'

At least the *barbacoa* was in the open air, to begin with at any rate. Ushered in to the usual glasses of sangría, they were shown to tiered benches round a sand-surfaced paddock and treated to a brief display of Spanish dressage. The young girls at least enjoyed this: the trim ponies, mostly pie or skewbald, the exotic, western-style tack with inlay of silver and mother-of-pearl, the handsome if pompous young riders.

It was all rather spoiled when a green Land Rover drew up at the far end of the paddock. Four Civil Guards got briskly down – cloaks, shiny black hats, moustaches, all a bit comic except that two had carbines. They knew the man they had come for, so did he. A waiter, standing near the rail and apparently at his ease smoking a cigarette and watching the display before going back to serve the meal, suddenly bolted up a slope of dry grass and immortelles towards a low dry-stone wall and a neglected olive grove. The guards shouted. Then one barked an order, the men with carbines crouched, the guns clattered with appalling noise, the waiter's body was scooped in the air as his legs were shot from under him.

They had a stretcher up to him in no time and one of the guards stuffed a handkerchief in his mouth to cut off his screams. All bundled back into the vehicle, which swung away down the dusty drive and under the arch which separated the *finca* from the main road. A siren diminished slowly in the thick air. The whole incident had lasted scarcely two minutes.

The French pulled down the corners of their mouths, pouted and shrugged. The Germans peered with expressionless blue eyes out to the coppery horizon and drummed nervous fingers on the cases of their cameras. Only the British seemed to have felt that something terrible had happened. The whole coachload from the Sol y Sombre suffered a wave of collective anger, though this was caused by shock and fright rather than by any real sense of moral outrage.

By the time they had been herded into the long whitewashed dining rooms of the *finca* and fed with charred steaks and as much *tinto* as they could drink the mood had shifted to one of sturdy self-satisfaction. The uncivilized impossibility of all foreigners had been unequivocally demonstrated yet again. Nothing like that could happen back home.

Not then. Not in 1973.

When they got back, Bob and Charlie sat up in the bar for another hour drinking *sol y sombres,* the speciality of the hotel, they were told. A couple of fingers of brandy, then a couple of fingers of anis poured through it so the anis settled on the bottom of the glass. You then drink the anis through the brandy, which takes off the sweetness of the anis, and a brandy over what is left of the anis, which takes off the roughness of the brandy. The perfect way of getting rid of those pesetas at the end of the holiday, the perfect way of getting hideously smashed.

Somehow Charlie got back to his room. Somehow Jane

pulled his clothes off. She stood by the bed in the dim light, dressed in the largely see-through floral nightie she'd bought at Marks, and looked down meditatively at the man she'd now allied herself to.

They had made a bargain, much of it explicit since they were adult, had been through it all before, knew where the pitfalls lay, knew pretty well what each had to offer each, and, more importantly, what neither could expect from the other. And what was not explicit was well understood. He might go to bed with other women, and she might know of it, and she would not mind: so long as they were virtually one-off events, did not cost, did not interfere with the running of Woolingham Storage Enterprises. He might, for instance, poke Connie, perhaps already had. Good luck to her. Jane looked with some amusement, even a sort of tenderness at his rather small, wrinkled prick with its awkward, out-of-proportion foreskin, flopped to one side to expose the soft silliness of his balls. Good luck to her if she managed to get him to use the thing properly. She, Jane, could also have one-offs – the difference was that neither Charlie nor anyone else was to know about them.

The trouble was, she thought, one-offs never work –they are always even worse at it than Charlie: if you get them up at all, they come too soon.

He's got good strong legs though, nicely tanned below the line of his crazy Bermuda shorts, and neat, small feet for his size. Basically he keeps himself well, and now much better, since she'd come into his life and sorted out the areas where he'd begun to slip. She liked that in a man: neatness, a sense of style, good clothes. There was a Daks lightweight in the wardrobe that cost all of sixty-five guineas. And that really was the basis of the bargain – the sex was quite unimportant. She'd keep house for him and do it well. Choose good-quality fabrics and furniture, give the establishment a touch of expensive style – modern, up to date, yes, but not flash: Maples, not Heals, and definitely not Habitat. Habitat went out with Dr J. Crathorne. Thus she'd make him respectable.

She sat down on the edge of her twin bed, leant forward and ran her hand – good strong long fingers, well-kept, good nails, – from his navel and slowly up over his domed tummy to his heaving chest, through the coarse pale yellow hair and reddish yellow hair, spreading her hand so the little finger rested on one nipple, the thumb on the other. She knew he was a bastard: greedy, selfish, cunning, even cruel; worst of all, he still had a foul and occasionally violent temper. But she did for him what he needed, and she knew he knew he was on to a good thing. And, with a little help (actually quite a lot of help) from brother Pete, who had virtually set up this new arrangement, he made money. A lot of it. And that meant security and a decent start in life for her kids. And let's face it, she had never met, has anyone?, a man who *made* money who was not a bastard. And the other sorts of money – not the made sort, the classier sort, the inherited or arty, clever-clever sort of money, even professional money – she knew, had learnt the lesson painfully with Dr James toffee-nosed Crathorne, was beyond her.

She was glad to have Charlie, even proud to have Charlie. In spite of the life insurances and a share in the business, things would not be so good if he snuffed it. And now he was cold to the touch, his breathing wasn't quite right. She pulled the sheet up round his shoulders, then the heavy, woven cotton bedspread and tucked them about him. Finally, perching a little ridiculously on the edge of the bed, she lay alongside him. After a moment he grunted and turned on one side away from her and she pulled herself in closer, enjoying the size and solidity of his back, even through the bedclothes.

For the next two days Charlie had alcoholic poisoning, which left his recollections of his last thirty-six hours in

Majorca fragmentary, elusive, and suffused with a nightmarish light that confused and conflated dreams and reality. In later weeks, months, the first experience that he could be sure of, as much part of the nightmare as the rest, was the flight home.

It was horrifying.

After all the black coffees he could persuade the stewardess to bring, he stood up to go to the toilet. Swaying with dizziness, he saw through one sound eye and one closing between bruises which were just beginning to colour up, tall pillars of cloud towering out of a lower base. They looked to him far too like those that support the mushroom clouds of our collective fear, and though they lacked the cap the sight of them still caused appalling dread to clutch at his diaphragm and spleen like the icy but remorseless hand of a zombie. But they were far off, perhaps over the Pyrenees. What he saw next was the sea, below the wing, an almost black sea minutely foam-flecked, with boats like tiny red ants, and vertigo now compounded the terror, became unsupportable . . . The stewardess, summoned by Jane, recognized the rare but disquietening symptoms and quickly provided a fast-acting and effective tranquillizer.

In later months this memory was always pursued, linked by association, with another one, which was of a dream, but not in any way more dreamlike or less real than the first.

Waking, in this dream, from a dream in which he wrestled with a heavy machine gun, whose belt of large-calibre ammunition sometimes dragged like a chain, sometimes whipped about his legs like a python while he struggled to get the muzzle in his mouth and his fingers or even toes on the trigger at the same time, in which he and the gun together presently became a black, sad bull, loosing gouts of blood from his nose, standing at the gate by which he had come in, waking from these dreams into another dream, he struggled on shattered shards of splintered bone to the balcony of the room.

There he looked out over the tiny cove, now filled with giant rollers that surged in accelerated succession up to the swimming-pool deck to crash amongst the thatched parasols, sending the sun-loungers (sun-lounger snitcher) and other furniture hurtling about in a melée of towels and wood and tubular steel that looked like the arms of desperate robots, smashed and drowning. He looked up at the night sky – a dreadful gale blew through it, had cleared the coppery haze to reveal a cosmos of galaxies, far more than any ever seen or photographed by the most powerful telescopes. And as he watched, these legions of universes began to form into separate and opposing patterns, began to move across the sky in endlessly receding phalanxes, one behind the other, towards a confrontation that would take place right above the hotel itself: it was, Charlie knew, the beginning of the nuclear war.

Waking in the morning, the coppery haze had not lifted. Half of the hotel's guests (the other half were up in the mountains at George Sand's house or swigging G and T on boat trips) drifted listlessly about the hotel wondering how to get rid of their last pesetas. Dust, cigarette packets, used tissues stained with lipstick like menstrual blood, or vice versa, collected mysteriously in the corners of the balustrades: mysteriously for there was no wind to carry them there. By some fluke of currents in the windless sea, a nasty, yellow, lacy scum was lapped into the cave on listless waves. Charlie, vainly seeking fresh air, peered over the wall and saw a dead, decomposing sardine floating in the debris of an emptied ashtray. He could not stomach the thought of another of those buffet lunches.

Bob, in towelling bathwrap striped purple, green and orange, with satin boxer shorts to match, beamed down to his side to boldly go with him where no man had ever gone before. With the absolute certainty that the still-drunk man with a dreadful hangover can bring to such perceptions, Charlie knew that he had expected him to appear, just in the way he did, either minutes before or as part of the dreams that had plagued him through the night. That is, if he wasn't actually dreaming now. Equally he knew exactly what Bob was about to say; or rather knew for certain that, even though he could not after all foretell it, he had already dreamt it.

'What I would give now for a Sainsbury's pork pie or an honest ploughman's.'

'I'll be glad to get back.'

'Like Christmas, you can have too much of it. I say, my son, you look a bit rough.'

'I feel it. Yet I didn't drink much. I remember that red wine at the barbecue.'

'But not the *sol y sombres* back here.'

'The what?'

'*Sol y sombres.* Brandy and anis mixed.'

'Jesus. Was I drinking that?'

'You had four.'

'No wonder I feel bad.'

They sat at one of the tables and the contaminated waves patted the concrete beneath them.

'Jane and Connie gone to Palma then?'

'That's it. With the kids. Your kids.'

'Not my fucking kids.'

Bob shrugged. 'With the kids. I'll tell you. I'll tell you what they'll come back with.'

Charlie at last realized that his interlocutor was both as pissed and hungover as he was. Well almost.

'They'll come back with. Back with. Flouncy dolls to put toilet rolls under. Paperknives shaped like swords. Fans with chrys . . . carn . . . bullfighters and flamencos on them, and personalized posters – you know, your name above that of El Cordobes.'

'They've got them already. From the shop.'

'Of course they have, my son. But that won't stop them getting more. And they'll, they'll not forget us. Oh dear me no. They'll bring cigarette lighters with playing-card things stamped on them. Like the ace of spades and so on. And. Cufflinks to match. I say, my son. Would you like beer? So would I.'

But something awful had happened to the Sol y Sombre. The lifts were not working. As they laboured up to the bar, they were aware of sandy foot- and shoeprints unswept in the stair carpets, of finger smudges on the brass handrail, and at the top the bar was shut.

'What's going on then.'

'Lord knows.'

Raised voices suddenly as somewhere a service door swung open, then near silence again. Other guests moved like the walking dead about the wide, dim foyer. An old pair who had been coming to Majorca for twenty years sat at a glass-topped table, unpolished, with an overflowing ashtray and two dirty glasses on it.

'Hullo there. What's happened? Can you fill us in?'

'Industrial action. Strike. Never known anything like it.'

'Why? I mean, what brought it on?'

'No one's too clear. But it's something to do with what happened in Chile.'

'In Chile! Why, for Christ's sake?'

'Some of the staff wanted to wear black armbands and management wouldn't allow it.'

'Wasn't he some sort of socialist? Well. I should think not. This is the last flaming straw. Over the top.'

'You're right. Right out of order.'

They drifted around the dying hotel, for that's what it was like – something out of one of those apocalyptic novels that were then so popular, about an earth where most of the population has been annihilated (by nukes, poisonous gases, ecological disasters, passing comets) and the survivors live on in a debris that still functions partially, like a wrecked body in an intensive care unit, with automated nuclear-power stations still working, with petrol still in the pumps, and tinned food in the shops, but all slowly winding down.

Sweating, head aching, lower gut heaving with cramps that never quite produced the diarrhoea that would be a relief, Charlie finally forced himself up all those stairs to his, and Jane's, room, aware as he went that somewhere in his mind an old lesson, once learnt with dynamic, epiphanous force, but since partially forgotten, was reasserting itself: the hotel with all its machines, its appointments and appurtenances was nothing, was dead, was useless without the elves – it required, just like everything else, the magic of labour to give it value. Which made it vulnerable, in spite of Franco and the Civil Guards. Charlie was no more prescient than anyone else and could not see that in the coming winter these awful truths were to become very real and immediate, with the three-day week, the miners' strike, and even dark rumours of the army doing a Franco if Labour got in – but he could sense that, while warehousing and storage reduced wealth-making to the very simplest form, by turning air into a saleable commodity, there was room for improvement. Computerized automation might well get the elves off his back for ever, or at least push them back into the unconscious, where they belonged.

He found aspirin in Jane's toilet bag, took four and drank a pint or more of tap water. Cholera would be a relief, he thought, as he collapsed on his bed and fell almost instantly asleep.

My ding-a-ling, my ding-a-ling, I want you to play with my ding-a-ling . . . He was in a large cavern, an actual cavern of natural rock, which was, extraordinarily, a disco. The largest space was a dance floor; but off it were smaller chambers, all eerily magical, lit in blues, greens, reds, which included a bar, tables, toilets even, and from one you could look down thirty feet to black water lapping in from the sea. And a party of fifteen or so from the hotel, determined not to let the strike spoil their last night, had virtually taken it over.

I want you to play with my ding-a-ling.

In a circle, sometimes holding hands, sometimes not, they bounced up and down to the obsessively repeated chorus, the lights drifting over sweating faces, shirts undone to the waist and glowing numinously in the ultraviolet, women's bosoms flopping to the beat, the brush of hair in your face as she turns away . . . but where was Jane? Back at the Sol y Sombre, wouldn't leave the kids there on their own, quite right, my son, but no reason why we shouldn't enjoy ourselves.

There he goes, that Bob Dobson, leering out of a patch of gloom, then back in the light, his teeth glowing like a hallowe'en mask; he sways away and now it's Connie, her hair plastered wetly but awrily over her forehead, sweat under her arms staining the red vest she wears bra-less over a red skirt that doesn't quite match, but never mind, no stockings and bare feet now, strutting and flouncing in imitation of the flamenco act they watched ten minutes or ten hours ago and *I want you to play with my ding-a-ling* she mouths to the music, but very specially at him. She twirls away into a patch of ultra violet that drains the colour out of her clothes and suddenly she is a ghost: Lissie's. Poor Charlie had quite forgotten the resemblance.

'Jesus, Bob, stop him. He's hurting. Charlie. Don't you see you old fool . . . Ow! *Ow!* He's trying to sodomise . . .'

Bang! On his ear.

Stars.

Again *Bang!* On his eye this time.

'I say. I'm most awfully sorry, my son. But she said you were hurting her. Can't have that.'

Sitting on the floor now, naked, knees drawn up, smarting ear, and eye really very painful and running with tears? *Blood!* Charlie gave way to a brief despair and sobbed.

'Christ, Bob. You didn't have to hit him with a *shoe.*'

'He's bigger than me, Connie. Stronger. Didn't want to get into a fight.'

Charlie choked on the sobs, converted them into racking coughs.

'Christ, Bob, he's going to spew.'

'Get him to the bathroom.'

They got him there but he wasn't sick, had not eaten all day. There was, though, a small cut over his eye, nothing much, but the sight of blood brought back a sense of . . . responsibility?

Charlie sat on the toilet seat. Connie leant over him, one hand under his chin, the other gently dabbing the cut with cotton wool and TCP. Her tiny breasts, still pert, moved inches from his face, and for a moment he felt that all he wanted was to pull her those few inches closer and lay his head there, but dimly, unverbalized, he sensed the gesture would be weak, not at all orgiastic. He kept aloof, hands firmly clenching his hairy thighs while her legs brushed against them, and so allowed her to make a fuss of mopping him up.

Through the tunnel vision of the very drunk he occasionally made out Bob Dobson in the background – a body noticeably older than his own, spindly legs and loose skin, stretch marks on his tummy. Once Bob had been tubby too, but had lost weight. No doubt the sort of silly sod who goes, what do they call it? jogging.

'There, you'll live.'

Awkwardly, at a loss, they moved back into the bedroom. Connie went to the dressing table, sat on the stool in front of it, put her head in her hands. Charlie, sitting on one of the beds, took in, dwelt on the long line of her brown back, pimpled on the shoulders, down the long spine to the tight, white buttocks, and mourned opportunities gone for ever.

She lifted her head, ran fingers through her black, glossy hair, turned from the mirror. For a moment she looked at both of them – Bob, her husband, old enough to be her father; Charlie, thicker, heavier, a bit of pot on him, but ten years younger. Her eyes were now quite expressionless.

'Two . . . limp . . . pricks,' she said, and turned back to the mirror, tipped a bottle of lotion on to more cotton wool, and began to clean her face.

Laboriously, with one eye almost closed and a tiny strip of plaster above it, one ear red and swollen so he looked a little like the last white man to come out of the corner for the third round against Cassius, whoops, Muhammad Ali, Charlie, for the first time wearing his Daks lightweight, checked through the sheaf of slips he had signed, so it appeared, during the previous fortnight.

He owed the Sol y Sombre (Prop: Charles Forte) five thousand, four hundred and ninety-eight pesetas. He had six hundred and forty-three. Around him a small crowd, all with that coppery tan, shifted irritably. They were laden with: china bulls, plastic bulls, bulls made out of some unidentifiable composition material; flamenco dolls, some small, some pretty damn near life size; posters – for bullfights and flamenco dancers, but personalized; donkeys, like the bulls in a vast variety of sizes and materials including straw, but all, every one of them, carrying two vessels slung one on each side of their backs, some of which were full-sized spirit bottles, some miniatures only; banderillas, swords, antique pistols; and bottles of Fundador, Soberano, Carlos Tercero, Carlos

Primero, La Iña, Olorosa, Ginebra and Ron – Bacardi, Dry Cane, Guarani, and every other make of Ron under the sun. The more with-it colour-supplement types had strings of garlic, Rioja wines, manchega cheese and even chorizo sausages. There were also leather hats, straw hats, ponchos, fishing rods, majolica 'pearls', majolica pottery, glass ornaments, cigarette lighters, decks of Spanish playing cards, and leather goods left imperfectly tanned so you could smell how 'real' they were.

'Yes well,' said Charlie. 'It does seem to be about right.' He leant forward conspiratorially. 'Will . . . you . . . take . . . a . . . cheque. Pounds. Sterling.' He searched for the word. *'Libra.'*

The clerk frowned, pulled a scribble pad across and wrote on it: 125.

Fucking hell, thought Charlie. I am about to be ripped off.

He sensed the warmth of Jane at his side.

'Trouble, Charlie?'

'A spot. I don't seem to have enough pesetas.'

'I think I have. I haven't spent all you said I could have.'

She delved into a peasant-weave bag and pulled out five green backs and one blue back. Dolefully the clerk counted out a handful of change.

'It's what wives are for, Charlie,' said Jane.

As the coach passed the sewage smell, Jason screamed, 'My fish, my fish.'

'What?'

'My fish. The one I caught. It's been drying on the balcony. I have to have it. I have to bring it home.' His face was darkening, a storm of passion on the horizon.

Charlie remembered the squidge between his thumb and forefinger when he snuffed the flapping, fluttering life.

Jason turned to him. 'Please get it for me, Charlie. Please tell the driver to go back so we can get it. Daddy. *Daddy*. Please *Daddy*. I want my fish.'

Charlie looked down at him, the little boy, brown now, bleached hair, who could outswim him, who was peeping tearfully up at him. Daddy. At last. *The fucking bastard.* Let his mother explain. She's bloody clever about everything. Let her explain why you can't turn a coach round, go back.

Part Six

1

Never forget how workers had to beg for the right to work and often did not get it; patients for the right to be admitted to hospital. Blood donors could not give their blood, children were locked out of schools, and mourners could not bury their dead . . .

A funeral. Woolingham Crematorium – a building which looked a little more like a miniature Guildford Cathedral than a monstrous public convenience, but not much. A bitterly cold day at the end of January. Yes, there had been a picket on the gate, two pickets to be precise, and they looked a very great deal more miserable than any of the mourners. Nor surprisingly really, since the latter had come to vapourize Councillor Swivel, who had at last succumbed to multiple cancers of the throat, lungs and liver. What's more, the pickets had courteously doffed their woollen hats knitted in the colours of Charlton Athletic as the cortège passed.

'The departed's life is one to be celebrated, not mourned; to be emulated, not forgotten; to be inscribed in the roll of honour of those who have served our community with diligence, skill, integrity, not . . . not . . . not forgotten. In his profession Arthur Swivel upheld the highest standards of justice . . . he defended the meek, prosecuted the guilty, and on humbler levels smoothed the way for hundreds of us in those aggravating problems that beset us . . .'

He let that dike get away with 263 Goldsmith Drive, incompetent creep.

'In his later years, as a councillor, he served without

reward in the highest, ah, councils of our community and particularly . . .'

Without reward! Bloody hell. I kept him in cigarettes for the last two years of his life, and Christ knows . . .

'And now the time has come to say, farewell, old friend. Keep a place next to you for us against the time when we come to join you . . . meanwhile, know that until then there will always be a corner in our hearts that is yours.'

Councillor Duxbury pulled out a huge, white, black-edged handkerchief and blew his huge nose. The last trump. The lights that illuminated the coffin went out and drained the colour from the flowers heaped on it. Suddenly the chapel was a dim cold place, lit only from the tall grey windows. Snowflakes oddly black against the lighter sky, were tumbling down outside so if you fixed your eyes on them you could get the sensation that the whole edifice was slowly soaring, like Swivel's soul, to a better place beyond the stars.

A dim rumble, a distant roar. So much nicer than that awful business of curtains and the actual sight of a hellish glow, and the heat. False bottom to the coffin, see. Drops him on rollers that trundle him into the jets. Progress. Can't beat it. And economical too – that coffin's been here before, will be here again, only the three-ply bottom goes in with the corpse.

House-lights up. Taped organ music playing a tolerably brisk march, get us out before the next lot come in.

Pressure on Charlie's elbow. Councillor Duxbury. Yes, older now. Head sunk a little into his shoulders, and where before his nose had seemed the logical, indeed triumphant, conclusion of the face that swooped towards it, now it dominated everything, a deformed excrescence on the body politic that was Duxbury. Duxbury in Crombie black with a velvet collar.

'You spoke . . . handsomely, Councillor.'

'The floral tributes are handsome too.' The voice more

sandpapery than before, occasionally fluking into an unoiled squeak. 'Shall we inspect them?'

Charlie felt all right about that. Jane had ordered a sheaf of red roses. Rightly enough, they did not surpass, the monstrous wreaths from the council, the Conservative Association, and the Leonine Rotationists (to the last two of which Charlie had contributed), but they more than held their own amongst those from private persons.

Duxbury muffled his turkey throat in a grey scarf, crowned himself with a homburg. They took their turn near the front of the slow line passing the tributes that had been heaped outside and which were already disappearing beneath the snow.

'We shall miss him at the Town Hall. Grievously. It is not easy to find right-minded people. People who understand how the cogs of commerce, industry and government should mesh and run with a proper smoothness to the benefit of all.'

They padded on through the whiteness that creaked beneath their well-shod, black-shod feet, round the side of the crematorium (a brief heat haze still bending the snow-laden air above its vent) and so into the carpark. Duxbury still kept his ancient Austin Princess. Charlie had a brand new silver-grey BMW. Seven thousand three hundred, but leased. Peter Coleman saw to all that.

'There'll be a by-election. Quite soon. I know the ward. It's next to mine. I could let your name go forward. What do you say? Think it over. Give me a bell.

Through avenues and streets on whose every corner black plastic bags were piled, most rent and spilling refuse for the rats and foxes, Charlie drove his sweet new car, and the normal brick red of his well-fed face glowed more shinily at the thought of the proposition. Councillor Bosham. Why not? Truth to tell, time had been lying a bit heavy on his hands. This might not be a bad idea, a step into the unknown. New worlds to conquer. He'd ask Jane, of course. She knew best about this sort of step, but she'd like it too, he felt sure. Of course she would. Councillor and Mrs Bosham . . .

Next day in Orpington Jane stood in the warmth of their spacious dining room and looked out through windows framed in heavy cinnamon-coloured velvet. Only a robin and a predatory cat had dared to smirch the snow-clad lawn. Beyond, laurels drooped at the weight of it all. Behind her, her reproduction Sheraton table gleamed as if Willie Rushton himself, clad in First World War flying gear (rather than the girl in a sari who did for her five mornings a week), had zoomed in with spray and cloth – gleamed and glimmered, reflecting the flicker of the gas flames licking up out of the simulated logs in the fireplace. A centrepiece of simulated gypsophilia, sweet peas and tea roses, set in a simulated silver bowl and sprayed with Wildflower Scents, added a touch of brightfulness and freshfulness.

She lifted the imitation-antique handset from its ormolu cradle and dialled.

'Peter?'

'Jane?'

'Has Charlie gone?'

'Yep. Out to a lunch with the Portakabin people.'

'Listen, Peter. Duxbury wants to put him up for Swivel's seat on the council. What do you think?'

'Bloody good idea.'

'Good. I think so too. But why do you think so?'

Silence.

Then: 'I'll be frank with you, Jane. I know, and you know too, who runs Woolingham Storage Enterprises. But it's getting more and more difficult to keep Charlie from knowing. Actually, he does know really. And that needles him. Drives him to interfere. No. You get him into politics and out of my hair, and we'll all make a couple of grand more a year each, just out of the wastage of time and resources saved. Do you think they'll take him?'

'I don't see why not. We've contributed enough to Association funds. They even asked me to open a sale of work back in October.'

'But there's bound to be others around, you know, like your actual party workers and so on, who'll be putting themselves forward.'

'I imagine Duxbury can take care of them. Else he wouldn't have suggested it.'

That evening, in the large stripped-pine kitchen (the only part of the house that still retained the Habitat look from the Crathorne era), Jane took the Martini jug from the cabinet fridge and said, 'Of course you should do it, Charlie. You've built the firm up so well it just about runs itself now, and Peter can keep an eye on it for you. We're never going to be short of a bob or two. You've got time now to do something important. To be someone. Get things done . . .'

'Duxbury says I could be spokesman on housing. You know. Push this sale of council houses lark. He reckons there's a lot of mileage in that.'

'He's right. You see? We've made our bit, now we've got time to really help people. In a way it's sort of a duty, really. Is the drink nice, pet?'

'Fine. Yes. Yes. You're right you know. I've spent a hell of a lot of time and a hell of a lot of sweat building that firm up. And as you say. It just about runs itself. I could do with a change. Branch out a bit.

Jane, dressed in silk and smelling like a thousand new francs (she had spent two hours getting herself to look right, feel right, be bright for this moment), moved as if on wheels across the simulated-marble floor and hung her long, bare white arm around his neck, let him rest his forehead on hers, then pecked a scented kiss on his mouth.

'You'll be marvellous, darling, you really will.'

She straightened his tie.

'You'll end up mayor, I shouldn't wonder.'

'I'm not sure they have mayors any more.'
'We-e-e-ll. You know.'

But it didn't work out. Swivel had picked up the ward during one of the worst slumps ever in Labour support. Moreover, there now were more ethnics in the ward than there had been, and the Labour Party had been taken over by an efficient team of left wing activists. Charlie lost the seat. He was mortified. And where another man might have said a plague on both your houses and gone back to business, he became utterly determined to prove himself, to get a seat on the council.

Duxbury himself added fuel to this, whether consciously or not, who can say?

'The trouble was not with you, Charlie. And not really with that Commie scum who took it off of you. But, and I tell you no lie, behind it all lay Mead.'

'Mead! Terry Mead! Why?'

'Well, I've heard it said he has it in for you. Tried to block your candidacy. And the faithful in that ward like him. Mrs Armstrong, remember her? And Mrs Grosscurth? and Mrs Goulden? Those ladies fancy themselves as gentle ladies and, where they'd get the vote out for a professional man like Swivel, they wouldn't be bothered with the likes of you. And especially not if there was a whisper Terry didn't want you in, whom they idolize on account of his late lamented papa . . . well, I should have seen it, you didn't have the back-up you should have had, deserved to have, was yours by right.'

Fuck you, Duxbury, thought Charlie. And you too, Terry Mead. You got me in this shit of having lost the Tories a seat on the council, now I'm going to find some way to get you to get me on, no matter fucking what.

We will oppose a slide towards state control . . . What we need is a calm but resolute return to the politics and economics of the Free World . . .

The opportunity arose surprisingly soon. Let us allow in our fiction one handy coincidence at least. Or, if not a coincidence, an apparent coincidence which need not be explained . . .

In late March, Charlie was sitting in his chairman's office on the fourth floor of a block that had been built, in part, on the site of his father's failed hardware store, wondering how to occupy his time until lunch other than by rating out of ten the fuckability of the bints who went in and out of Marks and Spencers on the other side of the High Street, when one of his phones rang.

'Bosham here.'

'Charlie? Alderson here.'

'Yes, George.'

'Charlie. Coupla sweenies in from the Met want to have a look at your facility out at Sevenoaks. It's not you they're after – but someone's got something out there.'

'Thanks, George. How long have I got?'

'An hour. Don't reckon on any more.'

Charlie replaced the private phone, swung round to his desk and pressed a button.

'Peter?'

'Charlie?'

'I've just had a bell from George. It seems Old Bill wants to look at Sevenoaks. ETAPDQ. Do we have anything sensitive there?

'Hang on while I get it up on the VDU. There. Unless someone is pulling one on us, and if they are that's their lookout, I can't see anything suspect apart from a couple of tons of Magicote Ultra Brilliant White Non-drip Gloss that Duxbury keeps there.'

'And nothing else.'

'Not at Sevenoaks.'

'Right, get it out. Shift it. To . . . let me think. What's it in?'

'Cube container.'

'Right. To Maidstone. Now.'

'Just as you say, Charlie.'

Business is business. Whatever unpleasantness might have existed between Bob and Connie Dobson and Charlie and Jane Bosham, following events in Majorca, had been well smoothed out in the interest of profit. Which meant that shifting two tons out of the Sevenoaks facility and on to a container truck destined for Maidstone could all be done in less than twenty-five minutes, thanks to computerized automation . . .

The changes are not leaps into the unknown, but those with which Winston Churchill led the country out of the dull, drab days of post-war Labour Britain, and set the people free . . .

'Another Martell, Councillor?'

'Why not, Courvoisier, I prefer.'

'And you, Charlie?'

'Pint of Waddies.'

'Cheers all.'

'Bottoms up.'

'That's where I like them.'

'Excuse I. Just need to make sure it's not dropped off.'

'Where's Councillor going?'

'Shake hands with his wife's best friend.'

'I could use a leak too.'

'Ah. Bosham.'

'Councillor.'

'Young Coleman tells me I'm in your debt.'

'Maybe. I took the liberty of moving some paint from Sevenoaks to Maidstone when I heard a couple of sweenies were about to call. That's all.'

'It must have cost. What do I owe?'

'Nothing at all, Councillor. All part of the service.'

They shook (no matter how you shake your peg, the last drop's down your trouser leg), zipped, and faced each other.

Christ, but he's ageing. The booze is really getting to him now and he's losing his grip.

'Come on, Charlie. I know you well enough by now, and what I know I respect. What do you want?'

'A seat on the council I can't lose.'

The sigh came like the drag of a receding wave across shingle on an ebbing spring tide.

'Have mine, Charlie. Have mine.?

Unless we change our ways and directions, our greatness as a nation will soon be a footnote in the history books, a distant memory of an off-shore island, lost in the mists of time like Camelot, remembered kindly for its noble past . . .

'That's lovely, isn't it Charlie?'

'What?'

'What she just said. About mists of time. And Camelot, and the noble past.'

'Who's Camelot?'

'What do you mean, who's Camelot?'

'Some silly bugger. I mean he must have been to get lost in the mist.'

'Charlie, you are an idiot.'

Grinning at his joke. Charlie got up and switched off the set. The image of the Leader, speaking at marginal Bolton, folded in on itself and disappeared up . . .

'Nevertheless, she'll blow it, you know.' He sank back into the deeply cushioned comfort of his chair, circumcized a cigar and stuck it in his mouth. His gold Zippo flared.

Jane looked at him with affection. Her man.

'Shall I freshen your drink for you?'

'OK. But you have something too.'

Cut-glass chimed. 'I'll have a chartreuse.' Then: 'Do you really think she'll blow it?'

'Good chance. Poll yesterday had the lead back to two per cent. From ten or nine per cent four weeks ago. Stock market didn't like it one bit. And the fat cats know. They know.'

'I don't see she's done anything wrong.'

'No. Not at all. Not a foot wrong. Can't be wrong-footed at all. But she's a bint and that's all there is to it. I just know the great British public will not vote for a bint. The polls show it.'

'Yes. But you're in this time, aren't you?'

His face flushed at the memory of the earlier humiliation. 'Damned right I'm in this time. No way will they keep me out this time.'

'And when you're in, we'll move back to Woolingham.'

'That's right, pet. I promised Duxbury we'd do that. And he's right of course. Can't approve blokes who sit on councils where they don't live.'

'I'll be glad to be out of here.'

'Of course, pet.'

She looked around the velvet curtains, peacock-blue in the lounge which picked up the blue in the Axminster; at the simulated beams, the fireplace with its steady purr and steady glow; the virgin fire irons finished in a sort of blue-tinged steel effect, supported by a little figure in medieval armour; the framed print of an orchid on the grating of a gutter; the drinks cabinet behind *The Complete Works of Dickens* (Fire-side Edition).

'It's not that I don't like the house. I like it a lot. But they're a stuck-up lot round here. They really are. It'll be nice to be back in Woolingham. Do you have any place there in mind?'

'No, pet.'

'Well, I wondered. I mean, I wonder if you'd like to look at this.'

From a magazine rack, gilded wires with hard plastic sides decorated with views of Canaletto's Venice, she pulled out an estate agent's sheet.

Baird and Skeffington. Well, I'm blessed. A glossy colour photo at the top, upmarket stuff, of an old-looking house, all gables and leaded windows, but obviously well done up, well taken care of. Small hall through to two large receps, large entirely modernized kitchen with breakfast room, conservatory, utility room, etc., etc., these last being recent extensions carried out in excellent taste. Gas-fired central heating throughout. Stairs (fine old oak banisters – a real feature) to four bedrooms, the master one having avocado bathroom en suite, also separate bathroom and w.c. Double-glazed throughout.

Double garage, loggia, two barns, ½ acre well-kept gardens, sunhouse, fishpond, etc., etc., with some old, well-established fruit trees.

This highly recommended property is situated on the southern borders of Woolingham, within easy reach of the North Downs. An added interest for the discriminating buyer is that the original dwelling, to which extensive additions have been made, is, as far as we know, the oldest in the borough.

Skerrit's Farm: £95,000.

'But there's an industrial estate all round it.'

'No, sweet. Only on two sides, and honestly you'd never know. It's very well screened off, and the access roads are a quarter of a mile off.'

'You've been over to have a look.'

'Yes, sweet.'

Charlie smoked, drank. A warm glow began to burn in his stomach, then rose to his chest on the fumes of alcohol, to burst in a star of soft elation. Skerrit's Farm. Oldest property in Woolingham.

'It might do. It might very well do nicely.'

Jane patted his hand.

'We'll go and view on Saturday, eh? When the results are in.'

High wages for hard work; just rewards for inventiveness, energy, foresight, and special skills; incentives for saving; the creation of real jobs paid in real money; and the nation safe from foreign attack . . .

Flurries of snow out of a wind-tossed sky, bitter cold, the coldest first week of May on record, tulips wondering what the hell they'd got into, hawthorn blossom staying more sensibly in tight little, white little buds, and Jane Bosham clad in furs standing outside a Portakabin. Unusually, that year many county and borough elections coincided with the general election. Beside her stood a girl, half Jane's age, dressed in a sheepskin coat; she had brown hair well cut to shoulder length beneath a lambswool knitted cap. They had got on quite well with each other for most of the afternoon, better than with the Liberal, a thin, ascetic man in a long mac. He had a blue chin and long boney fingers that gave Jane the creeps.

A Daimler purred up. A very young man leapt out of the driving seat, round to the passenger side and opened the door.

'Come on then, Margot, here we are.'

An elderly lady, very thin, dressed in a silk Yves St Laurent headscarf, suede jacket, immaculate slacks, with a crocodile handbag and shoes to match, allowed herself to be handed out.

'One of yours, I think,' said the Labourite girl.

Jane moved forward. 'Margot. So glad you could make it.'

'Jane. Yes. Well. Too absurd to have to come up here to vote. We've never been in this ward before. I should not have bothered if young Harry Mead had not brought me. Yes, dear, I will remember it's for the council too. Is this Charlie's ward? No. I thought not. He's got poor old Duxbury's place this time.'

Harry Mead was elated. 'I say, Jane. I do think the Dop is going to get in. Quiet confidence is the mood down at HQ. They reckon we've sixty-eight per cent of the vote so far.'

A double-decker pulled up fifty yards away. It was almost full: girls in scarfs (not Yves St Laurent) and macs, men in donkey jackets carrying snap boxes, five blacks and two turbans.

'But of course the other lot can never manage to get their vote out until the last moment. Typical, isn't it? I mean, of the oicks not to vote until the last moment.'

The Labourite girl suddenly blazed, 'Oh, come on! You can't mean that.'

'Eh. I'm sorry but . . .'

'You can't be so stupid. Not as stupid as that.'

'I say, I am sorry, but . . .'

The girl, whose face had gone from white to pink, said, very slowly, 'Our people. Vote late. Because they have been working all day. The same cannot be said for your lot. It's as simple as that.'

Well done, Jane thought to herself. She's right. The elves, Charlie calls them, the ones that work.

But Terry Mead did not regain his father's seat – indeed, against the national trend, the incumbent, a heavily built, florid man called Tom Murdish, who, apart from the hiccup in 1959, had held it since 1945 and was now Deputy Whip, increased his majority. When the result was declared in the Guild Hall, he made much of this.

'I have to say. No. Hear me, friends. Brothers and sisters. That this tremendous result is a vindication of the sort of socialism I stand for and believe in, the socialism not of Marx but of Keir Hardie, not of Trotsky but of Clem Atlee . . .' At which, uproar broke out amongst his own supporters and actual fighting too, so that Old Bill had to move in and knock a head or two together.

Early in the morning, three o'clock, Councillor and Mrs Bosham returned to their Orpington home, which, that very same day, was destined to be put on the market. With a large brandy, Charlie sat by his steadily flickering fire and grinned at himself with warm satisfaction. On the telly, tired commentators babbled to tired politicians while superimposed names and numbers flitted across their stomachs – all in silence, for Charlie had killed the noise with the remote control.

Thorpe's gone. Should bloody well think so. And there goes a big one. That Shirley Williams.

Jane came in with a plate of beefburgers in sesame buns, hot pepper relish. Freezer to microwave in, hey presto, six minutes.

'Pleased then, Councillor?'

Charlie struggled to suppress the grin that longed to split his cherry face in half, and finally managed it. Gravity, responsibility, these were to be the keynotes from now on.

'Thank you, Jane, yes I am. And thank you too, my dear. You are a great help. A very great help.' He patted her hand.

Jane was amazed. She looked twice at him, to be sure he was not taking the mickey, but no, his face was deadpan, the blue eyes flickering a little behind the lids, puffier than ever, but the mouth, bull-dog like, as steady as a rock.

'Well.That's all right then. I'm sure I do my best.'

'You do, dear. You do.'

Puzzled, she bit into a bun, then delicately wiped the relish from the corner of her mouth with a daintily tilted little finger. Tuchaclass, Charlie thought.

'Shame about Mead though,' she said, and swigged chartreuse from the tumbler she'd found for herself in the kitchen.

Charlie cradled the huge bowl of his brandy balloon, maintained the new-found stateliness of his delivery.

'Not really. You see, Terry, fine man though he is, one of the very best. Is not really the sort of person Woolingham needs. While. In his way. Murdish is. Terry lacks . . . toughness. Resolution. You know. A week back we found a couple of old biddies who were ready to swear the Labourites had told them they would be *forced* to buy their council flats if we got in. Buy or get out. They were terrified. Now Terry wouldn't use it. Refused to touch it. Thing is. It's a tough world, the world of politics. You've got to be tough if you want to get on. Murdish is tough and we respect him for that.'

'You are too, Charlie.'

'Yes, Jane.' He added, 'I don't mind Murdish. We get on.'

Murdish and his union people at Town Hall. Yes. Woolingham business had always got on well with them. Dockland redevelopment. No nonsense about the council employing its own construction workers or anything like that, decent sharing out of contracts . . . Mead was too bloody sea-green and incorruptible. Three years ago, when invited to speak at the Leonine Rotationists, he had actually had the nerve to say he thought Town Hall was due for a spring clean, he mentioned the Augean Stables, whatever they were, and in front of three elected councillors, one of whom was part of the Labour majority.

'But Mead lacks resolution. And responsibility. To those of us in the community who serve it by keeping things going. And it shows. I mean, he dropped votes today when everywhere else they've been picking them up. Honestly, Jane. Much though I admire him. Even like him. We were after all at school together. He's not the man for

Woolingham. He ought to stand down. I mean, I reckon those five hundred votes stem from his milk and water approach. Nothing more. Nothing less.'

Which was unfair and untrue, though it was being widely said across the constituency on that night. The truth was that, two years earlier, Woolingham's Labour council had accepted eight hundred overspill families from dockland north of the river . . .

They munched on, drank more. The voiceless faces came and went; nonentities fell, and nonentities rose to take their places.

'Bed?'

But Charlie was on a high. Councillor. Well. It was a step in the right direction. A new life. Get Peter Coleman off his tits. A new interest. Councillor Bosham and his wife.

'Freshen it?'

He waved his almost empty balloon in response.

Glug, glug.

'James Last?'

'Why not?'

This was code, what he had been hoping for. Twice before, this had happened towards the end of a celebration, at a time of self-congratulation: the opening of a new facility as far off as Eastleigh (airport, railway, M3 fingering its way towards the M27, twelve miles from Southampton Docks), and after the collapse of a rival. *Woolingham Stores the South.*

Jane found the tape: that smooth big-band noise – smooth but raucous too, brassy anyway, a great noise, a whoopee noise, and slotted it into the Akai. They let it flow for a track or two, munched more, slurped more, glug, glug, then Jane moved between his plump but still-strong thighs. Charlie lay back in the deep chair, shifted his arse forward an inch or two, and let her get on with it. Robin Day also mouthed on.

Where there is discord may we bring harmony; where there is error may we bring truth; where there is doubt, may we bring faith; where there is despair, may we bring hope . . . Now there is work to be done.

2

It was a brisk, cloudy, breezy, sunny sort of day – what you'd expect at the beginning of April – and Charlie, looking out through diamond-paned windows, wondered whether he shouldn't walk to the Wellington. More exercise, the quack had said.

Mind you, as a result, he and Jane were now playing badminton, using the courts at the new Sport for All Leisure complex that had been completed at the top end of Skerrit's Meadow where once had stood cottages. Very handy, only five minutes' walk, and as private founder members they were privileged to have first call on most of the facilities at a reduced price whenever they wanted. Poor old Jane wasn't much good – she'd played no racket games since school – but she was a great sport and took it in good part. Usually he let her win five or six points a game. Once she suggested a handicap, a five-point lead to her – and he got really puffed and dizzy with a roar and a pounding in his ears before he beat her, so they gave up that idea.

There were mixed sauna baths (a private franchise called the Roman Rooms) for afters. If you picked your time, you could steer clear of the oicks from the Flowers whose use of the Sport for All was restricted anyway; first, because founder membership was limited to eight hundred people, and the Leisure Committee at Town Hall, on which Charlie sat, had hardly had to supervise how that was carved up, having set the founder enrolment fee at one hundred quid per person, two hundred per family (thereby saving the ratepayer and helping to keep outgoings within Heseltine's norms); second, because if you were not a member a badminton court cost you two quid an hour; third, certain periods each day were member-only periods.

There had been a move from that new councillor Ken Langley to make it twenty-five pence for unwaged, and let them share membership privileges during off-peak, i.e., during normal working hours, but it had been defeated, because three of the councillors on the committee who had been elected as Labourites now called themselves SDP.

Councillor Bosham had made a good litte speech on Langley's proposal which had been quoted in the new Woolingham *Advertiser,* pushed through every letterbox in the borough whether you liked it or not. 'These men and lads should not be enticed by free handouts to waste precious hours when they should be on their bikes combing the hills and lanes to find again the opportunities they have allowed to slip through their fingers.' Jane was very good at that, he did freely admit: he had the ideas, but she had this gift of putting them into words you could actually say.

In point of fact his first two years as councillor had gone very well indeed. Both business and labour respected him from a distance; closer in, they discovered the advantages of having a colleague who could offer a discreet facility in warehousing and storage. The professionals too, the doctors, lawyers and retired civil servants, quite took to him – after all, he was an Old Sydneyan, had the right accent when it suited, and if he was a touch inarticulate, so what? Most of us are these days, apart from schoolteachers and talking heads on telly.

In the council chamber itself he had presence; his bulky but immaculate figure was imposing enough, his voice resonant. When he spoke, his left hand stayed in his jacket pocket, he waved his right fist or stabbed the air with his strong right index finger. He was well briefed in three or four areas – sale of council houses, making the leisure services pay, privatization of refuse collection and other council services – and always produced variations on the same speech on these topics whenever they were on the agenda, and very often too when they were not. There was nothing odd about this. If a couple of speakers managed to string together more than eight tolerably grammatical sentences, a retired colonel from one of the outer wards was sure to stand up and congratulate the chamber on the high standard of debate, the highest he'd known for some years.

With the defection of three councillors from Labour to the SDP in the New Year, the whole thing became much more interesting. Labour still nominally ran the show, so Charlie and his colleagues were rarely called on actually to take responsibility for any of the decisions the council made, but in some areas, particularly where ratepayers' money could be saved (thought to be a vote-winner), the SDP voted with the Tories, and, since Charlie often led for the Tories in these areas, he gained most of the credit.

He also enjoyed and went in a lot for fête-opening, fund-raising, and sat on the board of governors of two primary schools. He appeared on regional TV on four occasions and was once filmed uncorking a bottle of champagne from the basket of a hot-air balloon – the ascent marked the opening of a new facility for storing compressed gases. An even greater triumph got him into the *Sun,* the *Mail,* and the *Express,* as well as on telly. He organized a reunion of all the surviving members of a transport squadron that had been based on yet another disused airfield he was able to take off the hands of the MoD to the benefit of both. He hired a bugle band and a troupe of pubescent majorettes and everyone had a lovely time. The firm prospered too: as Coleman had prophesied, the less Charlie was in the office, the richer everyone became.

His only failure was with the blue-rinse brigade. These were the ladies, mostly widows with not very substantial incomes but pretensions to gentility, who provided the middle layer of the local Conservative Association infrastructure. They provided free if not always entirely competent clerical assistance at election times, ran coffee mornings and sales of work, and were occasionally rewarded by being made honorary this or honorary that. They had made quite a show of getting one of their number on the council in Duxbury's place when he announced he was standing down. This challenge, however, evaporated when the lady in question was assured she would be made delegate not only for the Conservative Women's Conference but for the National Conference too if she stood down in Charlie's favour.

Now, on this particular day in April, he turned back from the diamond panes and padded through the wide (widened) living room – that's what Jane called it now, not a lounge – towards the bright, all-mod-con kitchen, bending ever so slightly and quite unnecessarily below the beams, which he told everyone who came, were real, part of the old house.

It was amazing what Jane had done with it all: she'd scrapped almost everything they'd had downstairs in Orpington and spent hours going round the antique shops, the bric-a-brac shops, the stripped-pine shops, and even the junk shops, to assemble the sort of stuff she knew would be in keeping. There was a high-backed unupholstered armchair, a rocking chair, a stripped-pine dresser with blue and white plates, cups and saucers showing sailing barges and windmills – which they never used, they were too pricey – a large bureau with lid supports that you had to pull out by hand and a secret drawer, and best of all a grandmother clock with a sun and a moon that rose and fell appropriately. It had all cost a bomb, but was worth every penny.

In the kitchen Charlie poured himself a coffee from the ever-warm Rowenta and from a carton in the fridge freshly reconstituted natural orange juice into which he dropped a slug of Gordon's. He longed for bacon and eggs but Jane was adamant, and she really could be very adamant where his best interests were involved, and so no bacon and eggs, just a bowl of muesli. Actually he quite liked this if it had enough raisins and brazils, and no one was there to watch when he added dark brown sugar and gold-top. She was lying in as was her wont on a Saturday, with the kids watching *Superstore* in Jason's room.

Brazils. Wasn't there trouble with them? Something about those islands in the South Pacific. Bali Hai Calling. He unfolded the paper he'd brought from the front door. No. Argentina. 'Don't Cry For Me Argentina', that was the place. And the Falklands. A name to conjure with. Wasn't she a baroness or something now? Emergency debate this afternoon to be broadcast on Radio 4. Well, he'd be giving that a miss – his Saturday routine started with lunch at the Wellington, then snooker at the Woolingham Conservative Club. Jane liked to have Saturday with the children during termtime, both now at Philip Sydney. Funny they should have girls there – still, got to move with the times, and no doubt it meant less ball-bashing and buggery. They had kids' lunch together, fried chicken and chips, huge ice creams, and in the afternoon she took them to judo.

He turned a page. On a Saturday you often got a bum as well as tits. Yes. W-a-a-a-af. Great. And a big black leader opposite. Let there be no doubt. Let there be no namby-pambyism. British property, sacred sovereignty, our duty is clear . . . That really is a nice bum.

He reached over, touched a button and got in rich quadrophonic sound, from concealed speakers, so really you felt you could reach out your hand and touch him/her (Charlie never found out which and preferred to leave the point deliciously ambiguous) singing Mendelssohn's 'Hear My Prayer'.

The fact was that Jane had been culturizing him a bit, and

it was a process he had begun to enjoy. You could, after all, these days, if you choose the right night, see bums and tits at Covent Garden . . . not like that awful time he had taken Lissie when that fat wop had been singing and no one would serve him at the bar. No trouble that way nowadays. He even liked going to the Barbican to hear Mozart and Schubert, especially if you got a seat where you could actually see the guy's fingers and their reflection in the panel above, especially when it was old four eyes Alf who got in more notes than anyone else, and the tunes at the end were lively and jiggy, and you could tap your feet to them, even hum along when they came round for the fifth time.

Meanwhile, in sound far nearer, far more tangible, far more real than anything you got at Covent Garden or the Barbican, that swooning, swooping epicene voice:

'Hear . . .
pray . . .
my . . .
er . . .'

And then like young, naked feet running up steps:

ear . . .'
thine
incline
Lord
'Oh

followed by those flattened intervals and harmonies that actually did something to your blood, and then those strong, firm, masculine voices coming in behind, caressing the epicene voice, catching it, smoothing its marble skin, then letting it flutter on . . . 'Oh, for the wings, for the wings of a dove, far, far away would I fly . . .' till at last s/he is caught again by the men, brought gliding down into the darkness of their lust . . . 'And remain there for ever – and rest.' Two long organ notes at the end, the second held longer than the first, so real they make the glasses in the cabinet shudder, and it's over. Charlie, still in his pyjamas, made a long arm for a man-sized, and wondered if after all he might not grill some bacon.

Of course, by the time he'd had a bath, and some more coffee, and smoked three or four Mozarts for the throat, and dressed in Daks slacks and a pullover so generously silky it might well be vicuña, there was really no time for walking. He took a quick swig straight from the Glenfiddich bottle to sharpen up his sense of reality, called a fond farewell or two up the featured oak staircase, pressed the electronic switch which would unlock and open the double garage, and stepped out into the raw brisk air.

Obsequiously the daffodils nodded their heads as he passed and tulips in bud stood to attention. So they should. Duxbury had promised to start delivery of goods owed that very afternoon. During the snooker game. If it all worked out, then Charlie really would be on his way, and fuck you, Terry Mead.

3

'Heads I win, tails you lose,' said Charlie, smacking a coin down on the side of the table. Three other coins smacked down with it. Charlie, heads (he actually used a double-headed coin Jane had found in a junk shop), Duxbury tails, Yallop tails, Hibbert tails. The last three smacked down their coins again. Duxbury and Yallop heads, Hibbert tails. Christ, thought Charlie, I'm playing with that Hibbert, I'll have to pull out a stop or two if we are to avoid a hiding.

'Usual then', he said. 'Best of five frames, a fiver each on each frame played.' He smacked down the false penny again, and Duxbury called heads: he'd spotted the coin weeks ago. 'OK, partner,' he said to Yallop, 'you break.'

Joe Yallop was a master butcher enjoying a very comfortable early retirement, Dewhurst having bought out his three shops two years earlier after he'd contrived to get them and Baxter's into an auction situation. He was very big, had tiny red eyes and a nose that looked like a prize-winning strawberry. Derek Hibbert, on the other hand, was believed to be a gentleman – that is, he had no visible means of support. He was tall, thin, had sandy hair, a sandy complexion, and was occasionally caught in posh vowels. In fact, he operated on the fringe of the film world: two or three directors believed superstituously that their films would flop if they didn't have him around. They used him on the set to patch up awkward moments in the script; occasionally he got a speaking part of a line or two; sometimes he would be given a grand or so consultancy fee for nothing very much at all. He did all this under a pseudonym and used another for stories he wrote for pulp magazines about Green Berets saving the world from Communism. With a bob or two from a trust to top it all up, he didn't do too badly.

Duxbury, in a long cardigan that hung like a pelmet over what was now an enormous pot, was president of the Conservative Club, which was a totally meaningless title but kept him in touch with the local Association of which Yallop's wife was fund-raising secretary. Yallop, like Charlie, was on the council. Hibbert, who claimed a naval past (RNVR, ended his war as a lieutenant commander), ran the Empire Loyalists, the British Legion, and was a churchwarden. All three were much older than Charlie, in Duxbury's case thirty years older.

Joe Yallop broke confidently and skilfully leaving the white well in baulk and only three reds visible.

'Age before beauty.' said Charlie, and Hibbert took the next shot.

They settled into the rhythm of the game, the sweet run of the porcelain over the baize beneath the long light with its tasselled shade, the usual jokes: 'Thought I'd missed it' after outrageous flukes; 'Stuck it up for you' when a difficult shot had been left; and so on. Charlie and Hibbert trailed but Charlie got them back into the game with a break of twenty-eight – four reds, two blacks, two blues.

'What about this Falklands lark, then,' said Hibbert, chalking up his cue.

'Over the top, right over the top. No way can they be allowed to get away with that.'

'Quite right, my son. No way.'

Hibbert again: 'That debate'll be about starting. I shouldn't mind hearing a bit of it.'

'Why not. There's a wireless in the bar no one ever uses. I'll get Hoskins to bring it up.'

'Might as well fill up while we're at it.'

'My call, I think. Brandy for the president.'

'Courvoisier. And a panatella, if you don't mind.'

'Of course not. Be my guest. Joe?'

'Scotch. Water. Half and half.'

'And Charlie's a real-ale man.'

'No more. Quack said I should lay off the beer. I'll go along with Joe.'

This was a lie. The quack had actually said cut down the booze.

By the time all this had been organized and both drinks and radio arrived, Duxbury and Yallop had won the first frame by eight points. Yallop potting a tricky pink to nail it. They chalked up, cheered each other, drank, set up the table again. Hibbert tuned in the radio. If they stood near it, next to the scoring rack, they could hear it easily, but further off it was not loud enough to interfere with conversation or concentration on the game.

The people of the Falkland Islands, like the people of the United Kingdom, are an island race. Their way of life is British; their allegiance is to the Crown. They are few in number but they have the right to live in peace, to choose their own way of life, and to determine their allegiance. Their way of life is British; their allegiance is to the Crown. It is the wish of the British people and the duty of Her Majesty's government to do everything we can to uphold that right. That will be the hope and our endeavour and, I believe, the resove of every Member of the House.

'Bit low key, I thought,'said Yallop.

'Sticky wicket,' said Hibbert. 'I mean, it should never have happened and she knows it. I believe that Carrington did the right thing to resign. First of all he sells out the Rhodesians, then he gets too pally with the Arabs. Now this.'

'Mugs away,' said Duxbury.

Charlie cued off, slightly fluffed, broke more out of the pack than he should have done.

'Now for Wurzel Gummidge. Odds on, the unemployed

will be seen to be in for an extra bashing because of this crisis.'

'Poor old sod. Blind as a bat.'

It is a question of the people who wish to be associated with this country and who have built their whole lives on the basis of association with this country. We have a moral duty, a political duty, and every other kind of duty . . .

Hibbert's turn; he put down a red and shaped up for the pink.

'The blue's a better bet,' said Charlie.

Down it went.

'Now you've got the red on the top pocket.'

Duxbury, next to him, said, 'I have it on the very best authority, and I tell no lie, from the horse's mouth itself, I tell no lie, that old Tom Murdish is not about to survive this new re-election procedure the Labourites have brought in.'

'Good shot, Derek. Now the brown, eh?

'Actually I think I can just about clip in that black.'

Silly fucker, Charlie mouthed, and he missed. 'Seven scored, seven away, even stevens. Your poke, Mr President.'

They are faced with an act of naked unqualified aggression, carried out in the most shameful and disreputable circumstances. Any guarantee from this invading force is utterly worthless – as worthless as any of the guarantees that are given by this same Argentine Junta to its own people.

Stick that up your junta, thought Charlie as Duxbury went in off. 'Four away.'

'Reverting to poor old Tom,' said Duxbury, busily re-chalking the cue he blamed for his mis-hit, 'you can imagine what this means to him. For a quarter of a century he's given his all for this community, and now those militants you hear of are giving him the boot . . .' Charlie, in spite of all this, put away a red, a brown, a red, a green, a red, a black, and ended with a neat safety shot, almost a snooker.

'Ta muchly,' said Yallop. 'How the hell am I meant to extricate myself from this?'

'You can see a red or two,' said Duxbury.

'Oh yes. Indeed I can. But what to do with them, what happens to them when I've hit them, that is the question.'

. . . uphold the rights of our country throughout the world, and the claim of our country to be a defender of people's freedom throughout the world, particularly those who look to us for special protection, as do the people in the Falkland Islands.

'You know,' went on Duxbury in his gravelly squeaky voice, 'old Tom Murdish is a damn good bloke. We've always got on well with him, and the Labourite councillors who are of the same ilk. They know as well as we do. What oils the wheels of industry and commerce in this borough. On which the prosperity of all depend . . . but I doubt the same can be said of Ken Langley's lot, and he's the one they'll select. In fact. Not to put too fine a point. I'm damn sure they don't. My poke again? How many reds left? Four. Well, that's one more out of the way. Now what? I think I'll have a go at the brown but I'll need the furniture. Give us a hand, there's a good fellow. Did you see how he got money up, council money, ratepayers' money, to finance that Indian Co-operative restaurant up in North Woolingham? Crazy. Waiters getting a share of the profits instead of paying back the council. Whoops. Getting too old for this.' He meant the long rest and the long cue. He puffed and wheezed, hoisting his pot on to the edge of the bottom end of the table, squinted down the long pole on which his nose almost rested – not a fruit like Yallop's, but the sort of thing you find at the bottom of a cabbage with club-root – right hand pistoning under the chin. 'Still, there it goes. Now what? I'll take that one over the middle pocket.'

Even though the position and the circumstances of the people who live in the Falklands are uppermost in our minds – it would be outrageous if that were not the case – there is the longer term interest to ensure that foul and brutal aggression does not succeed in the world. If it does, there will be a danger not merely to the Falkland Islands, but to people all over this dangerous planet.

'Well done, old Wurzel,' cried Hibbert. 'I really thought he was going to try and stir things. I mean, damn it, he's a ban-the-bomber, isn't he? But not today. Real sense of responsibility.'

Duxbury agreed. 'You see,' he said, turning again to Charlie, 'these two sorts of Labourites. Most, however leftie they seem, are, at the bottom, Brits. And that's a fact. Only a tiny minority, and I'm afraid our Langley may be one, even though he has his name on the Duxbury Cup for Public Speaking, may be one of them. Sorry. Still my poke, isn't it? Green.'

'Cunning bastard,' said Charlie, as the cue ball kissed gently off the green, on to the bottom cushion to come to rest behind the brown, back on its spot, and the yellow which almost touched it.

'Biter bit,' said Yallop, with satisfaction.

British interest in that part of the world, in my judgement is substantial . . .

'Who's this?' asked Charlie, as he paced thoughtfully round the table, trying out how best to play the shot. The two remaining reds were close together not far off the side cush, about half way between blue and pink. Not a difficult target, question was, how to play it.

'Du Cann,' said Hibbert.

'Good bloke.'

It is substantial in the sea which has yet to yield up its treasures. It is also substantial in Antarctica . . .

Charlie smacked the white; it bounced like a wrestler coming off the ropes and clipped the nearer red hard so that it hit its neighbour and banged it into the top pocket.

'Thought I'd missed it', said Charlie, walking round the

table for all the world like a portly Hurricane Higgins, to pick off an easy black, and the last red.

'Jesus fucking Christ,' said Yallop.

Duxbury drank off what was left in his glass: 'You know, Charlie. I'm not sure I would have played it quiet like that . . . Still I suppose you now aim to clear the table.'

'I think it might be made to yield up its treasures', said Charlie, getting one leg over the side cush to take the blue and run the cue ball up into the neighbourhood of the yellow. The break went on.

We have one duty only, which we owe to ourselves – the duty to rescue our people and to uphold our rights. Let that be the clear and unanimous resolve of the House this day. Let us hear no more about logistics – how difficult it is to travel long distances. I do not remember the Duke of Wellington whining about Torres Vedras ('Hear, hear.') We have nothing to lose now except our honour . . .

Charlie fluffed the pink, but it didn't matter; he and Hibbert were now sixteen points ahead and Duxbury and Yallop conceded.

'One all. Well done, partner. Actually, you know, that bit about Wellington and Torres Vedras is horse manure. Torres Vedras is fifteen miles from Lisbon, where all the allied reserves and magazines were, and where the fleet was too. And in those days,' the lieutenant commander went on, 'Britannia really did rule the waves. No. Quite the boot on the other foot – it was the poor old frogs whose logistics were in a twist at Torres Vedras. Wellington, in any case, never took a chance with his logistics.'

Hibbert, Charlie and Duxbury sat on leather chairs beneath wall-lights – simulated cast-iron supporting plastic candles and flame-shaped bulbs beneath parchment-coloured lampshades – and, cues between their knees, smoked while Yallop fetched the next round, hear no evil, see no evil, speak no evil. Above them a framed photograph of Supermac and Freddie Mead taken in that very room, October 1959, the night Terry Mead procured a letter from his father's files, in order to get his sister out of a mess, fix her up . . .

'Of course,' said Duxbury at last, to neither of them in particular, but Charlie felt it was to him the old man was speaking, 'there is a step old Murdish has recourse to take if he wishes it. And when I spoke to him last night in this very room, I urged him to take it. And I think he will. Who's this? Old Enoch, isn't it?'

'I think so.'

'Good old Enoch. What old Tom Murdish must do, the only thing he can do if he is to remain a force to be reckoned with in this borough, is to go SDP. Ah. Joe. Good lad.'

There is only one reaction which is fit to meet unprovoked aggression upon one's own sovereign territory: that is direct and unqualified and immediate willingness – not merely willingness but willingness expressed by action – to use force.

'Which means,' said Hibbert, 'poor old Terry Mead will get the seat at last. No shadow of a doubt.'

Duxbury pulled himself to his feet, yanked his cardigan down, wiped his hands on a huge handkerchief. 'That's not how I put it to Tom. He thinks he can hold it under SDP colours.'

'No way,' said Yallop. 'Anyway, in a by-election perhaps. But he won't give up the seat until he has to. And he won't hold it in a general election. No way. Cheers.'

Duxbury nodded heavy, wise agreement, chalked his cue. 'Mugs away, eh? Then I'll take first poke.'

The Prime Minister, shortly after she came into office, received the soubriquet as the Iron Lady . . .

'So. Terry gets the seat at last,' repeated Hibbert.

'The Tory candidate, whoever he will be, stands a very good chance.

In the next week or two this House, the nation and the

Right Honourable Lady will learn of what metal she is made.

Fired perhaps by Charlie's outrageous fluke in the previous frame, or perhaps just bored with a game that can become tedious if everyone insists on playing safe, Duxbury gave the pack a good hard slam, making a total shambles of the entire table, but potting two reds. He took the blue, another red, the brown, before muffing his fourth red.

'Mr President,' Hibbert was reproving. 'Shoot me down in flames if I'm wrong but in our party we have no reselection procedures, I am profoundly glad to say.'

'Indeed, Derek. And so am I. And so am I.'

Duxbury's gamble was now revealed as the hollow gesture it was. Charlie was by far the best of the players there – a fact he tried to conceal: he had matured since his squash-playing days and had apprehended, even if he was not always able to carry it out, the precept that he who occasionally loses lives to be asked to play another day, whereas he who wins all the time, especially when there is money on the table, becomes quite quickly someone who seems to get left out. He was the best player because he had a table of his own in one of the converted barns at Sceret's Farm (Jane's idea to revert to the Domesday Boke spelling), on which he pushed the ivories about for at least an hour most days of the week. It was his den – there too he kept his now quite substantial collection of books about weaponry.

And now, after Duxbury's smash, a burning ambition was on the cards – a break of half a ton.

Charlie padded round the table, a little pale with excitement as the score mounted; the others watched, and Duxbury continued to talk over the noise of the radio and the click of the balls.

'Since Derek has raised the point, and it was he who raised it, not I. It is worth giving a moment's thought to this novel situation. That is. That our borough. So long a well-defined bastion of the Labourites. And they have not scrupled to make it so; we all remember the case of the overspill, and their insistence that the low-cost housing that would service the industrial estate should fall on our boundaries, and I for one don't blame them, I'd have done the same. Notwithstanding all this. Our borough's seat is now up for grabs.' He drank.

'Now. I am an old man. Retired from business. From politics. Neither a borrower or lender am I, in no one's debt, and no one can hurt me. I'm fireproof. Charlie, why not go for the pink. No. I'm sure you know best. But I do feel I have something to offer. To offer to the community. At large. Something I am uniquely privileged. From my present situation. Because the fact is I can speak now, on this very important subject without fear of favour . . .'

The Government have the right to ask both sides of the House for the fullest support in their resolve to return the Falkland Islands and the freedom of the Islanders to British sovereignty . . .

'Who's that?'

'David Owen,' said Hibbert.

'Piss-artist. And what I think we have to ask ourselves is this. Is the present holder of the incumbency as Conservative candidate for this borough the right one? When. It now seems. He might win. Horses for courses. The candidate for a lost seat is not necessarily the candidate for a winnable one. How many is that, Charlie?'

'Forty-three.' Shaping up for the black that might make it that magical half a ton.

'Forty-two,' said Hibbert.

Charlie straightened slowly, fixed the ex-RNVR man with a long, slow, burning look from behind his puffy lids, staring across the green baize, under the tassels of the long light, through banks of pricey smoke slowly shifting, out of darkness into darkness. At the same time Tam Dalyell, a raving leftie, was now trying to exercise his parliamentary right to persuade the good doctor to stint his flux for a moment and answer a question. The good doctor was firm in that plummy, righteous way that is so definitely one of his more endearing characteristics:

There is no question of anyone in the House weakening the stance of the Government.

Charlie pulled out a handkerchief and carefully wiped his hands and cue, chalked up, stooped and dropped the black. Then played a safety shot, tucking the white behind the pink on the top cush. He said, 'One red, one blue, one red, one pink, one red, one blue, one red, one brown, one red, one blue, one red, one black, one red, one yellow, one red, one black. Fifty. Your poke.'

Sir Julian Amery: *We have lost a battle, but have not lost the war. It is the old saying that Britain always wins the last battle. I seek . . . two simple assurances. The first is that we are determined to make the Argentine dictator disgorge what he has taken – by diplomacy if possible, by force if necessary . . . nothing else will restore the credibility of the Government or wipeth stain from Britain's honour.*

'Wipeth my arse,' said Joe Yallop, his turn now to pad around the table, cue held by the butt, sticking out in front of him like a medieval lance or a bull's pizzle. 'Up shit creek again without a paddle. Thank you, Charlie.'

'Personally,' said Hibbert, 'I don't see what's so wrong with old Terry Mead. He's a damned good scout, has toiled in the vineyard all his life; now, even if only by a piece of good fortune he gets his reward, well I say he deserves it.'

'Sod,' said Yallop.

'Four away,' said Charlie.

'No one, least of all I, would deny Terry his deserts. No way. But that's not the point. All I am asking is. Is he the man Woolingham wants to represent it in Parliament?'

'I don't see why not.'

'Nor do I. Nor do I. But I have to ask myself again – is he

what *Woolingham* wants? I also have to ask myself: is he what Central Office wants? Does he fit the new brand of thrusting, enterprising, feet on the ground, and ears there too, Members of Parliament and candidates, people who all can look to as one of us, only different in that through guts, hard work and enterprise they have done a bit, got on a bit? Or is he not rather something, well, just a touch . . . old-fashioned? Out of touch with the times? My poke?'

'The blue-rinse brigade lick his arse,' said Yallop.

'Just so. And how many of them are left in our midst at this point in time? Oh, I know Mrs Armstrong, Mrs Grosscurth, Mrs Goulden are fixtures, or we may assume so. But that power base is by and large drifting off. To Eastbourne, Hove and the environs of Bognor. I mean, look at Skerrit's Farm, that young Charlie has now. Sir Jas Mongolivy and his lady wife could not have done more for our Association, nor more for Terry than they did. But Sir Jas snuffed it and Lady Mongolivy now resides in Climping. Dear me. My poke again already? Only twenty-two on the table? Do we have a chance? No. Concede, Joe, what do you say?'

The routine repeated, this time Charlie went for the drinks. Once Old Bill had stopped by at the club to see that food was being consumed in accordance, it then being a quarter to four. They were youngsters. Duxbury had been matey: 'You're new on this patch, I think? had bought them a bottled DD each and sent them on their way. As the barman lifted glasses to the optics, Charlie took stock. A little care now in order. Silly to knock up a fifty if only because it now meant he and that wally Hibbert were now leading 2–1. If they took the next frame, they took the match, and that would upset old Duxbury.

Another lesson the maturer Charlie had learnt was that most people really do seem to believe that who steals my purse steals trash, but touch them on their vanity and they holler. Which, he thought, seems to be at the root of this Falklands cock-up. Trash has been stolen but loved I not honour more was the key of it. Amazing how the Labourites were behaving. It was surely clear to the most naïve babe-in-arms that the Thatcherites, who were already on the skids if you believed the opinion polls, were done for if they didn't get the Falklands back. Yet somehow the Labourites had been psyched into not saying this, not saying that survival of a Tory clique (he called it a 'click') was what it was really all about. At that point in time, Charlie had little time for Maggie.

'Here we go then,' he said, as he returned with the tray, 'Christ. What have you all been up to? You haven't even set them up. Too much jaw-jaw, not enough war-war.' And he went round the table spilling the balls out of the pockets.

The radio reasserted itself, as indeed it would, since war had broken out in the Commons itself. Above shouts and jeers, Raymond Whitney, a Tory, was striving to make himself heard.

. . . there are alternative ways in which the interests of the Falkland Islanders can be protected and I feel these can be achieved by negotiation . . .

Point of Order. Mr Speaker. Point of Order. If defeatism of this kind is to be spoken, should it not be done in secret session? Would it not be in order to spy strangers?

Howls. Caterwauls. The high, brave voice again.

It is not a question of defeatism – it is a question of realism and the avoidance of another humiliation for our country . . .

'There we are,' said Charlie. 'Your go again, I think, Mr President.'

But Mr Duxbury looked suddenly tired. The alcohol had shifted – the high fading, the tired depression coming on.

'Go on, Joe,' he said. 'You give'm a poke.'

I earnestly implore the House to think very carefully so

that we make sure that we are ready to take and answer the challenges of the questions that are there. They will not go away if they are not enunciated.

'Good shot, Joe. Now that, whoever he was, is the sort of Tory our Terry is. And, mark my words, their day is done.'

The game moved on, but, following Joe Yallop's near perfect break, very slowly. Duxbury, old and tired, began to lose his temper. He miscued, swore, called them all cowards for not breaking up the reds, but refused to do so again himself.

The radio too blustered: *The time for weasel words has ended. I expect action from the government; and I hope we shall get it . . .*

Hibbert tucked the cue ball right into the middle of the nest of reds in such a way that it was virtually impossible to play it in any useful way at all. Duxbury's age and physique did not help him. A pro, Charlie even, would have straddled himself on the table, just keeping one regulation toe on the ground, would have spread the fingers on his left hand in a high 'bridge' to give the cue something to rest on above the reds without touching them, and would have got out without disturbing them significantly, sending the cue ball off the top cushion and back into baulk.

All this was beyond Mr President. After a spell of huffing and puffing, he fished out the 'spider' – a rest of quite decoratively wrought brass.

The very thought that our people, eighteen hundred people of B-b-b-ritish b-b-b-lood and b-b-b-one, could be left in the hands of such criminals is enough to make any normal Englishman's b-b-b-lood . . . and the b-b-b-lood of Scotsmen and Welshmen . . . b-b-b-oil too.

Balls jumped in the air and one landed on the floor. Duxbury was helped down to *terra firma* and all present agreed, with a nod and a wink and a raised eyebrow, not to notice that he had nicked the green cloth with the tip of his cue, thus committing absolutely the worst crime available to an English, sorry, British snooker player. Even though it was the very tiniest of nicks, the Entertainments Committee would want an explanation in due course of time. Meanwhile only 'foul stroke, four away', but the shambles let in Charlie, and at the end of his break he and Hibbert were forty-eight points ahead.

John Silkin was also smooth: *I make one appeal above all others to the Government. Let us ensure that our dear fellow citizens in the Falkland Islands are kept in touch with us as much as possible. Let us extend our broadcasts . . .*

Joe played awkwardly out of the position Charlie had left him in, and Hibbert came to the table. He pondered for a long time . . .

When Galtieri says to us that he will respect the rights and property and above all the lives and freedom of our people, we have a right to wonder whether this is true in view of what he does to his own people . . .

. . . and then carefully laid an appalling snooker, with the cue ball in baulk and actually touching the brown, the green very close and the remaining reds clustered on the top cushion behind the black.

Poor Duxbury huffed and puffed, and his complexion ripened from strawberry to plum. Joe and Charlie offered helpful suggestions: Derek Hibbert, long, thin, leaned against the wall by the cue rack, and smoked an Embassy through a bone, silver-mounted holder.

Nott wound up: *If we were unprepared, how is it that from next Monday, at only a few days' notice, the Royal Navy will put to sea in wartime order and with wartime stocks and weapons? I suggest that no other country in the world could react so fast and the preparations have been in progress for several weeks . . .*(!!)

Duxbury played the cue ball without much force against the bottom cushion; it angled off to the right and kissed the yellow.

'Four away,' said Charlie, briskly, for he saw the danger very well.

'Hang about. Hang. A. Bout,' cried Hibbert, pushing himself off the wall and levering the filter out of his holder with his thumbnail.

'*Seven* away,' said Yallop, as firmly as Charlie had.

'Oh, come *on,*' said Hibbert, coming to the table and putting his splayed hands on the edge, his head sunk into his shoulders so he could peer under the fringe at the others.

'What the hell is going on?' shouted Duxbury. 'What do you mean "seven away"? Charlie, tell me, what are these hustlers farting on about?'

'I think, Mr President,' said Charlie, keeping his voice very even, standing very straight, cue held like a rifle in front of his body, head up, eyes glittering through heavy lids, 'I think the suggestion is you played a deliberately foul stroke.'

'Of course I bloody played a foul stroke. I hit the yellow. Four away.'

'But they think . . .'

'Think? I *know,*' said Hibbert.

'. . . that the stroke you played could never have begun to get anywhere near the reds, and you played it thus to avoid the possibility of hitting the black. So. Seven away. The penalty if you had hit the black . . .'

'Come on, Charlie. You know there's a sight more to it than that. He's also avoided leaving a free ball, which could well have let you in to clear the table. Now my reading of the rules is he can either forfeit the frame or at least give you that free ball.'

'Buggered if I will,' shouted Duxbury. 'I played a perfectly fair foul shot, four away.'

Impasse.

We intended to solve the problem and we shall try to solve it continuingly by diplomatic means, but if that fails and it probably will do so, we shall have no choice but to press forward with our plans.

'I'm sorry, Mr President,' said Hibbert. 'I think, and I think the other two agree with me. I think your shot was a deliberate foul, and the rules, as amended, are quite clear . . .'

'I'm not too sure I've ever worked out the full implications of that amendment,' said Charlie.

'Buggered if I even understand it,' said Yallop.

'A shot played foully, deliberately, to incur a lesser penalty, incurs the greatest possible penalty or the frame is forfeited. Since you won't accept the penalties, you forfeit the frame. Which means you lose the match 3–1. Which means someone owes me a tenner.' He twisted his cue into two, carefully wiped the pieces on a large yellow duster, which he then wrapped them in before zipping up the bundle in a cloth, leather-edged carrier. Quite the navy man.

Yallop gave him a tenner.

We can at least give to the armed forces the unanimous backing of the House in the difficult task that they are being asked to undertake.

Hibbert drank up. 'Thanks for the game. Very pleasant,' and he marched off.

Yallop looked at the large watch which was yet almost lost in the red hairs of his huge wrist. 'Well, it's later than I thought. There's an LVA dinner dance at the Prince of Wales tonight and Mrs Baker, you know, that holds the licence at the Orlando, has asked us to be her guests.' He had his own long black tin cue case hanging on the members' rack, and he slid his cue up into it. 'Heavy do's these LVA junkets usually are, so I think I'll get home and have a kip first. Ta muchly for the game, Mr President. Sorry it had to end like that. And you, Charlie. See you around.'

'Hoskins may still be here. Do you want a freshener?'

'No thanks, Mr President. I've still got half left.' Charlie pushed the unpotted balls into pockets around the table.

'You're probably right. If I'd had one less I might not have done such a fool thing. I owe you ten quid.'

'Skip it.'

'That Hibbert must be short of a bob or two to kick up like that.'

'Or mean.'

'Or both.'

Charlie pulled back the heavy velvet drapes that covered the large windows at the top end of the table. Yellow slanting sunlight from a cloudy sky cast beams through the dissipating smoke. They made the room that had seemed so cosy, so rich, so enclosed, so safe, albeit part of a world that had died forty years earlier, drab and tatty. He lifted the huge and heavy cover, baize mounted on a rubberized backing, off the windowsill, dropped it on the table, began to unfold it. Duxbury heaved himself to his feet to help him.

'What do you think of this Falklands caper then?'

Charlie had listened to enough of the debate to have cottoned on to the line. 'It's a case of *noblesse oblige* really, isn't it? I mean. We've got to be able to hold up our heads in the world.'

'Maybe.'

Charlie was surprised at the doubt in the old man's occasionally shaky voice, stopped and looked up at him. Duxbury, his colour settling back now, his nose resuming a more hominoid shape, glared back almost balefully. 'Young lads are going to die in very cold water.'

Charlie said nothing.

'That shouldn't happen for a few bits of crappy rock in the South Atlantic.'

'It's the principle though. The principle,' said Charlie. 'Can't let the Argies trample over Brits without we do something.'

They finished unfolding the cloth. Duxbury straightened, hands in the small of his back, ready to change the subject.

'I think I did you a good turn this afternoon.'

Charlie fingered out a Dunhill. His gold Zippo flared.

'You did very well.'

'Mr Alderson off my back now?

'He was never there as far as I was concerned.'

'So you say, Charlie. So you say. But you have his ear.'

'Oh yes, I have George Alderson's ear all right. And I'll put a word in it for you, never you fear.'

'How old is he now?'

'Two years older than me. Forty-three. Thereabouts.'

'Long way to go.'

'If the circs are right, he'll take early retirement.'

'I took late retirement, and won't last much longer if what the quack says about my ticker is right. So I can't offer him. But Dick Small wants to tighten his security, he could use an ex-copper on his board, that I do know. He owes me a favour or two. So let Mr Alderson know that, will you?'

'George would like that.'

The old man reached for his jacket.

'You know, Charlie, I still don't see just how you're going to bring this off. Terry Mead has got no reason to back down. The Association like him. He's well liked. He has a reputation for helping blokes down on their luck, does Legal Aid work and so forth. He's got a nice manner. How do you get a bloke like that on his bike?'

Charlie felt sweat break into his palms and his heart rate accelerated, but none of this was evident to Duxbury. In a very even voice, he said, 'I was at school with Terry.'

'Philip Sydney.'

'And saw quite a bit of him after. Rugby club and so on.'

He remembered the awful horseplay, naked in the showers. He remembered he and Terry tossing each other off in Skerrit's meadow on Coronation Day.

'His wife left him. Lives on his own. She took the kids and he sees them often. Grown-up now. Neither of them married again. I'm not saying he's an out-and-out poufter. But he's two-handed, to say the least.'

The sun went in; the dull, drab room with its low-wattage light bulbs simulating candles looked nastier than ever.

'You're a cunning bastard, Charlie. A cunning bastard. You'll go quite a long way. Yes. Yes. The blue-rinse brigade won't like that one bit if you can make it stick.'

'Throw enough mud, some sticks.'

'Too true. Well. Time to adjourn. See you around, Charlie. Put those lights out, will you? Switch is by the scoreboard. Cheers.'

4

Woolingham Guild Hall: eight-foot-high oak panels, then Byzantine columns soaring in relief to ornamented architraves and archivolts supporting an equally ornate vaulted ceiling, all done straight from the *Stones of Venice*. At one end the huge doors are set in an oak screen beneath the tiered gallery occupied by eight or nine punkish youngsters, on one or other of the current schemes for winkling cheap labour from unemployed school-leavers. For the next two hours they will drink canned lager, eat crisps, and maintain a level of behaviour precisely within the shady area that constantly tempts those in charge to throw them out without actually ever provoking them to do so. At the other end of the stage: the candidates, their closest supporters, agents, and so on, the Returning Officer and his minions.

Between these two poles there are long tables, and the counters, for the most part specially recruited bank tellers. At the back of the hall under the gallery, Old Bill is much in evidence, particularly near the doors where the black tin boxes have been stacked.

The atmosphere is uncomfortable, lacks the *alegría* of '79. There is no possibility of a change in government this time, and the fact that the seat will change hands is a source of shame rather than excitement. All have colluded, and as a result the social fabric may be destroyed – the whole kingdom may even be reduced to an uninhabitable wasteland. At all events, hardly anyone there expects much good to come out of what is now happening.

Of course this shame is most strongly felt by the Labour and SDP supporters – so much so that they keep at opposite ends of the stage, as far from each other as possible: Ken Langley, long locks shorn to a civic shortness, neat in a double-breasted suit in the style affected by Neil Kinnock, on one side; big Tom Murdish on the other, old and now with a Duxbury-like fume of decay coming off him, but a grander decay than the ex-councillor's. But the shame is present too in the Tory camp. At least half the Tories in Woolingham hate Thatcher almost as much as they do Charlie. They want Dual Key for Cruise, a sensible settlement in the Falklands, not a fortress, moderate reflation, a fall in unemployment, and so on. They want again to smile at the dustman, the jobbing gardener, the nice girl at the cash-out, and get a sheepish smile back. For more than a year now sullenness, even rudeness, has been the order of the day, not enough to frighten them, but it makes them feel a little sad, even a little guilty. Above all, this particular lot want their borough to be represented in Parliament not by a jumped-up warehouse owner and his common wife, but by someone they can genuinely respect, someone like poor Terry Mead.

A year earlier at Sceret's Farm.

'That'll be George. George Alderson.'

'Is it business? Do you want me to stay?'

'Stay a bit. To begin with. A snack if he fancies it.'

'Then go to bed?'

'That's it.'

Beefburgers in wholemeal sesame rolls, spicy relish, coffee, whisky, the Archduke Trio played softly on the Akai, and the real logs crackling in the wrought-iron fire-basket.

'Bloody cold for the time of year.'

'Funny you should say that, George. I was remarking to Charlie only yesterday, ever since we've had this holiday for May Day, we've had a really nasty cold snap.'

'Too right, ma'am. Shows what the great white weather man in the sky thinks of it.'

'Personally, I'd rather have the holiday on Shakespeare's birthday.'

'Or St George's Day.

'Why not?'

At loss for a moment Beethoven tinkled on, then Jane attempted what she took to be a line more suitable for male company. 'What about the *Belgrano,* then, George?'

'"Gotcha!" the *Sun* said, and that sums it up for me.'

'You're right of course. But I can't help thinking of those poor men in that cold water.'

The policeman shrugged at this evidence of feminine sensibility, put on the tone he used when reprimanding WPCs for acting soft: 'They were warned. They knew what they were letting themselves in for. If they don't like a poke in the eye, they should have never have got into it. Eh, Charlie?'

'That's right. George. Freshen you?'

'Thanks, Charlie.'

Jane made an effort to regain the men's esteem. 'Talking of the *Sun.* Did you see that bit where they sponsored the first missile to be fired at Galtieri's gauchos, they said, and that Jon Snow . . .'

'Tony.'

'Beg pardon?'

'Tony. Tony Snow, Jon Snow is something else again.'

'Thank you, Charlie. Well, anyhow, how he wrote . . .' She felt a blush coming but went boldly on: '"Up yours, Galtieri."'

'And today they knocked down a Canberra with it.' Charlie rattled the poker amongst the logs. Sparks flew upwards as surely as man is born unto trouble. St George, killing a dragon, on the fireback Jane had paid so much for, flickered into life with the flames, then died again.

Jane was puzzled. 'I thought they were ours. Well,' she

looked at her watch, 'The Labourites Party Political will be over by now. I'll go upstairs and watch the news if you'll pardon me.'

'How are these council elections going then?' George asked.

She was standing now: 'I think there's just a chance we may win the wards we need. It all depends on the SDP, whether they pull in the Labourite votes that put them there in the first place or split the vote and let us in. Charlie thinks the Falklands are helping us a lot, don't you, Charlie?'

'No shadow of a doubt. And not just at local level.' He was a little drunk, and very desperate to hear what Alderson had to say, but determined too to maintain the tone of civilized intercourse his wife had so deftly set. As often happened when ends conflicted, he became verbose. 'I mean, the war has definitely increased our world standing – I mean, I don't give a bugger for world opinion per se, but our standing in the world has been totally altered by this. It has made every other member of NATO say, "My God, the British are tough."'

Like most of his sort, with a Scotch or two in him, the hazy line between his party and his country had become quite undistinguishable.

George chimed in, 'No doubt of it at all. One needs clout, and the toughmindedness to use it. You learn that lesson in the Force.'

Jane now felt she could decently slip her moorings, and with all the grace of the QE2 (requisitioned that very day), manoeuvred her way round the stained-oak gate-leg tables and the Chelsea spaniel set as a doorstop. The stairs on the feature staircase creaked and she was gone.

Charlie rose, reached for the Glenfiddich, poured generous measures into the Waterford.

'Well, George . . . but first, has Dick Small been in touch?

'Yes, thanks, Charlie, he has. Something on the lines of

security adviser or consultant, on the payroll, with a directorship in due course of time.'

'And that suits?'

'Very well, Charlie, very well. I've always got on very well with old Dick. Right now. I'll give you the straight story of what happened.' He drank, wiped his mouth.'At about ten fifty-three last night, a certain Maurice Pagham left the residence of Terence Mead . . .'

'This Pagham?'

'Known perv. Gay rights. That crap. Mead got him off a soliciting charge, but what he don't know is we later found Pagham carrying cocaine, and that's our handle where he's concerned. He does what we say.'

'Go on.'

'He left Mead's residence and was immediately assaulted by two men . . .'

'Who were?'

Mock irony: 'How would I know a thing like that? Actually they're a coupla lads from the British Movement. Pagham screamed – he does a good scream – Mead came out of his house. He got pushed about a bit. Bloody nose, quite a nasty boot in the shin.'

Charlie turned away to hide his grin. George went on, 'At this point a patrolling squad car came by, and the assailants ran off. The officers invited Mead and Pagham to make statements. Both refused. Officers invited them down to the nick. Mead advised Pagham they should go.'

Alderson drank. 'There I interviewed them. Told Mead what he already knew: that he had a public duty to make a statement; can't let thugs go around beating up respectable citizens in upmarket residential areas. Not on. He took the point. He and Pagham made statements. And that leaves me clear to give the *Woolingham Advertiser* a short para. Straight factual report ending: Mr Mead, highly respected local solicitor, recently got Pagham off a soliciting charge at Woolingham Magistrates' Court.

'Back to last night. I then asked Mead if he'd give

evidence if we caught the assailants. He said no. I said why not. He said none of my business why not. I said, if we caught the villains I'd subpoena him . . .'

Charlie realized that Alderson had no time at all for the liberal solicitor who defended pervs, shoplifters and the like, who had, three times, extracted apologies from the police for being over-enthusiastic in the pursuit of their duties.

'He said he'd go to judge in chambers and have the subpoena overturned. On what grounds, I asked. He wouldn't say. But he knew I knew.'

'I'm not with you.'

'The only grounds judge in chambers would accept to overturn a subpoena are that it had been issued with malice to bring witness's name into disrepute.'

'Ah.' Charlie nodded, drank. 'He's rumbled then.'

'Oh yes. He's rumbled. Now I could go further, pick up those lads, charge them, subpoena Mead, and Pagham, have the whole history of their relationship out in court, and see the lads get off on a technicality. In short, fit him up in style. But he's a pro, and he knows something of what it's all about. It could come unstuck, and that could turn out nasty, very.'

'I don't think that's necessary, George. That para in the *Advertiser* and a good whisper across the borough should do the trick. 'I'll see those lads from the Movement get a pony each, and they can get round the pubs with a yarn about how they thought they were into a bit of straight queer-bashing and found they were kicking the shit out of the Tory candidate. You've done a good job. George. We've got him. Like the old *Belgrano,* it's a case of *Gotcha!*

He saw the policeman to the door, where he pressed the buttons that would release the steel gate at the end of the short drive – Fortress Sceret's – watched the three and a half litre Rover through the gap, then closed everything up behind it. Back in the living room, he poured himself another Glenfiddich, and a chartreuse for Jane, took them upstairs.

She was sitting on the pillow of the high large bed, which was covered with a heavy thick woven spread of ethnic design, beneath the unsimulated beams, eating chocolates, and watching the telly. Although she was now as fat as a Rubens goddess she was no less attractive either, though clad in an enormously frothy nightie, and with her hair groomed into a tempting wildness. At the sight of her, Charlie felt a little spasm of lust, and a quite large glow of pride: his most treasured possession. He'd tell her next day that she could go and get herself one of those newly launched MG Metros: she'd need a smart run-about when she was the candidate's wife.

But she looked worried, gestured at the telly, tapped the volume on the remote control.

'Old four-eyes again,' muttered Charlie.

. . . Sheffield. A type 42 destroyer. Was attacked. And hit. Late this afternoon. By an Argentine missile. The ship caught fire. Which spread. Out of control. When there was no longer any hope. Of saving the ship. The ship's company . . .

'The fucking bastards,' cried Charlie.

. . . abandoned ship. All who abandoned her. Were picked up. It is feared that there were. A number of casualties . . .

'The treacherous, fucking bastards. You hear that, Jane? The bastards!'

It wasn't clear to her what he meant. Were the treacherous bastards the Argies with their creepy Frog missiles or the crew abandoning ship? Possibly both.

Downstairs, Beethoven, unheard, switched himself off.

At the back of the hall is a small telly, a Sanyo portable, but with an indoor aerial faultily adjusted so the colour comes and goes, and snowstorms occasionally drift over it. The first results are in, in the Midlands somewhere, and it seems to be going the way everyone knows it will: a computer predicts a Tory landslide, a huge majority, Labour only a few per cent ahead of the Alliance but likely to get far more seats. A landslide! When the Tory vote is actually *down* on 1979. What an absurd system! Or so some talking head now asseverates.

Jane, a slimmer Jane, dressed in a longish, deep blue coat, with a star-shaped glittering brooch on the left lapel, and in a floppy velvet hat also deep blue, squeezes Charlie's hand. 'You're in, darling,' she whispers, 'I'm sure of it.'

He looks down the long, wide, dimly lit hall. The counters have now sorted the votes, the party officials are doing spot scrutinies, shortly they'll begin counting them into tens, then bundling the tens into hundreds. Not easy to be sure but everywhere out of the three piles one looks a little bigger than the other two. The gaudily crested heads of the punks in the distant gallery are pleasantly mute for once: polychrome gothic gargoyles.

There had been bad times for Charlie in the struggle to get himself adopted. Often, when sick of the whole business of fawning at ward tea-parties, of granting expensive, even dangerous favours to businessmen in a corner through the continuing avalanche of liquidations, of using Alderson's efforts yet again to get the agent off the hook for using his reprographic facilities to forge 'O' Level certificates for sons of Paki traders, he had thought to himself: better it is to die, better to starve, than crave the hire which first we deserve. Or something to that effect. Nevertheless he pressed on, was even to some extent pushed, for Mead's resignation had followed swiftly, and by early summer there was talk of an autumn election.

The worst had been lunch with Giles Marsh at the Athlone Club in St James's. The invitation, really it was a summons, came on the first Friday in July, the lunch to be on the Monday. For most of Sunday evening Charlie worried silently about what to wear. It quite took the edge off the enjoyment of *Conqueror's* return, with Jolly Roger and red bar flying to signify 'Warship Sunk'. In the morning he found that Jane had put out a quite heavy Austen Reed pinstripe, vintage 1974, his Old Sydeyan tie, now definitely the worse for wear, and the pair of black shoes he kept for funerals. He rejected the lot: the spell of good weather looked settled and he chose instead his silk and mohair lightweight, blue, but richly blue, a pale blue silk tie with bright pink clocks, and his cordoba-red elastic-sideds. He trimmed his sideboards.

Up West, he drove around for half an hour finding all the meters taken and all the carparks full. Finally he pulled in on a residents' permit slot in a square north of Piccadilly, and so arrived at the Athlone ten minutes late. A servant took him to a large lounge with tall sash windows, low leather chairs, portraits in dirty gilt frames, in fact the lot. Everyone wore a pinstripe suit, a tie that said 'I belong' rather than 'I cost a lot', and had not only bushy sideboards but often enough hair growing out of their ears. Everyone wore black shoes.

Giles Marsh too wore the uniform, but with some style. In twenty-four years he had altered hardly at all. His glossy black Maltese hair was still swept back in corrugated ridges; his face was thinner because he had lost his wisdom teeth; his skin was still pockmarked and sallow, his lips as full; and the gold ring still glittered in the black hair that covered the back of his hands and the first joints of his fingers. He rose to give Charlie a dry handshake, and a cloud of the very best cologne blossomed around him.

'Charles Bosham. How do you do? Parking problems? It's never easy, but with the train drivers' strike bloody impossible. Scotch? The Club Manzanilla is very sound. No? One Scotch, one fino.'

Did Giles remember they had met before? Was it

appropriate to bring it up? Charlie sweated. Not knowing, he felt disadvantaged, ill at ease.

They took their drinks into the dining room (thus accenting Charlie's lateness), and over smoked trout with horseradish sauce, a mixture Charlie found stranger than anything he had been asked to eat in Majorca, Sardinia or Barbados, the vetting began.

'You're in warehousing then. Storage. That sort of thing.'

'Woolingham Storage Enterprises.' Charlie picked brown flesh off spiky bones, then blurted out, 'Woolingham Stores the South.' The wrong note, that of the fourth-form braggart.

'Business good?'

'Can't complain.'

'I mean the recession and all that. Lots of small businesses going into liquidation, over a hundred a week.'

Charlie wiped his small mouth on a napkin, drank the club claret. 'Woolingham Enterprises is not a small business. And in fact the fall-back in consumption has aided us considerably. Manufacturers can't shift stock, they have to store it somewhere, it's as simple as that. And if they go bust, our contracts stipulate the Official Receiver pays our dues before he gets the stuff out. Can't lose.' That had been Peter's idea.

'And you're able to give the time needed for a career in politics? I mean, you know, you won't be able to put in four days a week at your office if they adopt you and you get in.'

'No problem. My brother-in-law is managing director. He's a very sound chap. If I can get to board meetings and have a private barney with him once or twice a week, that'll be fine.'

'And you built this up yourself. From scratch.'

Charlie was careful now not to brag overtly. 'You could say that.'

Giles suddenly grinned, white teeth flashing. 'The

Leader would like that.' He put on a passable invitation: 'We are looking for self-starters. We are looking for princes of industry. People who have fantastic ability to build things and create jobs.'

They moved on to the steak and kidney pudding.

'Better than pie, I always think,' said Giles. 'In a pie the pastry holds the gravy at a distance. Pudding absorbs it. It is, you might say, more co-operative.'

Claggy was the word that came to Charlie's mind as he felt the suety mess clinging to the chrome plate he now had to wear in the roof of his mouth.

'What about the Falklands victory, then?'

'What about it?'

'What significance do you think it might have?'

Charlie pulled himself together, cast his mind back to the coaching Jane had provided on the subject.

'I know one thing. As I go about my work. Which gets me about a bit in the borough. I can confidently assert there's a new self-respect abroad. A new self-confidence. A new sense of pride in ourselves has been born. A sort of re-birth.'

A sudden explosion of quite raucously hearty laughter, like thoroughbreds neighing, or, for that matter spavined old hacks, left Charlie bewildered, then angry. He did not dare look behind to see if what he had said prompted it.

Giles remained po-faced. 'A sort of new spirit, you could say.'

'That's the sort of thing I mean. I read what she said at Chesterfield . . .'

'Cheltenham.'

'Cheltenham. The Spirit of the South Atlantic.' He remembered his BMW parked a quarter of a mile away. 'Those train drivers need to get off their arses and think of the nation for once. What it comes down to is we fought to show that aggression does not pay, and the robber cannot be allowed to get away with his swag.'

'You're right of course. Met a French diplomat the other day at a party. He was saying we hoped he wouldn't do a Falklands on France because they'd had their wicked way with us over agricutural prices. He was joking of course, but it shows they're sitting up and taking notice.'

'Of course he was bloody joking. The Frogs have got enough Super Etendards and Exocets to sink the fleet twice over. They make them, don't they?' Charlie still felt very sore about the *Sheffield.* He went back to cleaning up the end of the pudding, pushing the last bit of paste round the plate, hunting the last drop of gravy. He looked up in time to see Giles's bushy black eyebrows returning to base. Christ, he thought. Shouldn't have said that. He blundered on, waving his fork: 'I mean, what it goes to show is that some elements in our defensive systems need a serious going-over . . . it's one of the lessons that has to be learnt from the conflict. Definitely.'

'The raspberries are just in. Or would you prefer strawberries?'

'Raspberries, please,' said Charlie. There, got that one right. Hope the pips don't get under my plate.

'And the workers?' said Giles, once they had helped themselves to dessert? sweet? pudding!? 'What about the workers?'

'The elves?' Charlie peered over a forkful (use your fork, Charlie, always a fork with your sweet, Jane had said), then laughed. 'It's my own word for'm.' They were well into their second bot of claret. 'They as always are the key factor in the equation. So long as the top ones are happy, the skilled, the technicians, and those with bottle like the miners, though nukes will see them off in the end, what it comes down to is we're laughing. I've seen it in Woolingham. It's a matter of pride. Top eight grand a year in your pay packet and it's buy your council house, face it with reconstituted Portland-type stone, change the front door to one of those with a fanlight and a brass knocker.

Catch a bloke who's done that much for himself voting Labour, and I'll kiss his arse . . . As for the rest, not more than thirty per cent of the whole country, well. It's time the British workman was liberated from the tyranny of the trade unions.'

This passed muster. Giles approved not only the content but the glibness with which it was spilled.

'Fine, fine. Now, if you don't mind, I'd like to run over your CV. Make sure I've got the record straight.' He pushed back his unfinished bowl of raspberries and cream, and pulled a leather-bound notebook from an inside pocket, complete with gold-encased, slim-line ballpoint.

'Born Woolingham, 1939. Father owned two hardware shops. Scholarship to Philip Sydney. Did well, but packed in at sixteen. Why?'

'Bored. Frankly. Bored.'

'Ever regret it?'

'No. Should I?'

'Apparently not,' Giles was wry. 'Estate agent's, then Belgravia Properties. Married. Felicity Mead.'

Charlie felt a chill. Giles tapped the leather with the gold. 'This is rather the nub. Coffee? Brandy? Club has quite a jolly Armagnac. You see, I do rather gather there might be bad feeling between you and the Mead family. I mean, this Mead girl was actually married to you when she snuffed it. Wrapped a car round a lamp-post, wasn't it? Coroner left the verdict open, could have been suicide. Have much to do with the Meads after that?'

'Not at all, Not a thing.'

'Any chance of all that surfacing? In Woolingham?'

'No.Only the Meads know and they're not going to bring it up. She was off her trolley, believe me. I should never have let myself be conned into it.'

Gazing emptily over the club dining room, his eyes went sightless and he remembered the long, long wet day at Wimbledon, watching the rain drumming on the covers long after the umpire had ruled no play today, then back to the thin white body, naked and cold in water gone cold, yet incredibly still alive. Nothing, after all, for him to feel guilty about.

A voice from the table behind him again: I thought McEnroe put up a bloody good show, don't you? The absolute gent. Personally, I'd have brained Jimmie bounce, bounce, bounce, bounce, bounce Connors halfway through his first service game. What? Eh?'

'No . . . overt bad blood between you and the Meads then?'

'Not at all.'

'Is it true he stood down because there was a rumour rife in your borough that he's a homosexual?'

Charlie chewed a nail for a moment. Then he spoke carefully with well-coached seriousness: 'I have heard that rumour too. And I utterly disown it. I mean, I totally deny its credul . . . credibility. No. The matter is both simpler, plainer and in a way more credib . . . creditable to Terry. At the height of the recent conflict, the newly selected Labour candidate, a young Ken Langley, well to the left of most Labourites, was interviewed in the *Advertiser*. He attacked the war in the strongest terms. The *Advertiser* then approached our member of Parliament, Tom Murdish, who now allies himself with the SDP interest, and Terry Mead for their own views on Langley's statements. Tom was outspokenly condemnatory of everything Langley had said. Terry less so. In fact he defended Langley's right to say what he wanted. Added that if the Falklands was about anything it was about making sure that our kith and kin continued with these rights of free speech . . .'

He slurped coffee, sat back with a brandy balloon cupped in his hands.

'Many leading members of our Association – it was just after the landings and the casulaties at Goose Green and so on – felt that it was not appropriate of Mead to take that sort of equiv . . . equivocationary line at that moment of time. I honestly believe this is what his subsequent resignation from the candidacy is down to and I applaud his adherence to principle while agreeing with the general body of opinion in our Association that it was an impolitic moment to air it.'

Word perfect. Or almost. Pheew!

'Yes. That sounds like a satisfactory cover.'

'Cover?'

'Who was that oick Giles was entertaining?'

'Aspirant from the sticks. Woolingham, I think.'

'We should take Woolingham if the Falklands factor holds up.'

'Virtual certainty. Sitting member has gone SDP.'

'Well then, I should have thought we could have found someone better. I mean, there are two or three good chaps whose seats are shaky with the boundary changes. The Blessed Norman for instance.'

'Oh quite.'

Charlie, crapping behind a locked screen, banged his head against the partition, overcome by anger, frustration and humiliation.

At the Hyde Park Car Pound he blustered at the sergeant on duty, 'You never tow off the little ones, the beat-up Minis, the bangers. You pick on decent blokes, with decent cars, up in Town on business, valuable time wasted . . .'

'The odd thing is, sir, every Mini owner we have in here tells us we should go for the Mercs, the BMWs and the Rollers. American Express will do nicely.'

Charlie signed the slip and muttered, 'That bloke Prudom has a point.'

He scraped the wing of his BMW on one of the concrete pillars and was lucky not to be breathalyzed on the spot, especially after the crack about Prudom, who had not yet been gunned down, was still living wild somewhere in Yorkshire. He got home without further incident but with the rotten taste of smoked trout bouncing up from his tummy. He watched Spain hold England to a draw in the World Cup and then told Jane that, if being a Member of Parliament meant mixing with a load of toffee-nosed bastards, then he'd rather not bother. In that case, she said, I'll not bother with aerobics.

A sudden cheer. 'We've got Lewisham. Price is out.' Again Jane squeezes Charlie's hand – with Lewisham gone, then Woolinghams is on the way. Charlie looks down the tables – the bundles of tens gathered into hundreds, the hundreds now being gathered into thousands, and feels a heavy sort of excited pride beginning to swell in the middle of his body. Toad-like he's about to be puffed up into . . . somebody. Bloody shame they don't have the telly here. Anne, Mother, Aunt Eliizabeth, if she's still alive, should be watching this.

Jane had taken the phone call. 'It's Anne.'

Charlie looked up from Jason's home computer on which he had been playing himself at 'Blitz'.

'Anne?'

'Your sister.'

'Oh. Anne. What the hell does she want?'

'To speak to you.'

He took the receiver.

'Well?'

'Charlie?'

'Speaking.'

'Anne here.'

'Yes?'

Pause.

'It's Aunt Elizabeth. She's dying. She wants to see you.'

Pause.

'I don't want to see her.'

Pause.

'She's got something she wants to give to you.'

'What.'

'I don't know. Oh come on, Charlie. Stop being so beastly.'

'What's she dying of?'

'Old age. Boredom. In actual fact, progressive kidney failure. Don't worry. It won't upset you.'

Not quite true. Aunt Elizabeth had always been thin, but now she was no more than a bundle of sticks, a *memento mori.* As Anne showed Charlie into the small ground-floor room (the once large salons of Balmoral had been subdivided four or five times), he felt sure that she had already snuffed it. But no, Anne, bigger than ever, but healthier-looking too, and wearing a Support the Greenham Women badge, slipped hands into her aunt's armpits and hoisted her into a near-sitting position, expertly plumping up pillows as she did so.

'Come on, Auntie. Wake up. Someone to see you. You've got a visitor. Charlie's here.'

At last the veined, purple eyelids flickered and watery eyes with cataracts appeared.

'Charlie? Here?'

'Yes, Auntie.'

'Bring him closer. Can't see him. Is that you, Charlie?'

'Yes, Aunt.'

'You're fat now. As fat as Anne.'

'Here, Charlie,' said Anne. 'Sit here.' She pushed a wicker chair, clearly a commode, close to the bed. Charlie, his buttocks cringing at the thought of what he might be sitting on or above, nevertheless did as he was told.

'I'll leave you now. For five minutes.'

Silence.

Aunt Elizabeth's breath grated, almost, oh God, *rattled*, her sparse white hair, frizzed out like a halo, stirred, and the eyes closed again. There were smells: air freshener overlaying oil used too often for frying fish, urine, death. Charlie very badly wanted to get up and go.

'Well. You came.'

'Yes. Aunt.'

The cloudy eyes were open again.

'I suppose . . . she . . . told . . . you . . . I . . . had . . . something . . . for . . . you.'

An extraordinary noise bubbled through her mouth, across her almost vanished lips. It could only be a snigger.

'Dad didn't want Edward to have it. I don't want . . . you to have it. But someone . . . Only you left now. No chance . . . Anne having children.'

Her eyes searched out the darkness of his bulk against the patterns of the flowered wallpaper.

'It's old. 1785. Been in the family since then,'

His pulse quickened. Anything that old must be valuable.

'In the locker. Anne put it ready for me. Old book.'

He found it. A thin leatherbound volume, badly worn round the edges, the corners of the pages tatty, it creaked as he opened it. Heavy black print in a fluid italic that at first sight was impossible to read. Then he realized it was all in a foreign language. Wop perhaps, or Spanish. Disappointment became irritation. The silly old bag, dragging him down to see her, just for this. He spelt out the title at the top of the page. *Lazarillo de Tormes*.

Anne pushed the door open and put one cup of tea on top of the locker, and a plate with two Nice biscuits. Charlie got up to go.

'Well, Charlie?'

'Thank you, Aunt.'

The twig-like fingers gestured dismissal. Thank God.

In the hall Anne paused at the large stained-glass front door.

'Don't you want to know how Mother is?'

Pause.

'Well. She's fine. She practically runs Goldsmith Drive for us. Up and down the stairs. Out to the extension.'

Charlie felt his pulse rate rise.

'She says she'll vote Labour if you're the Tory Candidate. I would too, but I can't stand Tom Murdish.'

'He's SDP,' said Charlie, without thinking.

'So he is. Well, that's all right then. Charlie?'

'Yes?'

'I'm sure you'll like the book Auntie gave you. And Charlie?'

'Yes.'

'If I were you I'd watch my blood pressure.'

'What was it then, Charlie?'

'Fucking *book!*'

'A book?'

'A book. A goddamn book.' He slammed it on one of the gate-legged, dark-stained tables. An ashtray built up out of a genuine horse-brass bounced.

'It looks very old.'

'It is very old. It's two hundred years old. But it's falling apart, and it's in Spanish.'

Again the binding creaked.

'Hey, Charlie. Look at this.'

'Why?'

'Charlie. Come on. Look at this.'

She had bent back the leather cover, exposing the spread of marbled paper at the very front of the book. From the right-hand leaf he read two inscriptions. The first, in a flowing italic, the hand version of the print inside: *Charles Edward Bosham;* below it in steel-nibbed scrawl that tried to be copperplate: *Joseph Bosham, Third Viscount of Bosham in the County of Sussex.*

'Charlie . . . you really are someone. You must be!'

Apart from checking that there really was a village called Bosham in Sussex, on Chichester harbour, to be precise, they left it at that. 'After all,' said Charlie, 'I don't want to find I've got a seat in the Lords that bars me from the Commons, at this point in time, do I?'

It really was – well, no *not* amazing – in fact utterly predictable the difference it made. There are Labour peers who insist their children put 'The Hon.' in front of their names; there are dukes who do not do a lot except be dukes who would be mortified if they didn't get their KGs and KTs; there are ex-ministers without children, and not likely to have any, who will follow you anywhere if you give them not a life peerage but an hereditary one . . . what sort of people are these to be so lacking in self-esteem, that these things count? Our leaders no less. At all events, it did for Charlie – the discovery that he might be a viscount, and after all Grandad had always claimed that it was so – just what was needed to get him through increasingly frequent confrontations with the toffee-nosed bastards.

The two peaks were the Brighton conference and a long weekend in what was said to be a country house but turned out to be just the sort of over-heated hotel with over-rich food (Lymington crab, devilled in the spices of Grenada with New Forest Rosemary from our own herbarium; haunch of Lyndhurst Venison marinated in our own red currant jelly and vintage red Burgundy) that Charlie and Jane went to for an occasional off-peak mid-week break. There, various notables, including You-Know-Who and Whatsisname, and Giles Marsh again, gave Charlie and other young hopefuls hints on how to comport themselves in the trials to come. Charlie got on quite well with most of the prospective candidates, self-starters for the most part, finding them not above a game of snooker, half an hour with a video nasty or *The War for the Falklands*.

Giles's position was ambiguous. He acted as master of

ceremonies, chairperson, but seemed basically to be linkman between an advertising agency from which he had been seconded on full pay, Central Office, and even Downing Street itself. He certainly seemed to be In The Know. 'Of *course,* his secretary is in the club. His wife knows, the whole ruddy party knows, but the laugh is that She-Who-Must-Be-Obeyed does not, and no one dare tell her.' 'Of *course,* acceptance of Cruise, and support in the Lebanon are part of the tab she has to pick up for Ronnie's help over the Falklands, but believe me you get very angry if you hear anyone say so. It's a stance you should practise, for there's worse to come. In the Caribbean if nowhere else.'

Yes, once he'd found his sea legs Charlie (Viscount) Bosham really began to enjoy it all, took to it like a duck to water. His voice became deeper, his face shone as if roast swan was his staple diet, his handshake became firmer, and podgier, his clothes hit exactly that perfection of heavy cloth, 'good' cut, the whole ensemble expensively, but not ostentatiously ornamented. He swiftly became a man of real, permanent, traditional substance.

And now the apotheosis approaches, although the group of Tory supporters in the middle of the stage has shrunk. Mrs Grosscurth has gone home, so has Mrs Armstrong and so has Mrs Goulden. Amongst those left, the two lads from the British Movement who suggested Charlie should give them a tenner each to make sure no Labourites tried any aggro on him, loom more obviously. But there are still Labourites and SDP supporters in plenty. What once had been a safe Labour seat goes Tory with the SDP ex-Labour candidate coming a goodish second, and one of the SDP side makes the mistake of offering a cheer. A dark-haired man in a leather jacket, whose pinched face and frayed jeans declare him to be one of Maggie's Private Army, bursts out of the Labour camp, heads straight for the SDP man, a youth, a student, and thumps him heartily on the nose.

Ken Langley follows to pull clear his overenthusiastic supporter and Old Bill lumbers up from the back of the hall. Apart from the punks on the balcony, who cheer and whistle, as the dark-haired unwaged character is frogmarched out, order is restored. The punks, it seems, are actually card-holding members of the SDP – a fact that becomes apparent when Charlie asks to have them ejected.

The count is almost over. Scrutineers have a last poke or two at the bundles of votes. Totting-up commences. Thousands, hundreds, tens, units. The Returning Officer, who is also the Chairman of the Borough Council, gives his chain a premonitory hitch. Almost as if he is drowning Charlie suffers recall of the campaign:

No man is an island. Entire of Itself.

Bosham's gotta lotta bottle.

What is needed is not consensus, not compromise, but conviction, action, persistence, until the job is well and truly finished.

There is a new way, a classless way. Let us end the class war, let us break the mould.

The emancipation of the workers from trade union exploitation is our aim and purpose.

1980 saw the greatest ever one-year decline in British output. Deindustrialization, a massive increase in unemployment, a surge in the export of capital, decrease in real wage incomes, tax concessions to the rich . . . those, brothers, are the figures for 1980. They will be worse in 1981 and 1982 and 1983.

Bosham's gotta lotta bottle.

America, Ronald Reagan, means to win the Third World War in Europe. That's what Cruise means.

What is needed is real British Government, a return to home-made leadership that bears the once formidable impress of equal . . . I mean quality: Made in Britain.

Bosham. Charles. Edward. Twenty-two thousand and forty-three votes. (Four thousand *less* than Terry Mead scored in 1979.)

Langley. Kenneth. Twenty-eight . . . Sorry. Eighteen thousand four hundred and twenty-eight.

Murdish. Thomas. Twelve thousand, eight hundred and sixteen.

I hereby declare the above Bosham, Charles duly . . .

May God the Master bless our fare
And give those here the lion's share
As gathered here in friendly glee
We share it round quite equally
Hurrah!

'Charlie.'

'Yes, pet?

'You owe yourself a holiday.'

'Yes pet. But where?'

'Grenada?'

From the tiered gallery a chorus breaks out; to Charlie, it seems as if, absurdly, they are singing the words of a commercial for the high-fibre breakfast cereal Jane now makes him eat instead of muesli.

Tasty, tasty, very, very, tasty . . . He's tasty!

Then two of the punks moon – that is pull down their jeans and expose their bums over the rail, and the words come through more clearly, loud and clear:

Nasty, nasty, he's very, very nasty . . .

The lads from the British Movement flank Charlie and Jane as he moves to the front to make his speech of acceptance. The chant ends on a shout:

HE'S NASTY!

All these books are available at your local bookshop or newsagent, or can be ordered direct from the publisher..

To order direct from the publisher just tick the titles you want and fill in the form below.

Name ______________________________

Address ______________________________

____

Send to:
Panther Cash Sales
PO Box 11, Falmouth, Cornwall TR10 9EN.

Please enclose remittance to the value of the cover price plus:

UK 45p for the first book, 20p for the second book plus 14p per copy for each additional book ordered to a maximum charge of £1.63.

BFPO and Eire 45p for the first book, 20p for the second book plus 14p per copy for the next 7 books, thereafter 8p per book.

Overseas 75p for the first book and 21p for each additional book.

Panther Books reserve the right to show new retail prices on covers, which may differ from those previously advertised in the text or elsewhere.